ALMOST

MORTAL

"The verdict is in – Attorney Christopher Leibig offers a legal thriller for the ages. Realistic yet unpredictable, with a clever metaphysical twist, *Almost Mortal* is a thrilling roller coaster ride!"

—ROBERT DUGONI,
#1 Amazon, *New York Times* and *Wall Street Journal* Best Selling Author of *My Sister's Grave*

"A poised protagonist leads this serpentine but engaging legal tale."

—KIRKUS REVIEWS

"When *Almost Mortal*'s cynical, brilliant but big-hearted public defender offers to take on a legal conundrum worthy of a John Grisham thriller, he uncovers surprising details about his own past and is confronted with a mystery reminiscent of the magical realism of a Gabriel García Márquez tale. A page-turner that you'll probably want to read twice."

—PATRICIA MCCARDLE,
author of Amazon's award-winning novel, *Farishta*.

"Leibig invites readers into the creative, chaotic, and often caustic environment of criminal defense work while presenting both its intensely real, human side and engaging our fantastical, supernatural curiosities about good and evil."

—SARAH BURKE,
capital mitigation investigator and managing partner of Virginia-based investigative firm, Burke and Associates

"...You will sit down with *Almost Mortal* and not want to put it down."

—AuthorsReading.com

"Everyone who investigates and litigates serious criminal cases has had that one case they'll never forget, the one that haunted them, seduced them, or just turned in a completely unexpected direction. This book is about that case."

—Phil Becnel,
Private Investigator, Managing Partner of Dinolt, Becnel, and Wells, and author of Principles of Investigative Documentation and When Your Lover is a Liar

"Chris Leibig's quick moving legal thriller mixes accurate insights into the world of criminal defense attorneys with the unusual and unexpected twists of the novel's surrounding events. It's hard to put down and leaves you with much to think about."

—John Kenneth Zwerling,
Nationally known Washington, D.C. Criminal Defense Attorney

"After narrating five of his books, Chris Leibig has become one of my favorite authors. They're smart, entertaining, engrossing and addictive. His latest, *Almost Mortal,* is the jewel in his crown and lives up to all these adjectives. Needless to say, I recommend it highly."

—Steve Carlson,
Audible audiobook narrator, actor and author of Heaven, Almost Graceland, and Final Exposure.

"Chris Leibig takes readers on a surreal and sublime journey to catch a serial killer through the eyes of wickedly clever and cunning hero..."

—Anne Marie DiNardo,
2011 Rod Serling Screenwriting Competition Finalist.

Almost Mortal
by Christopher Leibig

ISBN 978-1-63393-179-4

Published by

◣ köehlerbooks ™

210 60th Street
Virginia Beach, VA 23451
212-574-7939
www.koehlerbooks.com

ALMOT
MORTAL

A LEGAL THRILLER

CHRISTOPHER LEIBIG

VIRGINIA BEACH
CAPE CHARLES

DEDICATION

This book is dedicated to Janis Elaine Leibig.

You shall have no other gods before Me.

EXODUS 20:3 (NKJV)

PROLOGUE

AUGUST 13, 2015, HAVANA, CUBA

Other than the famed Zapruder film of the JFK assassination, it was probably the most viewed video clip of a true-life murder in world history. Rarely had a killing been perpetrated at a moment when its victim was already the focal point of dozens of state-of-the-art cameras and thousands of curious eyes. The perfection of the angle, the crispness of the color, the starkness with which a viewer could watch the transformation of a human body from a vibrant vessel to empty flesh had never before been achieved—at least not publicly. All the networks—local and national—got the footage. But it was the local ABC 7 News that scored the ultimate prize—the shot that actually captured the eyes going blank a fraction of a second before the body collapsed. More spellbinding than the quality of the film, though, would be its significance. It was the mystery that made people watch the clip again and again.

In the days since its making, the lawyer, despite having been a close eyewitness to the event, had never watched the clip. Nor had he taken part in the international debate, fostered mostly by cable news and religious groups, about whether the victim could possibly have survived the brutal bullet wound. People had survived being shot in the head—but not like that.

The lawyer gazed across the Plaza Vieja. Three elderly women, evenly spaced, walked slowly across the square through a foraging flock of pigeons. He had never met or seen any of the trio before, but he instinctively knew that all three were widows who had probably been friends since childhood. He could tell from their strides, their pace, and the gestures of the chubby one in the middle, who was likely telling a boring old story about her deceased husband again.

The lawyer looked down at his tablet. His finger hovered over the link that would show him the video clip of the famous murder. He may as well watch it now. The clock in the corner of the screen showed it was two twenty-five. He sipped his coffee and took a long drag from his cigarette.

He wondered from which direction his guest, or guests, would approach. If at all. In any other similar situation, he would instinctively know whether someone was running late for a meeting, was not going to show up at all, or whether the person he planned to meet even existed. But here, he knew none of the above for certain.

He opened the folder in front of him and saw the neatly clipped sheaf of papers the old priest had given him. He would read until his guests arrived, or until he figured out where in his past he had seen that writing before.

CHAPTER 1

"I JUST SCOOPED HER—just kind of scooped her."

As he spoke, Jonathon P. Scarfrowe swung his arm slowly, as if to underhand a softball. He stopped for a moment and focused intently down at his twitching middle finger, which darted out from his hand like a practiced tentacle. Scarfrowe's pursed lips and excited eyes revealed that he was reliving the event he sought to describe. Deputy Public Defender Sam Young watched Scarfrowe closely. He always marveled at how some of his clients, like Scarfrowe, knew with such utter certainty who they were. They simply lacked the ability to feel self-conscious. Scarfrowe, short and round with a boyish face and red hair, blinked innocently back.

The lockup deputy, a beefy sheriff's department veteran named Plosky, leaned against the wall with his arms folded and rolled his eyes at the ceiling. The dank, cement-walled room between the Bennet County, Virginia courthouse cells and the courtroom could barely hold the small group, given Plosky's gut.

Scarfrowe's gesture had revealed so much more than he likely knew. His lawyers had merely asked him to explain how he knew the surprise witness, whose testimony they were about to face on the last day of trial. Yet Scarfrowe's dismissive gesture operated as a confession of sorts— perhaps not to the crime for which he was on trial, but to a way of life. Scarfrowe had served time for rape at age seventeen and aggravated sexual battery at twenty-five. And now, at age forty-seven, he was on trial for tackling and groping a woman on a bike path. A quick grope, really, but the victim had described in detail how Scarfrowe's practiced fingers had found their way down the front of her pants in mere seconds. Scarfrowe's problem, aside from his criminal record—which set him up for mandatory life in prison, if convicted—was that he had worn a black ski mask at the time and was immediately apprehended by an off-duty cop out for a jog. To make matters worse, eight other women in Bennet County had recently reported similar groping by a masked little pervert in the same vicinity.

Once tackled by the cop, Scarfrowe had apologized profusely for attempting to grab the woman's purse. That piece of obfuscation laid the groundwork for his defense—that he was guilty only of simple abduction, not abduction with intent to rape—which would count as a third violent sexual assault and guarantee a life sentence. Scarfrowe was one of those who learned his true nature early and stuck with it, despite the costs.

"I didn't make me this way," he once said.

Sadly for Scarfrowe, the prosecutor had just come up with a surprise witness—a detective who had interviewed a twenty-four-year-old Scarfrowe after a grope and run at a local mall back in the early 1990s. Scarfrowe had similarly claimed an interest in the purse on that occasion—a statement belied by the victim's testimony that Scarfrowe had spent considerable energy jamming his hand into her crotch; thus, the emergency lockup conference.

Sam shook his head, glanced at the deputy, and made eye contact with his co-counsel, Amelia Griffin, a new public defender. She was now second chairing her first big case. And it was about to blow.

"She's full of it, Sam," Scarfrowe said in a crisp whisper. "I swear to it. I never tackled her. It was more of a scoop." He then seared the moment into Sam's memory by repeating the scooping gesture with a bit more flair, his tongue wiggling out to mirror the flailing finger.

Sam pushed Scarfrowe's hand back down to his side while glancing at Amelia, who blushed but appeared stern and serious, hand on her chin.

"This is bad, Jon. Real bad."

Scarfrowe frowned. "I never tackled her. I scooped her—"

"Jon, it doesn't matter whether you tackled her or scooped her." Sam rubbed his hands over the top of his shaved head and sighed. "The point is the pattern of claiming you just wanted the purse. Follow me? The jury is not going to believe you went for a purse and got crotch—*twice*."

Sam could sense Amelia's heart rate spike. She was not used to it yet—the emergencies and things not going according to plan, which was always. He put a hand on Scarfrowe's shoulder.

"You should have told us you tried the purse gambit before."

The odd thing about Scarfrowe as a client was that he always acted like the whole thing was a television show. With him there was no desperation, no pleading, no embarrassment, no blaming the cops or his lawyers. He was who he was. *I just kind of scooped her.*

"I'll cooperate," Scarfrowe said. But they had been over this before. Scarfrowe regularly offered up the idea that he would become a cooperating witness in exchange for a sentencing deal. The problem was, he didn't know anything about anyone else's crimes. He didn't hang out with drug dealers, scammers, fencers, or any criminal types. He was the apocryphal cable guy who lived alone and kept to himself—most of the time, anyway.

Scarfrowe leaned close, tilting his head suspiciously towards the deputy.

"Suppose I got information on the murders." Sam could see an excited light in his eyes over his usual amused smirk. "A guy on our block confessed to me."

If true, Scarfrowe's plan could work. Lead the cops to the only serial killer in Bennet County history, right? Three murders. Three savagely butchered women in three months in the relatively wealthy Washington, DC suburb. Despite the police department's best efforts, the press had anointed the mysterious sicko as the *Rosslyn Ripper*, a blend of the infamous Brit and the business district just over the bridge from Georgetown.

"Who confessed?" Sam asked.

Scarfrowe hesitated. "Suppose I told you it was Morris Talberton."

"Won't work. Morris Talberton has been locked up since October. He couldn't have murdered anybody."

As a seven-year veteran of the Bennet County public defender's office, Sam knew most of the regular clients and a lot about their pending cases. "I'm sorry, Jon."

Scarfrowe shrugged. "Nah, I'm sorry. Shouldn't have tried to bullshit ya."

"That's okay. You're under a lot of pressure. I get it."

"Don't worry about me. We're gonna win. Five years. I can see it from here." Scarfrowe rubbed his fingers against his chin, exuding a creepy confidence. "Juror number six, Ms. Buttertree, and Juror number nine, William Hasbrow—they're dead sure I was going for the purse. Ain't no changin' their minds. And Hasbrow's likely to be the foreman. Them others are lost souls."

"I hope you're right," Sam said.

"Strange days," Scarfrowe said, more to himself than to Sam. Scarfrowe loved to say *strange days*. He used the phrase casually, the same way a hipster might say *good times*.

While Sam and Amelia waited for the deputy to buzz the door open, Scarfrowe spoke up again, raising, as he often did, a topic that had nothing to do with the problem at hand.

"Hey, Sam, I hear you're gonna represent Gilbert Hogman."

"I haven't heard that. Who's Gilbert Hogman?"

"Got booked last night. He's at the jail. Mental health unit. *That* shitbird's crazy. So watch out."

"Thanks for the advice."

Deputy Plosky buzzed the door, allowing himself, Sam, and Amelia to re-enter the courtroom. "That guy's a piece of work," Plosky said.

"We're all pieces of work," Sam said.

He flipped through his notes. He had about five minutes left to craft a cross-examination of the cop who would likely sink the case against Scarfrowe.

As he and Amelia crossed into the courtroom, Sam heard Scarfrowe speak to the deputy.

"Court's gonna go late. Can you call over and have 'em save my dinner?"

His dinner. Back at the jail. Funny.

• • •

One hour later, with Scarfrowe's chances of dodging the sex offense conviction severely reduced, Sam and Amelia stood in front of the courthouse, reflecting on the miserable trial. The sticky July day started to cool. Sam smoked a cigarette as Amelia rattled through ideas for her closing argument. The courthouse lights went off, all but the large, round spotlights that illuminated the high columns atop the front steps.

"At least the judge gave us until Thursday to prep for the closing argument," Sam said.

"Let's say I end with the reasonable doubt part. They have a choice between two equally viable options, and with no particular reason to choose one over the other, they have to choose the one that favors the defendant," Amelia said. "That's our system. It's better that ten guilty persons go free than one innocent suffer—"

"Work on that, Amelia," Sam said. "Make sure you have enough emotional stuff in there, not just legal concepts. Sympathize with what's her face. Be her, even. They have to like you. They can hate me; they can even hate Jon. But they have to like you. Be sympathetic. You can only imagine how horrifying it is to be attacked like that, at night, alone, from behind. What's her name shouldn't even be expected to remember *exactly* how it happened. And do *not* say the thing about the ten guilty people. The do-gooders on the jury don't agree with Blackstone on that one. They hate the idea of guilty people on the loose."

Sam studied Amelia under the fluorescent courtyard lights. He impulsively reached out and lightly touched the side of her head, adjusting her wig. The otherwise flawless, straight blonde hair that Amelia had sported for the last six months had slipped out of place ever so slightly, perhaps due to the humidity and her animated gestures.

She looked down. "Oh."

"You'll be great. Don't stay up all night on this; you have all day tomorrow to work on the closing. Get enough rest, and besides—"

"Sam, you fucking promised!" Promised never to refer to her illness. Promised never to feel sorry for her. Sam held up his hands defensively.

"Mr. Young?"

A woman stood near them. Just far enough away to not be rude, but close enough to politely interrupt the conversation. Had she come from the courthouse?

"My name is Camille Paradisi. I work at Church of the Holy Angels."

She extended her hand. She looked about thirty-five, if that, and wore a black beret and a long, dark tunic that hung loosely around her figure. It obscured, judging by her thin face and lower legs, a svelte, fit body. Long black hair twined around both shoulders as if blown there from behind. *Holy Angels?* Her sultry pose—hand on one hip, back slightly arched, and one high heel aimed off to the side—did not match her church employment. She was a beautiful young woman who conveyed a confidence beyond her age. Maybe the body language was learned. Part of an act, like cursing too much, speaking too loudly, or chomping on gum to affect the overdone nonchalance displayed by lots of young lawyers and cops. But Sam didn't think so.

The woman shook hands with Amelia as Sam studied her.

"Pleased to meet you. I know you two are in the middle of a trial. Sorry to bother you." She reached toward Amelia. "Hey, your necklace is slipping off."

Amelia blushed. "I'm a hot mess."

She grabbed hold of the necklace, which had somehow come unclasped and slipped down onto her suit jacket.

"No prob, I got it."

The woman stepped behind Amelia, cleared Amelia's hair from her neck with a gentle brush of her hand, and carefully clipped the choker necklace while Amelia held it in place, too flustered to object. The woman met Sam's eyes while she stood behind Amelia, fastening the necklace. Once the necklace was clasped, her hands lingered on Amelia's shoulders for an extra moment—longer than necessary, but not long enough to be too strange.

Amelia stared at the ground, frozen, and seemingly afraid to move.

"Thanks," she said softly, as if to herself—as if she thought no one else in the conversation was listening to her. "I'm gonna go. I'll see you, Sam." She picked up her briefcase and walked out of the courtyard, leaving the two standing together, watching her as she left.

"I heard you were here, and I wondered if I could have a moment of your time," the woman said. "You're kind of hard to catch up with. You know Father Andrada, right?"

Father Andrada? A priest at Sam's childhood church. A church that, like all other religious institutions, he had not visited since high school. Sam waited for the woman to fill the silence. She didn't. And when he looked up after one second too many, her eyes were resting on his.

"Are you all right?" she asked.

"I'm fine. Tired, I guess."

"I'm sorry. I don't mean to bum-rush you during a big trial." She flashed a smart smile, one signifying that she meant for him to know that she was not a woman who often used phrases like *bum-rush*. "But I need your help. Father Andrada said I could drop his name. He was close to your mother. You could say it's kind of an emergency, and you're the only person who can help me. Help me to help him, that is. He told me he's sorry he lost touch with you, which I guess was—"

"Sixteen years ago," Sam said. "But I was the one who lost touch with him. He's got no reason to feel bad about it."

Sam's mother had passed away when he was eighteen. She had indeed been a well-known activist at the Church of the Holy Angels. Nevertheless, it was odd, this woman popping up to mention his mother out of the blue. And Father Andrada? He remembered. Andrada had been his mother's friend. He even remembered the last time he had seen the guy—the day of his mother's memorial service. The woman's eyes crinkled at the corners, conveying a question, perhaps to herself. *Do I have the wrong guy?*

Even with all the thoughts of Scarfrowe's case, his other clients, and his desire for an overdue drink, Sam knew one thing for sure: he did not want to be the wrong guy. He summoned his courtroom energy, leveled his eyes at the woman, and took a quiet but deep breath.

"I'm sorry. I'm just a little out of it. Can we meet, let's say, tomorrow maybe? Or I could call you later, Ms . . . ?"

"Paradisi. Camille."

Sam accepted her business card. She touched his arm lightly as she turned away. "I know you're busy, but I think you'll be interested in this case. And time is, I guess you could say, of the essence. Can we definitely meet tomorrow?"

Sam took a deep breath. The warm air felt a little stifling now. "Sure."

"I remember your mother, too, Sam. A really nice lady. Smart. That's what Father Andrada always thought. He told me the other day that *he* actually learned from *her* about what it really meant to be a Catholic. I thought you might like to hear that."

Sam shrugged.

Her hair blowing behind her, Camille Paradisi walked away with a remarkably straight posture, her long torso resting comfortably above her swaggering hips.

"My cell is on the back." She rounded the corner, leaving Sam alone in the courtyard.

"Hey, Young!" Deputy Plosky, now in street clothes, approached from the side exit. He shuffled towards him, looking from one side to another as if to check for surveillance. Even when Plosky could wear whatever he wanted, he favored tight button-down shirts that accentuated his gut. His long sideburns, which blended into his 1950s country-cop persona, suggested more of an Elvis impersonator when Plosky wore street clothes. Sam steeled himself for the inevitable petty scolding he was about to receive. *Don't smoke in the courtyard. Can you clean off the counsel table at the end of the day in case the judge has an early hearing? Will you please stop giving Scarfrowe gum in the courtroom?* But when Plosky got closer, Sam could see that he looked nervous, which was not the norm for Plosky. He reigned with well-practiced authority in his little fiefdom upstairs.

"Can I talk to you for a second? A personal thing."

"Sure, Plosky."

"Irwin," he said, acknowledging that Sam did not know, after years of acquaintance, Plosky's first name. "It's about my son. He's a knucklehead. Goes to the community college out in Fairfax. Anyway, a cop out there stopped him and his friends, and Irwin got charged with possession of ecstasy—the dipshit. I raised him better than that, but, well, I know you're only supposed to do cases appointed to the public defender's office, but I guess I kinda heard that you sometimes—"

"I got it, Irwin." Sam wrote his cell phone number on a business card and handed it to Plosky. "Tell Irwin Jr. to call me. I'll take care of him. I promise."

Plosky grinned. "Thanks, Sam. You know how it is. We're not supposed to hire local attorneys for personal stuff. That's what some of the bosses say. You know, it could lead to—"

"I know." Plosky was taking a risk by allowing a defense attorney who regularly appeared in the courthouse he guarded to learn personal things about his family.

"It'll come out fine."

And Sam knew it would. Sometimes he just felt, at the beginning of a case, that he knew what was going to happen. He had that feeling about Irwin Plosky Jr.

"Thanks," Plosky said. "You know, it's funny. I was all worried about this, and now I can tell it'll be fine. You know what my wife said? 'Fuck the bosses.'" Plosky chuckled a heartening, old man's guffaw.

"Smart lady." Sam shook hands with Plosky, who walked towards his car with an extra bounce in his step. Sam, still holding the woman's card, flipped it over and read it.

Sister Camille Paradisi
Director of Religious Education
Church of the Holy Angels Parish
Bennet, VA

Sam had felt it the second Paradisi touched his arm. He had noticed such things before when certain people touched him— small bursts of energy, like connective electric jolts, almost always with women. Maybe he was just in a strange mood, but if he were not mistaken, Paradisi's touch had conveyed something important, like warmth that dissipated when she removed her hand and left completely when she rounded the corner out of his presence. Or maybe it was nothing but his mother's connection to Andrada that made him feel that way. Or it could simply be that he always felt strange during trials, as if his senses were on high alert, possibly susceptible to the fallacy of over perception. Like thinking he could read a lie from a witness, and turning out to be wrong. Sam lit another cigarette and walked out of the courtyard towards the bar. Jonathon Scarfrowe, Father Andrada, and a hot nun. All in one day. Strange days, indeed.

CHAPTER 2

SAM'S EYES OPENED, AND he was afraid to look at the clock. He gently massaged his head, took a deep breath and glanced at his cell phone on the bedside table: *9:49 July 29, 2015*.

Not too bad. He thought back over the night. When had he quit remembering? Ten? Twelve? Hangovers weren't unusual, but a complete memory blackout on a weeknight? He groaned, and then looked for his phone. Sometimes he was able to piece together a night by looking at his calls, texts, and e-mails. He found his iPhone on the floor face down between his bed and the bathroom. When he picked it up, his right knee throbbed. He must have bumped something. No calls in or out after ten. That was good.

His back ached. He took a deep breath and felt like puking. Instead, he lit a cigarette, which made him feel worse. He turned on his computer. At least he could e-mail the office and tell Amelia he would be late.

His homepage listed *Breaking News*. As usual, it contained uninformative updates about the Rosslyn Ripper investigation, including an anecdotal puff piece about how so many women in

Bennet were buying firearms at a local sporting goods store that the background checks were taking an extra day. The news was not *breaking* at all, just the same old noise about the scariest case in town. Actual breaking news would be if they caught the guy or if another murder happened.

After e-mailing the office, Sam's eyes fell on the pile of junk he must have dumped out of his pockets and onto his desk the night before. Two lighters, a crumpled cigarette pack, random change, and a business card. *Camille Paradisi*. Cell on the back.

He said her name aloud, "Paradisi." His phone rang.

"Sam, this is Sister Camille. Any chance we could meet today? Father Andrada is with me now. I'm at the church."

Sam studied her name on the card while she spoke. He ran through excuses in his head. *Have to prep with Amelia for Scarfrowe's closing argument. Client meetings all day. Not allowed to take cases not appointed to the public defender's office.* He turned the card over in his hand.

"Well?" Camille said.

•••

Sam sat in his car in the parking lot of the Church of the Holy Angels. He steadied his breath. This was his childhood parish, though he'd never returned to it after his mother had died. Marcela Young, a PhD in Religion from American University, had practiced her own brand of Catholicism. She had been pretty close to Andrada. "At least he has an education," she would say of him—meaning to contrast him with the average priest.

Sam's father had died before Sam was born. His mother's death when he was only eighteen had left Sam with no family—no siblings, no grandparents, no cousins, no uncles, no aunts, and, at least for now, no religion. Although he had not thought about his mother's connection to the church in a very long time, he thought about her a good bit. Often when he became stressed out during a frantic day, he would think of her words of advice. *"Relax. The simple things are the most beautiful."*

But he could remember her at a desk late at night, still there with the light on when he would get up in the middle of the night and walk past her room on the way to the bathroom. She would be leaning over her desk, flipping pages, always reading and jotting notes. She did not seem very relaxed during her late-night study sessions, or very simple. Sam's mother was loving and as close to him as anyone else's parents he had known. But she had always been an enigma of sorts to him, what with her quirky religious studies and eclectic friends from the university who drank wine and danced in the living room while Sam was supposed to be asleep. In the three years before she died, she had traveled abroad constantly on various relief efforts. Africa. Central America. India. During those years, Sam had attended a boarding school in New Jersey, yet somehow they had remained as close as ever.

"Your mom thinks she has to save the world," one of his teachers at Ambrose Academy had said to him.

Sam thought back to the day he sat in an estate lawyer's office and learned that his mother had left him a trust—enough to pay for college and then some.

"From where?" he asked.

The lawyer shrugged. "Who cares? Obviously she was planning for you."

Sam's phone buzzed. "This is Young."

"Sam, thank God!" Sam knew the voice right away. It was the mother of Sherita Owings, a regular client and a crack addict who just could not stop using.

"Sherita got pinched last night. She's locked up. I've had it, I'm telling you. If she really did this shit again, I'm done with her."

"Joyce, relax." He counted a few seconds until he spoke again to make sure Joyce ended her rant. "Take a deep breath. I'll see her today and call you later."

"Thanks, Sam."

Sam entered the church through the main doors and made his way through the gallery into the administrative offices.

"Camille Paradisi, please," Sam said to the receptionist, an elderly woman sporting a beehive hairdo.

Before the woman could respond, Camille appeared from behind him and extended a hand.

"Sam, thank you so much for coming."

Today, she was dressed like a stylish corporate lawyer. A button-up, loose-fitting skirt suit showed off her legs but made no effort to draw attention to her waist or torso. For the first time, Sam noticed an ever-so-slight accent. From where? *Don't forget she's a nun.* He shook her hand. "No problem. Intrigued."

Indeed, he was intrigued. He had no legitimate reason to meet with this woman, especially since he was supposed to be at the office helping Amelia prepare for her closing argument for Scarfrowe. Camille turned sharply on her heels, and he followed her down a corridor to her private office.

It was decorated simply: a framed undergraduate degree from American University; a framed commendation from a local hospice; a bold, metal crucifix hanging dead center behind her desk. No photos. A clean desk. Plain. A servant's office. Sam pointed at the diploma.

"My mother went there."

"So we have something in common."

He waited for his client to describe the legal problem. The first explanation often conveyed more than they knew.

"I'm not the potential client," Camille said.

"So what's going on, Sister Camille?"

"Just call me Camille." Her eyes narrowed with intelligent scrutiny. Almost like an old police detective who has been calculating angles for so long he forgot how *not* to do it. But Camille's quizzical look was a softer query, unassuming and comfortably nonthreatening.

"It's Father Andrada. He has a legal problem."

As Sam considered this, Camille's eyes flickered away from his. He cleared his throat.

"I remember him. From when I was a kid."

"He left Holy Angels in 1987. Served at two other churches since then, including one in Mexico City, and then returned here to become pastor again only three years ago. I've been with him, well, most of the way. He's been a real mentor to me, both at school and in my career. So much so that I followed him to Mexico and then back here."

Sam's memory of Andrada was of an athletic guy who joked around with his mother. He had lacked the intimidation factor that seemed the norm for priests when Sam was growing up. The memory, though, likely came not from himself but from stories relayed to him by his mother—especially if Andrada had left Holy Angels when Sam was seven.

"Should I be speaking with him directly? And . . . privately?"

"Not quite yet."

"So where do we go from here?" He wasn't sure Sister Camille understood the whole lawyering thing . . . or maybe she did.

"Sam, I know you aren't particularly religious, but I also know you understand the faith. The rules. The oddities, even. How about I present you with a hypothetical question, and you present me with a real answer? A legal answer."

"Go for it." Sam crossed his legs and put on his courtroom face. He had been told the face was angry. To him it always just felt alert and smart.

"I've been here just two years, the first nun assigned to this parish in decades."

Sam raised an eyebrow. "I don't recall any nuns here when I was a kid. Frankly, I've never met a nun under seventy."

Camille smirked, but in the way of one sharing a joke.

"Nuns aren't normally assigned as full-time employees to a parish. Father Andrada kind of worked out a special situation for me here so we could keep working together. The younger priests, well, you know, I hate to say it, but they're usually a bit odd. Strange birds in one way or another. In Father Andrada's day, in the Hispanic culture especially, things were different. Priests were regarded with more respect, more reverence. And, believe it or not, they were considered manlier. Father Andrada is old—old school. As a kid you most likely couldn't have really gotten to know him, but maybe you've met a Jesuit priest? They think of their mission as a call to war. Soldiers. They're willing to die to make the world a better place. These younger guys, most of them just don't get it. They don't understand that authority-pleasing priests have been a moral stain on the faith for the past two centuries. But Father Andrada and I have always understood each other. In any event, Father speaks fondly of your mother. He's heard of you as a lawyer and said that any son of Marcela Young just might be the right fit for this—to say the least—unique set of circumstances. From what he has said about her, I agree."

Sam had endured many, many lead-up speeches from clients. Often, they were boring precursors to a wishy-washy acknowledgment of the real problem. Sam preferred the clients who just blurted it out all at once. *"I sell coke." "I shot the dude."*

"I'm guilty." "Can you get me off?" He had learned to perceive the look in a person's eyes, the body language, and the subtle intensity that comes from a person right before he coughs up a disturbing truth. *Here comes the kicker*, it seemed to say. Sam waited for it.

Camille's voice carved and polished her words in a way that created a sweet melody. It made you want to listen intently, so as not to miss a single note.

"So you see, this is the type of man who believes that breaking a clear-cut rule of the faith is unforgivably weak. He may do it, but not, as you would say, with premeditation and deliberation. His sins are accidents. And while all of us here live in an ivory tower of sorts, when reality steps in, the strong of heart must meet the challenge. Of course, that challenge most commonly occurs when a rule of the faith conflicts with moral duty. Or, as in this case, a legal one."

"Fair enough."

"What if Father Andrada has been hearing a man in confession, and the man has made certain admissions to him? Admissions of horrible, repetitive sins?"

"May I interrupt?" Sam asked. Camille raised her eyebrows and nodded. "I see where this is headed. Virginia law recognizes a limited clergy-penitent privilege, enforceable by either party. In other words, Father Andrada is not legally obligated to disclose things learned during confession, and his penitent holds the right to prevent him from testifying about such private communications. There are exceptions, just like with the attorney-client privilege. For example, a lawyer or a priest must disclose information about a *future* violent crime, as opposed to a past one."

"So I have a question for you," Camille said. "You're saying that a priest is under no legal obligation to disclose information about a penitent's past crimes, no matter how heinous?"

"Right. But plans to commit a crime in the future can be different. I'd have to hear the details. It's sort of a case-by-case analysis with these privileges."

"Here we have a penitent who swears it will never happen again."

"I wouldn't worry about it anymore, except to say one thing. If it came out that Father Andrada told *you* about the man's confession, then that could be enough to pierce the privilege. In fact, he's already broken his vow, hasn't he?"

Camille did not respond. She stood, folded her arms, and walked to the window behind her desk. She then turned and faced Sam.

Here comes the kicker.

"The man seeing Father Andrada claims to be the Rosslyn Ripper. He confessed, was forgiven by Father Andrada, and swore it would never happen again."

Intense, to be sure, but the high-profile nature of the crimes did not change Andrada's obligations under the law. Besides, lots of people falsely claimed responsibility for notorious crimes.

"The murderer first confessed to Father Andrada six weeks ago. That was after the second killing. He has since confessed to killing Joni West *after* his initial disclosure to Father Andrada. Andrada truly believed the man would stop."

Camille turned sideways. Again, her posture was perfect, spine straight yet relaxed. She approached the desk and leaned on it with both hands, her face now much closer to Sam, her eyes directly on his.

"I don't care about protecting the murderer. My problem is that Father Andrada is considering turning himself in—as an accessory. What I need to know from you is what will happen if he goes to the police now." She paused and stood up straight before speaking again. "And perhaps more to the point, whether we can figure out a way to stop this killer without harming Father Andrada."

"Whoa." Sam leaned back in his chair. "I'm a lawyer, sister. A defense lawyer. You sure you don't want a private investigator? Or why not go to the cops?"

"Because they'd come down on Father Andrada the second I told them what I know. *He* is still the only one who knows the identity of the murderer. Or at least . . . ," she hesitated for a moment, "the only one who's seen the guy. And there's something else."

Sam sat quietly.

"We have also received a journal."

"From the killer?"

"Not sure. But one section of it arrived at the church,

addressed to no one in particular, no return address, postmarked from DC, the day after the second murder, and then another the day after the third. It's something of a rambling narrative. It appears to be selective chunks of some kind of a personal journal. I have no idea what it's about, but the timing and the sheer oddness of the narrative itself makes me think it could be related. Like a clue or something."

"A clue to what?"

"If it's written by the killer, maybe there's something in it that could, well—"

"Identify the killer," Sam said. "Get him caught and save Andrada from ever having to admit that he knew about the killer and did nothing." *And save yourself in the meantime.*

Camille looked away.

"I get it," Sam said. "If the murderer is caught, legal problem solved. We could drop the journal on the police anonymously. On a case this big, they'll run the guy down. That's what most lawyers would probably say to do."

"That won't work. The journal says nothing about the murders. Its storyline begins decades ago. I can't tell you if it has anything to do with the Rosslyn Ripper. People send all sorts of things to churches, actually. Confessions, threats, religious diatribes. You name it. I just think you should see it."

"Let me talk to Andrada and check out the journal. See what I can make of it."

Camille hesitated for some time before her eyes met Sam's again.

"Okay. But we have to do something soon. You've told me what some lawyers would do. I also know what most priests would do. Break the privilege. But Father Andrada is not most priests, and I don't think you're most lawyers. We need to do something, as they say, outside the box."

"How in the world would you know what kind of lawyer I am? I haven't been in contact with Andrada, or this church, for years."

"I've looked into you. We minister to Catholics in the jail. We know people. We hear things. I know you know how to look at things, I guess you could say, in a complicated way. The right way, as far as I'm concerned. I don't need a black-and-white thinker snooping around this situation. And I know you do every kind of case, no matter what it entails. And, like I said, Father Andrada thought your mother was a very special woman."

"That's not exactly accurate, that I do every kind of case. I don't do death-penalty cases."

Camille walked around her desk.

"Father's not looking at the death penalty, is he?"

"No."

"Then follow me."

CHAPTER 3

SAM FOLLOWED CAMILLE DOWN the cool, dimly lit hallway, noting the religious art on the walls. Religion aside, churches were simply a good place to relax. Camille turned right, and they passed what Sam knew to be the offices of the various parish priests, with Father Andrada's office at the far end of the hall. Camille knocked softly, opening the door as she did.

"Father?" she said softly into the room.

"Come on in." The voice from Sam's memory was a deep and scratchy baritone, the kind of voice that proved its words heavy with meaning—one that sounded awkward, even silly, when discussing mundane matters. It was like that of the guy who narrates the trailers for ninety percent of Hollywood's dramatic movies. Camille swung the door wide open and stood aside.

Andrada wore his non-liturgical clerical garb, all black with a white collar. Sam and Camille sat in the two wooden chairs in front of his desk. Father Andrada extended his hand. Sam tried to place his age. He had a full head of thick, gray hair, but his tight grip and vigorous manner bespoke a tough man of robust health. Sam glanced quickly behind Andrada at the office décor.

A small, framed, signed, black-and-white photo of Mohammed Ali knocking out Sonny Liston hung among Andrada's various degrees and awards. Sam remembered something about him then. Andrada had been a boxer. He had discussed it with his mother, finding it funny that a priest would get into a ring and try to knock people out. As Sam met Andrada's eyes, he remembered something else about the man. Something he had never noticed as a kid but had seen when he was eighteen, when Andrada spoke to him after his mother's memorial service. The guy had different colored eyes. One brown, one green.

"Sam, I remember you well as a boy and a young man. I've always been sorry we didn't keep in touch. Marcela was a real great lady. And I mean the real deal. She helped us with everything from accounting to development of the Spanish language liturgy that was way ahead of its time. But I guess you know all that."

"I know she cared a lot about you, too. Anyway, maybe I can be of help to you now. I hear there may be a problem?" Sam felt awkward around the priest, like speaking to him might dig up an old annoyance or worry, like an old high school friend with whom one no longer had anything in common. Or, maybe, like a reminder of something one would rather forget. Maybe religion just annoyed him.

"Has Camille explained the situation?" Andrada said.

"She has, but I need to get a lot more detail and do a little research before we really get into it. Before you talk to me about the case, I think we should be clear on the rules so you don't accidentally put me in the same dilemma you're currently facing. To put it bluntly, my first concern is that if you tell me about this murderer, you may have destroyed your own privilege to not have to reveal it in court. Secondly, *I* could incur an obligation to come forward."

Camille stood. "And Father Andrada has confessions and meetings all afternoon." Andrada nodded, but it was not at all clear to Sam that he knew he had confessions and meetings all afternoon. "May I suggest we talk early tomorrow?"

Sam stood as well. "Sounds good." Though it didn't sound good, or at least normal, if Andrada was really the client. "Good afternoon, Father." They turned to leave.

"Sam," Andrada said, "I hope we can move through this quickly."

"Of course, sir."

Camille walked Sam out without speaking. His car looked far away and alone on the old gravel in the back of the lot. The air had become still and light, with the thorough lack of pressure that precedes a thunderstorm. *Strange.* He hadn't even noticed parking so far away while all the closer spots were open. Sam noticed that Camille carried a thin manila envelope at her side.

"I have to ask," Camille said. "What do you do when a client tells you a story you don't believe? Do you go with it or not?"

Sam continued walking without answering. He had always been good at reading people. He could already tell a few things about Sister Camille Paradisi. She played mental games like he did; she wanted him to wonder what was going on, to know she was holding back on him.

"Believe it or not," he said, "it doesn't matter what I believe. It's all just narratives. The point isn't whether *I* believe the narrative. It's whether the narrative is believable. Whether it fits into a theory of the case that works."

Camille ran a finger along the haunch of Sam's car.

"Nice ride."

"Don't get the wrong idea. I'm as poor as anyone working for the public good. That car came to me for free."

The 2013 Cadillac Escalade had come to him from Barnabus Farley, a former client—or rather, a permanent one.

"So public defenders can accept expensive gifts? Fancy cars? So much for God's work."

"Gifts, no."

Sam dug for his keys. Camille stood in front of him with her feet crossed like a loafing teenager and her hand on a cocked hip. She let the silence sit in a way that made him feel the need to speak. Camille didn't play by normal social rules. She looked at people a moment too long and didn't fill silences with idle chatter.

"I bet my client we'd win his case. He bet we'd lose. So the car isn't a fee or a gift at all. It's gambling. I've always been great at it."

"I read that on the Internet. Made it to round three of the World Series of Poker. Impressive. What would you have owed if you'd lost the bet?"

Sam looked down for a moment before smiling at Camille. He pulled out a cigarette from his pocket and lit it.

"How old is Father Andrada now?"

"Sixty-eight, but tough as a Spanish stallion. It's not his physical health I'm worried about." Camille moved closer to Sam, closer than the normal American-speaking distance. Sam let the silence hang.

"I worry about his state of mind," she said. "You'd never guess it, but he gets very, very upset and angry sometimes. And he drinks. A few weeks ago he punched a hole in the office wall and couldn't—or wouldn't—explain why. I hung the Ali-Liston photo to cover the hole, kind of making light of it for him. But still, I'm worried. It's like somehow, even after a whole life of service, he feels some sense of deep guilt, like maybe he wants to punish himself or something. You know, like by turning himself in for not reporting the Rosslyn Ripper."

Camille took a step closer to Sam, into his personal space, like Eastern European clients did when they wanted to tell you something important. Usually he stepped away. This time he did not.

She placed the envelope in Sam's hand.

"The journal for your review. Check it over, see what you can figure out."

"This is an original?"

"It is. I kept a copy. But remember, Sam, this may have nothing whatsoever to do with the Ripper, or anything else. It could just be somebody's life story. A parishioner, a nutcase? Who knows. They're in plastic, each section, to avoid contamination. Let's talk tomorrow, and we can also deal with the matter of your fee."

"I get it about the journal. It may be nothing. I'll check it out. We can take it a little slow on the fee for now. I like to have a longer conversation with the client first, to make sure he knows how it works. The process, the decisions. Stuff like that."

"What do you want to discuss?"

"I mean with the client. Andrada."

Camille's eyes narrowed. She gazed across the parking lot, sort of in the direction of the church, but beyond it, as if she were looking for inspiration from the landscaped suburban neighborhood surrounding the Holy Angels grounds.

"For now, you can think of me as the client. I want to help Father Andrada. He doesn't deserve this mess."

"Well, Camille, that's not how it usually works."

Camille stood in silence, her hand on her chin, watching Sam.

"Look," he said, "there's no court case involving Andrada right now. Hopefully, there never will be. Let's think of it as a consultation for now. Between us. Frankly, the chances of Andrada being exposed are pretty slim, even if we do nothing. They'll catch the guy, and even if he rats out Andrada for knowing, that'll never be convincing enough to go anywhere."

"Why are you so sure they'll catch the guy?"

"Believe me, they will. The crime scenes are too messy. The press is too hot. Somebody will probably stumble across something and turn him in. This is Bennet County. They're good. Murders don't go unsolved. What's more, all the victims were killed on federal property, so it may be a federal case once it goes to court. That means the perpetrator is screwed, blued, and tattooed. It means he'll never be able to beat the case. Seriously, Camille, you should consider not even hiring me."

Camille frowned. "And you should be able to see I have a dual motive in hiring you. I want the guy caught *sooner*. Before he strikes again. At the end of the day, I want to protect these women. It's something I feel I must do, without harming Father Andrada, of course. And I'd be interested in your view on the journal, even if it has nothing to do with our problem."

"Why?"

Camille shrugged. "I don't know. Maybe I'm just bored."

Sam pulled his keys out of his pocket.

"One thing you should know about the payment," he said. "I'm a public defender. I only represent clients appointed by the court. Some people, let's say, maybe even some people who matter, think I don't accept money from outside clients. You understand that part, right?"

"But you represent drug dealers who gamble with sixty-thousand-dollar cars? Fascinating. I'm learning so much already," she said teasingly. Sam met her eyes and moved ever so slightly closer to her. He was not sure why, only that something about the woman pulled him closer, as if she were surrounded by a comfortable energy field he wanted to be in.

The pre-storm wind had begun, and the first light drops began to strafe the gravel and ping off Sam's car. Sam did not move to open his car door, instead inviting the first warm raindrops to splash onto his face and arms.

Camille shifted her weight, her high heels digging into the gravelly parking lot, partially turning away from him to head back towards the church.

"I'll bet you sixty thousand dollars you can't stop the serial killer before he strikes again," she called out to him. Her voice cracked, a bit like a child's, mixing with the growing wind.

Sam lifted his chin towards Camille before she fully turned away, indicating he had one more thing to say. She stopped, face turned back towards him, serious now.

"My mother died sixteen years ago, Camille. If you've only been at this parish two years, how'd you know her?"

Camille nodded as he finished speaking. "You ask good questions." Sam watched her until she disappeared inside, her gait relaxed and confident as she crossed out of the gravel and closed the distance over the new pavement. He stood alone until his vibrating phone reminded him it was time to drive away. Sam spun his car onto Annandale Road towards the highway.

"This is Young."

"We've got court Thursday," Amelia said. "My biggest closing argument ever, dude. You do remember that, don't you? 'I was just going after the purse' and all that shit. Where the fuck have you been?"

"Busy." Then he said, "Sorry. I'm on the way. Relax, Amelia. You'll do great. Besides, what do you need me for? You've been ready for this for months."

"It's not that. Broadas called. He has a final rebuttal witness. From the Forensic Science Department. DNA. Claims they just got a result from the swab of Scarfrowe's hand. Says it proves Scarfrowe touched vaginal fluid."

"Bullshit. Not this late. DNA evidence mid-trial? Never. That won't fly."

"Call Broadas. Now. I'm freaking out."

"On it." Sam pulled onto the Rosslyn exit, just minutes from the office. "I gotta run over to the jail first. Then I'll call Broadas. Sherita Owings got arrested last night. You know how she is."

"Yeah, I do," Amelia said blandly. Sam could feel her emotions through the phone. She wanted him at the office. But she was a true-believer public defender and wasn't going to question a jail visit to a poor crackhead.

"Oh, and no big deal," she said, "but the *Post* called. They want to talk to you about the case."

"The *Washington Post* called about Scarfrowe? Talk about a slow news day. Which reporter?"

"Lexi Shapiro. Said she wants a quote from you on whether you think the jury'll find him guilty of the attempted rape or the attempted purse snatching. I thought it was a stupid question. She doesn't even have the names of the charges right."

"You're missing the point. Reporters always get the legal shit a little bit wrong. Think big picture. You'll do the quote. Shapiro is very smart and aggressive, but she's also pretty honest. You have to *make* her promise to quote you exactly. Word for word. Call her back right away, and get a pen. Tell her this, exactly this."

Sam waited as Amelia shuffled around, presumably searching for a pen and paper.

"Go."

"Unfortunately, it doesn't matter much which crime the jury convicts him of. Both are serious felonies, and if he gets convicted of either charge, he is going away for a long, long time. Read it back."

Amelia read it back with an edge of annoyance in her voice.

"Sam, that's the dumbest quote ever. We're hardly even asking the jury to find him not guilty of either charge. I'll sound like an idiot."

"You know when you won't *look* like an idiot, Amelia? When we win. And say *long, long time*, not just *long time*. And be sure to make Shapiro read it back to you."

Amelia hesitated, and even through the phone Sam could feel her mood shift as she got it.

"Okay, boss."

"One more thing. Who's the DNA scientist?"

Amelia shuffled more papers. "J. Kim."

"Okay, I've got this. Relax."

"Thanks, Sam." Sam could already feel the release of tension in her voice. "By the way, what was up with that chick last night?

She practically gave me a therapeutic shoulder massage last night. That was weird."

Sam paused. "It's about to get weirder."

He hung up, swung his car into the closest space to the Bennet County jail, ignored the parking meter, and walked quickly up the stairs. After a brief credential check and cursory pat down, he found himself in the attorney-client visiting room, facing a crying, three-hundred-pound African-American woman in a tight jumpsuit.

"Sherita," he said, "please relax."

"I can't, Sam. I can't. I'm losing my shit. Seriously."

"I know, I know. I'll get you out of here before anything happens with Tamela."

"You sure? If I don't get out, my apartment's fuckin' history. I'll be kicked out of public housing. I'll get fired. They'll take Tamela away again. Oh God, my mother will send her to DSS if I'm gone more than a coupla days. It'll be over, Sam. My recovery, everything. I'll . . . I'll . . . I don't know what I'll do."

"Stop right there, Sherita," Sam said softly.

He reached across the table and grabbed one of her huge hands with both of his. Sherita was a regular client. Always crack. She had been recovering successfully since her last drug program, so he was surprised to hear she had been arrested the day before. Dealing this time, not just possession.

"Whatever happens, you'll get through it. I'll help you."

"I'm going to fucking prison. I sold to a cop. You know what the crazy part is? I hadn't even used yet. I scored three rocks, was walking home, and this dirty-looking fool walks up and offers me triple the price for one rock. Must have watched me score. And you don't know the half of it."

"Triple the going rate? You know better than that."

"I know, I know!" She sobbed into her hands.

"What's the other half of it?"

"I'm fuckin' pregnant. I was about to smoke crack even knowing I was pregnant! I'm a seriously fucked-up person. I was thinking about killing myself this morning."

Sam glanced down at her immense waist and torso. They blended into one colossal bulge, only a third of which could hide behind the bolted-down metal table. Some women showed sooner than others. With Sherita, visual observation could never prove it.

"You sure? How many months?"

She shrugged. "Maybe four, five?"

"But you still haven't used. You're still in successful recovery. This cop saved you from relapsing by busting you."

"I guess so," Sherita moaned. "Who gives a fuck, Sam? I sold him a rock! I'm a goddamn dealer now. And a terrible mother. Oh dear God."

"No, Sherita. You're not. These kinds of things happen. You have a disease—you're an addict. And you shouldn't even *be* in general population when you're pregnant. Maybe not even in jail. I can work this."

Sam already felt the beginning of a plan. He knew exactly which prosecutor he needed for this one.

Sam stood. "I gotta finish a trial Thursday. I'll get you out the next day, at the nine-thirty arraignments. I'm having you drug tested first, a piss test through pretrial services. When they come in, don't refuse."

"Why? I thought it was better to be a user. That's why I sold, right? That's the game."

"Let me worry about that. And Sherita?" She looked up at him with red, teary eyes. "Has it ever occurred to you that God put that cop in your path last night? To stop you from using? To save your recovery? To save your baby? Working in mysterious ways, you know?"

She finally smiled, a sassy grin that popped out every now and again.

"I'll buy that shit when the motherfucker gets me up outta here."

Sam took one of her huge hands again. "You're not gonna kill yourself, Sherita."

"I know. I got a baby comin'."

"That's not why."

Sam bounded down the stairs. It didn't matter whether he or Sherita believed God had turned her into a drug dealer to save her baby. The important part was that Assistant Commonwealth Attorney Sally Ann Richards, an annoyingly outspoken born-again Christian, might believe it. Sally Ann loved to crush the bad guys; she even used the phrase "eye for an eye" in court. But she would love this divine intervention—God working through a vice cop. She thought the world worked that way, angels saving the sinners.

Sam jumped into his car, pulled out of the jail lot, and headed for the office. He speed dialed a number in his phone. Dr. J.

"What?" an agitated voice said.

"Hey there."

"What the fuck, Sam?"

"You sound happy to hear from me."

"Hah! Happy to be coming to court tomorrow on this bullshit Scarfrowe case? Hasn't anyone noticed there's a serial killer out there? I've been working all week on the Ripper case, and they want me to sit around at court all day tomorrow?"

"I hear you," Sam said. "My sentiments exactly. What's the result on Scarfrowe? I may be able to get you out of this."

"Partial profile. A mixture. Perfect match at both genetic markers on ten loci. Major dropout on the rest."

"A mixture?"

"More than one person's DNA on the swab from your guy's hand. Probably from the last woman he groped. So what? He's going down anyway, right?"

"No comment. Listen, call Assistant Commonwealth Attorney Broadas and make sure he knows that you can't testify that the DNA came from vaginal fluid. It could just as well be sweat, skin cells, snot, saliva, whatever. Tell him the mixture's weak, there's lots of dropout, and you'll have to admit the DNA could have come from Scarfrowe grabbing at the purse. Tell him that if the DNA mixture from the hand swab were vaginal fluid, you'd expect to see a stronger result."

"Hmmmmm." Dr. J's signature response when suspecting someone may be up to something dodgy.

"The prosecutor deserves the truth, both the good and the bad. I know he wants you to say it's vaginal fluid, but you can't scientifically say that, can you?" Sam already knew the answer to that. The lab simply did not conduct tests that could really distinguish one bodily fluid, besides blood or semen, from another.

"No."

"I'll call him five minutes after you do. I'll get you out of it. But you have to call him now."

"Hmmm."

"Can I meet you later this week?" Sam said. "Pick your brain about a case? Drinks on me."

"Friday?"

"Tomorrow."

"Get me out of court, and you're on."

Sam parked in the office lot and lit a cigarette. He needed to kill five minutes so Dr. J. could talk to Broadas before he did. Broadas would exaggerate the DNA evidence to Sam, overstate the value of the evidence, either because he did not understand DNA or because he understood it a little but was accustomed to the state lab scientists saying pretty much whatever prosecutors wanted them to say. Once Sam called Broadas out on his overstatement, Broadas would agree not to use the last-minute DNA evidence. He would want to save face. Shit, Broadas thought he was going to win the case anyway. *Too late, not fair to the defense.* How terribly wise and fair Broadas would be. Statesmanlike. Sam could even hear him saying the words.

Sam felt the brown envelope in his pocket. He pulled it out and carefully removed the sheaf of papers. There were several sections, each sheathed in clear plastic. As he often did with documents prepared by a client, a witness, or an unknown person, he spent a moment looking at the document itself. White, lined paper, well-preserved but crinkled with age, and tight, rather precise, cursive script. First sentence of the paragraph indented. Neat margins. One side only. Each line written to a uniform width. Written in pencil, oddly enough. Numbered pages. No scratch outs, at least not in the first few pages. Pages were neither clipped nor stapled yet neat and square, as if the author had written them on a pad and torn all the pages out later.

Sam returned the stack to the envelope without reading a word, picked up his phone, and dialed.

"Broadas here." The prosecutor spoke in a clipped, manic chirp. Everything was an emergency to him.

"DNA? The last day of trial. You're kidding, right?"

"We've got your man, Sam. Vaginal fluid all over his hand.

We've got him nailed. *Purse* my ass. You should plead this guy out tomorrow. I'll give you twenty-five years if you take it now."

Sam flicked his cigarette butt out the car window, watching it arc like a tracer in the soft dusk. He took a deep breath, then lowered his rear view mirror and examined his face. His eyes always felt wrinkled late in the day, when the workday was winding down. He stared at himself for a long moment. At his eyes. One brown. One green. Strange days, indeed.

CHAPTER 4

FEET UP ON HIS living room coffee table, Sam held a cool glass of ice water to his forehead and began to read. Each entry was dated.

FEBRUARY 10, 1957

I begin this manuscript as a brief record of important events on our journey, even as I realize my life could easily end on any given day. True for all of us, but somehow a truth that looms large over me. If I am killed along my path, I suppose it is possible that someone will read this and see it as a historical record of my efforts to understand. I may read this journal years from now and experience it as no more than silliness—of a time when everyone thinks themselves unique, only to realize later that each of us represents only more of the same.

I was born in June 1942 in Bariloche, Argentina. I think my last name comes from my mother's choice and really has nothing to do with my nationality. My Argentine countrymen are so very taken with their fancy European heritage. But despite my name, I am no white Italian or blended Spaniard. My mother told me we are part of those special people without a home: the fortunetelling, trick-turning, dice-loading carnies she called *Roma* and Westerners call Gypsies. We were magical, she said. I can remember sitting on the rim of the sink in our kitchen, my mother holding me close from behind as we looked out the window together at the night sky and the dark mountains. "Shoot for the sky," she said. "If you miss, at least you'll land on the mountaintop." She would squeeze me, and I would laugh.

I knew early on that our mother was different. She had grown up in the city, in a family of immigrants who worked on a wealthy Italian family's estate outside Buenos Aires. It was only from a series of poor decisions that she wound up a peasant in Bariloche. Her words: "A series of poor decisions." I never knew the exact nature of these decisions, but I did notice while very young that others in the slum mockingly called her Virgin Maria. Later, I learned that she indeed had confided to an older woman in the neighborhood that she had never been with a man before arriving in Bariloche—a fact belied by the existence of my older sister, Trinity, and myself.

My mother made us learn English and speak it in our home. We read magazines and American books she had from childhood. It was fun, reading fancy old magazines. "Don't mutter this local trash," she said, speaking of the Indio-Spanish spoken in Bariloche. She made her mouth like mush when she imitated the neighbors' children speaking. What I remember most is that she always told me I was going to America. That I would need to get out of Bariloche before it was too late. I've always had it in my head that America is the mountaintop.

In some of my earliest memories, my mother walked with me along the dirt roads that crisscrossed amongst the Bariloche shacks. If time permitted, on an afternoon before Miguel returned home, we held hands at the base of the mountain, which sprang towards the sky just outside our barrio. "Slow time," she would say. "Observe." That was how she put it. At first I just stood still, pretending the heavens were filling my brain with the secret knowledge she seemed to possess about our surroundings. But soon I learned it was true, and that whether she directed my attention towards a tree, a rock, a dog, or, eventually, our neighbors, she was right. I could see the meanings and histories behind people and things.

"It is so strong in you, maybe even stronger than in Trinity!" she said. "You must be careful to show no one your gift. People will be afraid of you, maybe even hate you, maybe even kill you, if they know. It's hard enough to see things you don't want to see. Mostly you should keep them to yourself. But someday, maybe you will show the world. Maybe you will scream it from the mountaintop. But not until the opportune time."

The opportune time. My mother used that phrase only once, but it has always remained in my mind. It makes me feel both hopeful and sad. She thought her opportune time would never come, yet believed mine would.

"You can endure anything, you're so strong inside. Like Job from the Great One's Bible," my mother said to me one day while we pushed a wheelbarrow of water jugs across Bariloche towards our home, each holding one handle and grunting and laughing along the way. Mischievous, she was, borrowing water from behind the café downtown. "We'll return the wheelbarrow, of course we will. We're no thieves." She smiled at me, sweat running down her brow but doing nothing to dampen her beauty. My mother often referred to God as the Great One, and the Bible as his.

"Who's Job?" I said, wanting, of course, to be as strong inside as this Job but needing a point of comparison.

"The Great One's servant who was betrayed by him. Despite Job's faith the Great One ruined his life, and Job fought back. He challenged the Great One. Sued him to expose his injustice."

"You mean like in court?"

"Sort of like that."

"Did he win?"

"Of course not."

"Did you just say the Great One was unjust?"

My mother sighed and put down her side of the wheelbarrow. She was no longer smiling or laughing and clearly meant to end our discussion about Job.

"This is the sort of thing you must learn on your own, strong one."

My sister. One of my saddest memories is when Trinity ran away from home. Or so Miguel said one evening while my mother sat stone still, eating soup and staring blankly away towards the open window of our shack. Trinity was five years older than me, and while my mother and her magic lessons were my truest companions, Trinity would dance and sing and make me laugh when she returned from school each afternoon. She taught me to toy with Miguel by moving his stacks of coins, wine bottles, and other trinkets from one place to another so we could laugh inside while he searched, scratching his head in bafflement at why he could not remember where he put his grubby junk. Trinity also ran with a pack of older children from the barrio, earning my mother's scolding late at night. Maybe they never knew I heard all of it from my bed.

"She ran off, and I doubt she's coming back," Miguel said. And that was the end of it. My mother just kept staring out the window, one arm hugging her bulging stomach.

Our little barrio outside Bariloche was all we knew. It was a very poor place, with open sewers and a wooden statue of Jesus on the cross—a place where ten year olds just ran away and stupid drunks could capture magicians. The same year my sister ran away, my mother died during the birth of my younger brother, Paul. I was five. While I had never known a father, Miguel—perhaps Paul's father—inherited both of us the day she died. I was nervously throwing rocks towards the road when the midwife ran, crying, out of our shack. I remember staring at my mother's body. It was covered by a sheet on the bed. Miguel, on his knees by the bed, held Paul in one arm. When he saw me in the doorway, he turned towards me.

"It's just us now," he said. I spit on the floor, right in view of my mother's body. That was how my adult life started. Spitting towards Miguel in a dirt-floored shack, looking at my mother's dead body, and hearing my little brother's first cries.

I realized from a very young age I was different. At first I noticed the peculiarities in my memory. I simply lacked the ability to forget things—big or small. Once I began to socialize with people my age, it became even more obvious. But I soon knew it was much more than just a good memory. People use the term "mindreading" to denote listening to the precise thoughts of another—as if thoughts come through as crisp sentences. Of course, no one actually thinks this way, at least no one in

Bariloche. Thoughts are a muddled morass. I would thus not call my gift mindreading, but rather an ability (a curse?) that allows me to see the framework, for lack of a better word, through which a person operates. What a person will or will not do flows from this framework, more like a math equation than anyone would believe.

This week, I turned fifteen. Miguel promised me a gift, which he claimed would arrive on Saturday. I couldn't really imagine what sort of gift he meant, but I was still curious, and indeed, even mildly excited about it. Saturday came, and as the day wore on, Miguel declined to mention the gift. Before beginning Miguel's dinner, I went out to look for him. We had a small shed behind our shack for storing tools, no bigger than a large outhouse, really. Miguel told me he always kept it locked and ordered me never to approach it. This time I did and opened the unlocked door. A gruesome odor emerged, much like the smell of a dead dog's pen. Miguel was kneeling down in front of a young boy who was strapped to the wall, masked, and softly moaning. I knew what Miguel was up to (did I ever!). I turned and calmly walked away. That night, Miguel spoke to me about the matter as if it were as trifling as my having forgotten his dinner. He warned me to say nothing to anyone about the ghoul out in the shed. In Spanish it sounds much more elegant—*demonico* was the word he used.

Miguel's ghoul didn't horrify me. That he would kidnap, sexually abuse, and eventually kill innocent young boys was so utterly predictable that it barely caused a ripple in my psyche, and this scares me. I also understand and empathize with the ghoul's suffering, but I can't cry for him. His suffering was just a fraction of the nearly bottomless amount of human misery that took place during that week. Very, very nearly irrelevant to anyone except the ghoul—who himself surely found others' suffering fundamentally meaningless. I am worried I am a monster too, like Miguel.

That night, I pushed a knife into Miguel's heart while he slept. His eyes opened, and he fully comprehended my act several seconds before his light went out. Though his fists and fingers had dealt liberally with me for years, he declined to resist as the sharp blade eased between his ribs. I wondered if his eyes would say sorry before going dead, but instead, they said *thank you*. As always, it was all about him.

I hiked with ten-year-old Paul out of town, front pocket bulging with the three thousand pesos Miguel had somehow managed to hoard. We trudged down a long dirt road towards the mountains. I wanted to get high enough to see the glistening lakes on both sides of the divide. As we sat quietly, taking in the grandeur of those views, I realized that I hadn't killed Miguel because of what he did to that boy or because of what he regularly did to Paul and me or even because I had always doubted that Trinity had really run away. The event had simply been coming for a while, for a thousand reasons, and we both knew it.

We made our way across Argentina towards Buenos Aires on a motorcycle I stole from a roadside vegetable stand. Paul laughed as we sped away, the motorcycle's owner yelling after us hopelessly. He called us maggots, parasites.

I sit now, near Paul, in the center of a large, empty field by the dirt road. I hope no fellow travelers approach us, because I have no idea what to say or do. Sometimes I think that much of what I see is not even real, like the dirty aura darting around a lying street vendor's head or the angelic glow around Paul's when he sleeps.

My mother had come to me the day after she died. She let me touch her, caressed my head, and promised me that no matter what I felt, I was never really alone. I hate that she believed she had to go. To leave me again. But as she put it, resurrected ones should never linger for too long. "Jesus knew that, and so do I." Her promise to always be with me in my heart was not very consoling. As quickly as she had come, she was down the mountain road and out of town. Despite what my mother said, I feel so alone and scared. I wish I were an angel, like I feel my mother may have been. But I worry that I am just crazy. Or even a demon.

Maybe those like my mother or me are always born to a chosen or forgotten people.

CHAPTER 5

"WE, THE JURY, IN the case of the Commonwealth of Virginia versus Scarfrowe, find the defendant, Jonathon P. Scarfrowe, guilty of the crime of simple abduction."

The jury foreman folded the verdict form in front of him. His fierce gaze triumphantly lanced Scarfrowe. An outraged scoff burst from the victim's father, who sat in the front row behind Broadas. Her mother cried out, "No!"

Scarfrowe raised his arms in the air like goalposts. "Praise God!" He then began to dance a small, slow-motion jig.

The judge scowled and shook his head. "Cut that out, Mr. Scarfrowe."

The jurors looked confused by the various courtroom emotions. They were not permitted to know, until after the verdict, that because they had found Scarfrowe guilty of regular abduction instead of abduction with intent to sexually molest, he could now receive only five years in prison instead of a mandatory life sentence under the three-strike sex offender law. He had already served nearly a year, and with good-behavior credit, he would be out in about two and a half more. Amelia had successfully sold Scarfrowe's going-for-the-purse ploy without alerting the jury to the colossal sentencing difference that would follow if they found a reasonable doubt on the purse-versus-crotch issue. Strange days, indeed.

Sam congratulated Amelia and told her he would see her later at the bar, where she would undoubtedly go to celebrate with the younger lawyers in the office. He then leaned close to her.

"Nice job on the quote," he whispered. "The foreman read it. The prick read it. I can see it all over his face. You're the best." He could feel Amelia's heart glow with pride.

Sam phoned Dr. J. as he raced down the steps two at a time. "How early can we get together?"

"I'm meeting with FBI scientists at four; not sure how long that'll be. Really, it's a little crazy right now."

"All this time to get one result?"

"More than one result. I can't really go into it right now. The whole state is watching. Shit, Main Justice and the national media are watching. They're keeping the whole lab on this Ripper case all the time. I've got nineteen untouched, overdue files from other cases stacked in my office. Seriously."

"I hear you. I'll be at Luigi's at seven thirty. If you make it, you make it." Sam stepped out of the courthouse and lit a cigarette, listening to the silence over the phone.

"Hmmmm."

CHAPTER 6

SAM WALKED INTO HARPOON Hannah's, a cheesy, touristy bar across the street from Luigi's. Barnabus Farley already had vodka, straight, on the bar for him. They hugged. A pro-forma hug, more like a show of respect than affection.

"Samson," his client said. Somehow, Barnabus was able to not look out of place standing at a bar, holding a drink, a cigarette behind his ear, while wearing head-to-toe hospital-issued scrubs. His new day job, a nurse's assistant at Bennet County Hospital, while admirable to be sure, could not possibly pay for a quarter of his lifestyle.

"Hey, what was that thing you told me the other day about the Titans?" Barnabus referred to an old conversation they'd had about pro football. Sam knew it was just small talk, leading up to the kicker.

"I said I'd never take heavy action against an opponent of the Tennessee Titans because their team name is dumb. The Olympians overthrew the Titans—Greek mythology one-oh-one. I couldn't believe they named the team after losers."

Barnabus was about six foot five, three-hundred-and-fifty pounds. Sam had to admit he didn't look like a bookie and drug dealer. He looked like an oafish, funny, fat guy. His appearance had served him well over the years.

"Why'd you learn all that shit about the Greeks and Romans and stuff?"

"Because I hate math. But never mind that. I've got a date across the street in an hour. What's wrong? What happened?"

Barnabus smirked goofily, signifying he had done something he knew was stupid. Barnabus did not accept the proposition that being a rather big-time cocaine dealer was stupid, only that it was stupid to make little mistakes doing it, stupid to get caught.

"I've told you before, half of Bennet County drug users are snitches. You need to get a new racket, dude."

Barnabus turned his attention to the wide-screen television above the bar and clapped. "Yeah, baby!" On the screen, a Washington Nationals player rounded the bases. "You know, that's a nice TV. High-def. You like it?"

"Of course I like it, Barnabus, but you think we should talk about your problem?"

"I just won ten of 'em. And you got one comin'."

"Great." Sam meant it, but he felt awkward about Barnabus Farley funding his life with expensive gifts. But Barnabus believed, possibly accurately, that he owed his freedom to Sam. A nice little place to be. "But you really need to stop selling. It's not a viable long-term strategy."

"I know, I know. But this is something else. Look, I don't have a charge. Not yet, anyway. I rented this warehouse, you know, more like a big storage room. At one of those little places."

"Ugh, Barnabus, you can't use storage places. The owners of those things are all working with the cops."

"Okay, okay, but it wasn't drugs. Anyway, they searched my storage place, and now they want me to come in for questioning."

"About what?"

"They say they found two thousand cartons of cigarettes."

"They say?"

"They found two thousand cartons of cigarettes."

"Where'd you get them?"

"Bought 'em."

"Legally?"

"Tax stamps from Virginia and everything."

"Where?"

"A bunch of different stores—Costco, Super-Buy, those kinds of places. All fully legal, Cochise. I got receipts."

"This isn't the cops; it's the FBI, isn't it?"

Barnabus took a hasty sip of his beer, spilling some down his chin while he fished into his pocket and pulled out a rumpled business card. *Donavon Moncrieffe. Alcohol, Tobacco, and Firearms.*

"ATF, FBI, same difference. It's federal."

"Does that mean I'm fucked?" Barnabus finished his beer, bobbed his finger at the bartender for another, and winked.

"Maybe, maybe not. Theoretically, there's nothing wrong with you having cigarettes."

"I hear you. I smoke a lot, coupla packs a day. Maybe I can explain that to 'em."

"You know, the level at which you're full of shit is utterly staggering. You're not going to speak to them, Barnabus."

"If I don't speak to them, they're gonna assume I'm guilty of something, right?"

"They already know you're guilty of something. The only question is whether they can prove it. They're not going to believe any explanation, so there's no point in giving one."

Barnabus frowned. "So I'm fucked."

"You're not fucked. It depends on what other evidence they have."

"They don't have shit. It's the first time I've bought cigarettes like that."

"Ever?"

"Ever, bro. Except once before, last year, but there's no way they know about that."

Two thousand cartons. Barnabus had been fixing to make at least fifteen, maybe sixteen, dollars per carton selling the Virginia-taxed cigarettes to street salesmen in tax-heavy New York or Boston. Chinatown, most likely.

"You know what I've always wondered? How do the guys in New York get away with selling so many individual unstamped packs?"

"That's above my pay grade, Cochise. Besides, if I were to answer that question, you might think I have some knowledge of illegal activity." Barnabus winked.

"You know I'm not supposed to take cases that aren't appointed through the public defender's office. It carries a risk for me."

"That's all bullshit. You gonna help me or not?" Barnabus raised his eyebrows twice quickly, his way of humanizing himself as the endearing goofball. "And I don't forget favors. You know me, bro. I guarantee, you do this for me, one of these days I'll bring you the biggest case you've ever had."

"Barnabus, you've got to quit this shit. No more cases."

"No more cases for me. But mark my words. Hey, I know a lotta people. I'm your gift that keeps on giving, chief."

With Barnabus's generous fees and constant need of legal help, that was certainly a true statement. Ever since Barnabus had sought Sam out two years ago, Sam had earned more from doing side cases for Barnabus and his associates than his actual public defender salary. Sam put two fingers on his lips, as if pondering an important question.

"I guess now is a good time to talk about my fee."

Barnabus lifted his glass for a toast. "Fuck the fuzz."

• • •

Sam sat at a table alone, staring at the sweat on his first beer at Luigi's.

"Thanks, Crystal," he said into his phone. "Yes. Test Sherita Owings before court. Don't let her refuse. Yes, I agree to it. A full urine test."

Sam hung up and dropped his phone onto the table. He glanced towards the door. No Dr. J. He took a long swig of beer, feeling it hit his stomach and then pulsate through the rest of his body. He stared back down at his folder and pulled out his pen. Articles about the Rosslyn Ripper. As always, the police were holding back critical facts about all three crimes so as to eliminate copycat suspects and test the veracity of any informants or confessors who stepped forward. Even so, the police press office had put forward a compelling portrait of pattern killings.

Victim Number One: Mary Beth Schneider, age twenty-seven, single. No family in the area. A dental hygienist. Killed in the woods near the D-Day Memorial, about seventy-five feet from a public path down the hill from the monument itself, on May 10, 2015. Head almost completely severed by a sharp object. Face unrecognizably mauled. No forensic evidence at all—at least none that was being released.

Victim Number Two: Carol Kingsley, thirty-three, divorced. A paralegal. Body found only five hundred yards from where Schneider's had been. Also on D-Day Park property, but much further into the woods, on June 6, 2015. Face unrecognizable.

Victim Number Three: Joni West, twenty-eight, social worker, single. Killed behind the barricade separating Highway 1 from the D-Day Park on July 2, 2015. On her way home from the subway. Head found nearby in the woods. Sam envisioned the murderer hacking it off with some kind of weapon and tossing the head into the woods, maybe swinging it around by the hair first. Sam looked at Joni's picture. She was smiling broadly, her arm around an older woman in some kind of beach setting.

No wonder the investigation was being pursued by the FBI as well as state authorities. All three murders were on federal property.

Sam broke out of his trance just in time to see Dr. J. bustle past the hostess. Her thin frame and long, bouncing, black ponytail stood out in any crowd. In addition to thinking too fast, Juliana walked faster than any person Sam had ever met, her skinny legs effortlessly cranking out extremely long strides for a person who stood only five foot one. No knockout by normal standards, but beautiful nevertheless, a brainy, unpretentious, almost clueless kind of beautiful.

She gave Sam a mock frown and slumped into her chair. "Sorry. Late." She swept up the drink menu and looked around for the waitress.

"Not a problem," Sam said. "Any big news?"

"You wouldn't believe it." She ordered a wine, leaned back, and took a deep breath. "Or maybe you would."

Sam raised his eyebrows.

"You're weird like that," she said. "By the way, congratulations. I hear you got your creep off after all."

"Amelia did a great job." He took a long sip of his new drink, a vodka tonic. "So fill me in. The Ripper."

Juliana leaned forward, looking around. She whispered, not only to prevent others from hearing but also to make the point that what she was saying was, in theory, a secret.

"The FBI is involved. This is, like, *really* classified, or whatever. Seriously, the entire lab staff from Main Justice is on this."

"So that means you can't tell me until we get back to your place?"

Juliana turned away. She breathed deeply again and for a rare moment, sat perfectly still.

"A few drinks first?"

• • •

Juliana's skinny legs gripped Sam around the waist. As they became more and more frenzied, Sam sensed the onset of her signature move. Her ankles hooked together on top of his back for one final squeeze before she climaxed. She had the manoeuver down to a predictable science. It was a sexual proclivity that stuck in his mind during the days or weeks between his visits to Juliana's condo.

Sam rolled off her, his upper body and hair soaked with sweat. He reached for a glass of water on the side table but instead got the second half of his beer. He downed it, knowing he was pushing his absurd level of dehydration even higher.

Juliana climbed off the bed and sauntered into her bathroom. "You have an early day tomorrow?"

Sam laughed. "Don't worry, I'm leaving." His lungs hurt—the scratchy, chalky feeling of another day on cigarettes, coffee, and booze.

Juliana yanked the door open. "That's not what I meant!" She stood off-kilter, so unselfconscious in all her skinniness.

Sam liked it that she knew he'd gotten her. It had been exactly what she meant, her soon-to-be ex-husband, a local cop, and a jealous one, probably scoped out her apartment regularly. The last thing she needed was a hungover guy creeping out of her place in the morning, especially a local defense lawyer who knew the ex.

"Bullshit," Sam said. "But first, the Ripper. Whatcha got?"

"It's the weirdest thing." Juliana now lay on the bed, hands behind her head. She spoke into the air like a patient on a therapist's couch. "You know how the basic DNA typing works?"

"The basics, yeah. I can read the typing chart and the underlying documents. Even the, what do you call it, the allele call sheet. But I can't follow how you guys come up with the DNA profile in the first place. That's out of my league."

"Let me just explain the basics real quick. Otherwise you won't understand."

She sat up, her impending explanation yanking her back into work mode, frantic gestures and all. She loved talking about her job. When it came to the biggest case she had ever had, she would likely appreciate the listening ear of anyone she trusted. Maybe she chose to share with Sam because she and her husband had shared an interest in debriefing each other about crime fighting at the end of long workdays. Or, more likely, because they had not.

"After you extract DNA from genetic material, let's say blood, you run it through a process, either capillary electrophoresis or a computer version of that, and you multiply the genetic markers many times over. They appear sort of like peaks on a chart, with various heights depending on which marker is present at a certain location."

"I get it. The loci."

Sam realized she wasn't just talking for the bare human contact of it. She was rehearsing for meetings, and eventually for court.

"Don't interrupt." She softly slapped his thigh with both hands, but her eyes were far away, concentrating.

"Humans have exactly the same DNA at almost all genetic locations. Only in certain locations of our chromosomes does our DNA generally differ from person to person. Most of our DNA does not differentiate us from apes, or even from reptiles. And only a very small percentage of it gives us our unique characteristics. The human genome project that some of you may have heard about—"

Sam looked around. "It's just me here, Juliana."

"Shut up, please. The human genome project concerned itself with the portion of DNA that is common to all humans.

From that, they attempt to learn things about humanity in general, about our origins, our penchant for diseases, anything and everything, really.

"Forensic DNA analysis is concerned with something totally different. It focuses on that small portion of our genes in which humans generally differ. Instead of seeking commonality, it seeks to exclude. That's how we determine that a certain sample of blood could not have come from a certain person, or that it could have."

"You're doing great. Only reminding you that it's twelve thirty-seven in the morning. But please continue."

"The way it works is that in every location in our chromosomes—and there are many millions of locations— each of us has two genetic markers, called alleles: one from our mother, and one from our father. Since each parent has exactly two markers at each location, a child has a fifty percent chance to get either one. Virginia's DNA typing system, called Powerplex 16, maps the genetic markers at fifteen loci that are known to differ from human to human. If the suspect differs from the sample at even one of the loci, or at any one of the thirty genetic markers, we know the suspect could not have been the contributor of the blood sample. If, on the other hand, the suspect matches at both markers on all fifteen of the Powerplex 16 loci, the suspect cannot be excluded as a contributor."

"I have a question," Sam said.

"I know you've heard a lot of this shit before, but bear with me—"

"I know that once someone cannot be eliminated as a contributor, you guys run statistics on a database of hundreds of random DNA typing samples to extrapolate how many other people on Earth could not be eliminated. It usually comes out like one in six billion or something, thereby allowing the prosecutors to argue that their suspect must have been the guy. My question is, Dr. J. Kim, the statistics are bullshit, aren't they? I mean you can't really extrapolate all the profiles on Earth from a couple of hundred samples, can you?"

Juliana sighed. "You're dying for an answer to that, and you won't get it from me. Look, Sam, I know you probably have some client in prison whose DNA matched and you just can't believe he did it, but if he matched on all fifteen Powerplex loci, it was him, statistics aside—unless he has an identical twin brother. Anyway, back to the Ripper. Here's the deal. I had dozens of swabs from the crime scenes and for weeks got nothing. Then I asked the detective to bring me all of the crime-scene evidence, including from the autopsy. And I'm looking through these bags and boxes from Joni West's apartment, everything. And then I open the box with her clothes, and I can't believe I didn't do this before. Her bloody bra is sitting right there. I'd swabbed it for the blood, which was obviously hers, but this time I cut pieces from the straps, the non-bloodstained sections, and finally got a foreign profile. Ten alleles at six loci. Weak, but not nothing."

"What can you do with it?"

"Right now, not much. I ran it against the national database, but it's such a weak profile, it hits too many people. Most of them are in prison in other states, and the detectives looked into one or two who were out, but nothing viable. It's too weak to make a meaningful inclusion unless some other evidence links the person to the scene."

"Okay, but tell me if I have this right: those ten alleles at six loci could exclude a suspect, right?"

"In theory. But we'd have to have a suspect to compare it to or it's worth nothing. All I can say right now is that somebody other than Joni West touched that bra since it was washed. I can exclude specific people, but that's about it."

Sam stood, stepped into his pants, and began to gather his other clothes from the floor.

"Sam, can I ask you something?"

Sam looked at her.

She smirked. "I'm not ready for anything serious, don't worry, it's not that question. My question is, once we catch this guy, you're not going to represent him, are you? I mean, you could catch the case, and I'm sharing things with you about my career, and—"

Sam held up his palm. "Never." He held her eyes to accentuate the promise. "Besides, it's probably a federal case. Federal property. My office doesn't handle those cases. Unless the guy starts killing people somewhere else, the feds will get the case. So don't worry. You'll catch him soon." Sam buttoned his shirt.

"Can I ask *you* something?"

"Maybe." She leaned on her elbows on the bed, still naked and legs unselfconsciously spread.

"If I have a DNA profile I want checked against the bra snapper, will you tell me if it's a potential match or an exclusion?"

"Hmmmm. What are you on to, Sam? If you're sitting on a lead from the Ripper case, you'd better tell me and—"

"Not a lead, an unsubstantiated personal hunch. Not police worthy yet. But I'll call you about it. Will you check it?"

"You'd better. And maybe."

On his way down the stairs, a text buzzed in.

Sam, please call me. Truly an emergency. Would not bother you this late if it were not, though I rather guess you are used to being out and about at this hour. SCP.

Sam pulled onto the highway before calling Camille. His buzz had pretty much worn off, but he didn't want to be on his cell while driving in town. Sam would never break his promise to Juliana. He could never represent the serial killer, even if they caught the guy. Even if the case did not go federal, and even if the court appointed the public defender's office. What Sam could not tell Juliana, at least not yet, was that he was going to help her catch the guy.

CHAPTER 7

"I REALLY APPRECIATE IT, Sam." Camille shook Sam's hand in the foyer of the clergy's living quarters, a large, single-family home that stood far across the parking lot from the church building. Soft, low-watt lighting filled the high-ceilinged entryway, covering the furniture and paintings with a mild-fluorescent gloss. "It makes everything look holy, does it not? Even at two in the morning. This is our lobby of sorts. I'm in the carriage house around the back."

"Fancy," Sam said. The carriage-house comment made him think of a Jane Austen novel, not that he had ever actually read one.

"It's plain." She ushered him into a side room. "Vodka, right?"

Sam sat down on a long couch. The faux royal décor reminded him of something. Like a museum intending to portray Louis XVI's sitting room but with cheap furniture—red cushions, gold trim, lace, large mirrors.

She poured Sam a vodka tonic from a small rolling bar and sat next to him. Her long fingers gripped the glass near the top, the way they train waiters not to do. She leaned back on the red couch. Despite the poor light, Sam saw for the first time the very faintest hint of wrinkles at the corners of her eyes. Had he not been this close to her before? Camille's distinctively narrow face and straight posture reminded Sam of a hypnotizing and, indeed, oddly beautiful serpent—like a cobra emerging from a basket. Her hooded eyes watched him watch her.

"You don't drink?" Sam said.

"I like it well enough. My desire comes and goes. But we have a major development." She slipped off her shoes, pulled her legs up underneath herself, and repositioned her body to face Sam, arm over the back of the couch. A serpent still, coiled at the bottom now.

"Another confession?"

"Father Andrada's confessor called him. Asked if he could come to confession tomorrow morning at eight."

"You still don't know who this guy is?"

"Like you said, that would ruin Father Andrada's privilege. And Father Andrada would never put me in that position. If he even knows the man's identity."

"He's already placed you in that position, hasn't he? Dealing with me? Creating another witness?"

"That's protected by the attorney-client privilege."

"Maybe," Sam said. "But a lot of lawyers would break the privilege to stop a serial killer. The state bar would likely be rather understanding. Frankly, I could probably be disciplined at this point for *not* coming forward against you and Andrada. Every day that goes by places all three of us in a more difficult position, especially if, well, you know."

Without answering, Camille took hold of Sam's empty glass and walked to the bar. She faced away from Sam as she poured. She roughly massaged one shoulder. She flexed her back, then turned and walked slowly back to her place on the couch. Sam had been attracted to plenty of clients before. He always felt it was okay—thinking, but not acting.

Camille met Sam's eyes, having caught him, he supposed, watching her.

"It's where I carry my stress—the shoulders. So, what do you suggest? What is someone in Father Andrada's position supposed to do?"

"The murders all happened about a month apart, so there's at least some reason to believe the Ripper won't strike again in the next few days. I say Father Andrada should do the confession. Get a read on the guy if at all possible. We'll move on from there. If Andrada can get this guy's real name, I could go to the DA and cut a deal guaranteeing Andrada immunity for not coming forward before."

Camille's back arched. Her posture stiffened slightly, reflecting, perhaps, worry. Or something else.

"I get it that that doesn't solve the whole confession-breaking moral thing for Andrada," he said. "Fine. But like I said, the shelf life on this secret is very short. Look, let's do this. I'm going to stake out the church and take a look at this guy. I have court at ten and can't be late because I'm trying to get this pregnant lady out of jail. As long as he shows up on time, I'll get a good look at him. That way I'll know who he is but not through Andrada. From then on, I'll take care of it. I know people—cops, prosecutors, FBI agents. I'll stop the guy from striking again the right way, the legal way. Nobody needs to know anything."

"But you wouldn't know this if not through Father Andrada. You need his permission. I mean, isn't it privileged? That you only know about the confession through your client?"

"Come on, Camille. He broke the privilege by telling you, and you decided to tell me. We're deep into the gray zone here. I can handle this without involving Andrada. Shit, Andrada can go until the end of his days without thinking he broke the vow. I'm not even sure he did by telling a nun."

Camille shifted in her seat.

"So what do you think?" Sam asked.

"Telling anyone about confession breaks the vow."

"So? He's already broken the vow. My plan works, right? He breaks the vow, but I shield him from ever having to testify or be publically known as the way I got onto the serial killer."

Camille slowly rolled her shoulders, which seemed looser now.

"Okay, I think I get it. You see the guy, try and figure out who he is, and we'll go from there."

Sam stood, rubbed his temples, and stretched his arms above his head. He could feel the stress ooze out of his back.

"I should get home. I'll be across the street from the church at eight fifteen. I assume this guy arrives here in a car?"

"I've never seen him arrive. I've never seen him at all. I'll leave the surveillance to you."

"Three more things, Camille."

"Yes?"

"Tomorrow, when what's his name arrives, you have to get his DNA profile."

Camille's eyes widened. *"Really?"*

"If you're rejecting my other ideas, then you gotta do this. Just be around. Offer him a cup of water while he's waiting for the confession. He'll be nervous. Dry mouth. He'll take a sip, believe me. Then put the cup in a plastic bag and give it to me. Plus, you'll get a look at him."

"The second thing?"

"Does Andrada use a cell phone?"

"Not that I've ever seen. He's stuck in the '90s. And I mean the 1890s."

"What about caller ID?"

"Not that I've seen."

"Then I need his landline record for whichever phone received that call. He can get it online, through his provider."

"Why?"

"Isn't it obvious?" She appeared lost in thought. "Camille, I know people who can track down that number. The guy might have called from his own phone or one that gives us a clue. People are dumber than you think."

Camille sighed and looked away.

"And the third thing is I need the names of everyone who works at the church. Just write them on this, it'll be easier."

Camille accepted Sam's pad and pen.

"Three priests, me, and a janitor," she said, scrawling out the names. "So what do you think of the journal?"

"What about it?"

"Just anything. Do you feel it resonates with the case or anything else about it? I'm interested in your opinion."

"I'm a lawyer. I'm looking for objective indications that the journal has anything to do with our case. So far I don't see anything. I see a story about a poor, messed-up kid from a shitty family killing his crazy stepdad. Happens all the time. In fact, I've had that case. Twice I think. Other than that, it doesn't resonate."

Camille took a step past Sam towards the door.

"I'm taking your silence on the phone record as a yes. By tomorrow," Sam said.

"So, is it easy to get pregnant ladies out of jail?" She opened the door for Sam to step out.

Sam stood in the doorway, looking down at her.

"Easier than non-pregnant ladies. Why?"

"Sometimes I just like to know things." She held her index finger to her lips. Now that he was outside, they risked waking Father Andrada through the upstairs windows. She softly shut the door. Sam walked towards the Escalade, which again stood alone in the empty gravel lot. Halfway to it he turned back and looked at the rectory. It was plain, a suburban priest's house; yet inside, despite its gaudy décor, it felt like an ancient cathedral. A dull light shone from upstairs. Andrada probably, doing whatever priests like him did at half past two in the morning.

Sam's phone buzzed. He recognized the number, though no contact name appeared. *Torres, Dr. Fred Torres, father of a recent juvenile client.* A small case that had resolved easily for some community service. But why would the guy be calling so late?

"This is Young."

"Sam, I'm so sorry to call so late. It's not about Nate. It's about me. I really messed up. I think I need your help." The doctor's voice cracked, like that of a man unused to holding together under stress, perhaps an upright citizen just arrested for something serious.

Torres was an OB-GYN with a nice solo practice in Fairfax. He spoke like a gentle physics professor, always taking the time to make precise pronunciations of medical terms in his native Spanish.

"I don't care what it costs, I need to see you now. Can you please meet me at my office? Please!"

Sam took a deep breath. He glanced back at the rectory. The upstairs light was out now. He clicked his key fob, and the Escalade's lights flashed red like a buoy in the darkness.

"Address?"

• • •

"I can't believe how stupid I am. I can't believe how stupid I am. I can't believe how stupid I am . . . " Torres repeated the same phrase through tears in his normally elegant Dominican lilt. Shattered glass covered the floor of the windowless examination room, and a large piece of expensive-looking medical equipment, a scanner or EKG machine, lay smashed on the floor. Torres sat on the examination table with his hands on his head, rocking back and forth like a tortured prisoner. Sam stood near the table, arms folded, taking in the room, relaxing his mind, and trying to get a read on the source of Torres's desperation. The white, metal cabinets along the walls were the only remaining trappings of a normal doctor's office.

"Take it easy, Doc." Sam put his hands on Torres's shoulders. He felt the tension throbbing inside the man. Sam closed his eyes, and then stepped away. "Tell me, Doc, tell me slowly. We can solve this."

"You have no idea. The stress, I can't take it—"

"Stop it, Doc." Sam forcefully gripped both of Torres's shoulders.

"His name's Buterab. Steve Buterab. He's—"

"I know who he is." Sam saw it, Torres's whole issue. The smashed equipment, the crying, and the thoughts Sam could feel twisting and turning through Torres's mind, thoughts of his wife and his daughters and his nice suburban home.

"How much? Whatever it is, we can solve it."

Torres tried to muffle his wail with both hands.

"Two hundred, maybe a little more. The interest doubles it every few months." Torres rocked back and forth, arms around himself.

Two hundred thousand? Sam tried to remain expressionless. He could have made a long meeting out of the questions spinning in his head—*How did it start? Why not go to a bank? How did he meet Steve Buterab? Is he an addict? Or is it gambling?* But Sam decided not to. He knew Torres as a kind, smiling, law-abiding guy. A good, stern father and a doctor people really trusted. Whatever it was, Sam was sure he had his reasons to use a loan shark.

Sam's former client, Steve Buterab, was a Hungarian guy in Bennet County known for his lucrative bookie business and was reputed to be a pretty big pot dealer. Steve's father, Raj Buterab, whom Sam had only met once, was a rather notorious loan shark and an even bigger bookie that always seemed just legit enough to stay a free man. It was courthouse lore, true or not, that Raj was indirectly responsible for the bulk of the contributions to Mayor Douglas's campaigns. Raj carried himself with the old-school manner of a polite mob boss and resembled an elderly version of the wrestler and movie star The Rock. Huge, fit, and with a full head of white hair, he could have played a successful Southwestern rancher, an Italian gangster, or the president of a Latin American country.

Years ago, Raj had stunned Sam by approaching him at a local coffee shop about representing his son on a drunk-driving charge. When Sam heard the astonishing fee Raj was willing to pay, Steve had become his first off-the-books client—the first of many referrals from Raj, including Barnabus Farley.

Sam had successfully defended Steve and eventually became a regular at Steve's poker games in Bennet, a real game, with decent money at stake and a cut to the house every week. Sam had always known it was kind of sketchy, playing like that while working as a public defender, but he had appreciated the practice against opponents with real skin in the game. Steve came across as a nice guy, about Sam's age, and had started to refer cases to Sam. But it was all a bit too coincidental that a doctor in a neighboring county who had hired Sam to represent his son was now in the hole to Steve Buterab. Not impossible—but not likely.

"Doc, did you by any chance get my name as an attorney for your son's marijuana case from Steve Buterab?"

"I guess he did suggest it to me. I figured a criminal would know about such things. But I tell you, meeting you is the only good thing that's come out of my dealings with that, that vulture! If I don't come up with what I owe, he'll destroy the office, my practice, and then my marriage. It's over, Sam. I'm so far in the hole, and Renata knows nothing. You should see me, diving to hide the mail with the extra mortgage and credit cards. Oh shit! And I had an emergency delivery early tonight. A woman's life was at risk from preeclampsia, and I was so stressed about my own problems my hands were shaking. Pathetic. I'm pathetic!"

Sam was about to ask why he had needed the money in the first place, but he did not need to. He could already tell it was nothing sinister. No drugs. No gambling. Just a guy trying to be a successful doctor with a little less-than-successful income. The cars, the home, the private schools, all a bit too much for his nice, quiet, solo practice.

"Tell you what, Doc." Torres's face froze. He stared expectantly at Sam. "Give me about a week. I'm going to try to take care of this for you. Cut a deal. Maybe get them to take less, at your pace. I know Steve. I know his father, Raj. Maybe they can be reasonable if they see you just need more time."

Torres shivered, but straightened up.

"And I don't break legs. I'm just a lawyer."

"If you do this, I'll never forget it. I'll make it up to you no matter what it takes."

Sam patted Torres's shoulder. "I know you will. Just out of curiosity, what's preeclampsia?"

Torres looked puzzled. "A condition where a pregnant woman's blood pressure spikes," he said. "Sometimes it requires emergency early delivery, why?"

"Sometimes I just wanna know stuff."

CHAPTER 8

WHEN SAM ARRIVED HOME just after four in the morning he flipped through a stack of mail. Credit card bills, as always, but Barnabus's new case would take care of them and then some. He opened the envelope from You Keep the Key Storage, where he kept the six boxes some friends had packed up from his mother's bedroom and home office after she died. Sam had been paying the bill on the small storage space ever since—sixteen years. He thought about the boxes every once in a while, about looking through them, saving a few things, and getting rid of the rest. But instead, every six months, when the bill came, he paid it. This letter was different. State law had changed, and he had to personally appear at You Keep the Key Storage within sixty days to sign some paperwork. *Whatever*. Maybe he would pick up the boxes. Maybe he would just sign the papers.

One glass. Just one. He dumped vodka on some ice, making sure to give himself a nice pour since, after all, it would be only one. He sat with his drink in the soft leather chair in his living room. The journal, half in and half out of its brown envelope, lay in front of him on the coffee table next to his laptop. He pulled on a pair of blue, tight-fitting latex gloves, a box of which he kept in a drawer for just such situations. He picked up a cardboard-bound notebook, a small one, like those used by television detectives or reporters. He kept one in every big case: a personal notebook, not part of the file, not part of any formal record at all, just something for his own thoughts. Often, they were notes to no one—not the client, not the client's next lawyer, not some nosy secretary. Sometimes, when Sam looked back at his personal notes on a case, months or even years later, he was astonished by his prescience, or lack thereof. Always, though, it was an interesting peek into the past of how his mind worked—or failed. He inscribed *Andrada* on the cardboard cover, flipped it open, and placed it on the table next to Camille's journal. He quickly scanned over the small portion he had already read as he opened a Google browser. The Internet made things so easy; it was hardly even challenging anymore. It certainly evened the playing field, eliminating the difference between the truly knowledgeable or hardworking and all the rest. Any fool in an office cubicle could learn the history of China while on a phone call.

Bariloche—a town in southwestern Argentina, in Patagonia, which was believed in the 1520s to be the land of giants, since its indigenous people were taller than Europeans. Argentina, originally a Spanish colony, gained independence relatively easily, and Patagonia, Bariloche in particular, was settled largely by Germans—Nazis in fact. Swiss, Italians, and French. But Gypsies? *Roma?* The foreigners naturally would have become the elite of the region while the indigenous population suffered below them, but why would a European, an Eastern European at that, wind up living in a slum in Western Argentina?

Roma—The Romani people, originating in India but dispersed throughout the world, especially in Eastern Europe, but also in the Americas. Orange dots representing Roma, a subgroup of Romani, appeared on a population-density map. They clustered throughout Eastern and Central Europe in various pockets. Roma were variously persecuted throughout European history, most notably during the Holocaust. And yes, here it was: many were deported to Brazil during the colonial period.

Roma Girls' Names—T. Talaitha, Tshilaba, Tsuritsa . . . Trinity.

Sam began to take notes. Many believed Roma, or Gypsies, originated in Egypt. An apocryphal story has them exiled from Egypt for harboring the infant Jesus. Many fictional depictions of the Romani people present romanticized narratives of their supposed mystical powers and habits of criminality.

Clearly, Camille's mystery man knew of these special Gypsy powers; indeed, he narcissistically claimed them. Sam had a case a few years back, an unmedicated schizophrenic charged with murder, whose rants touched just enough truth to make one wonder, a sick but curiously brilliant mind. His former client had repeatedly complained about the medication he was ordered to take while awaiting trial. *It makes me dead inside.*

Sam conducted several more searches until he found what he needed: *The Romani people are present in Argentina with a population numbering around 300,000. They mostly live on the trading of used cars and jewelry, traveling all over the country. An Argentine soap opera called Romane, based around the Romani people in the 1980s, featured Chilean-born Romani speaking their native language with Spanish subtitles.* Of course, the mystery man, whether Roma or not, could have learned all about them from his couch as his diseased mind evolved. And all that had nothing to do with whether he was really the Rosslyn Ripper. Certainly, a person can gain more than enough knowledge both of the Roma and the Ripper murders to pass initial muster. Even with the cops.

Sam scanned the journal and plucked out a few more terms to Google for significance.

The third hit was a Bible verse, the Standard American Bible. His computer screen depicted the words in an overdone Gothic script. Sam copied it down. Luke 4:3-8, and then 13.

The Devil said to him, "If you are the Son of God, command this stone to become a loaf of bread." Jesus answered him, "It is written, one does not live by bread alone." Then the Devil led him up and showed him in an instant all the kingdoms of the world. And the Devil said to him, "To you I will give their glory and all this authority, for it has been given over to me, and I give it to whomever I please. If you then will worship me,

*it will all be yours." Jesus answered, "It is written,
Worship the Lord your God, and serve only him." When
the Devil had finished every test, he departed from him
until an opportune time.*

Maybe the mystery man likened himself to either Jesus or
the devil in the old story about Jesus's ability to resist earthly
temptation. *Maybe people like my mother or me are always
born to a chosen or forgotten people.*

Sam walked into the kitchen to pour another vodka. He then
wandered into the bathroom. He rifled through a few drawers
until he found some Q-tips and then returned to his work. He
carefully swabbed the edges, front and back, of the top three
pages of the unread section of the journal. He similarly swabbed
the journal portion he had already read, knowing it would likely
have his own DNA, which would distinguish swab one from
swab two, since he had not touched the second journal piece
from Sister Camille.

*The writer sure doesn't seem like a teenager. Especially
not a teenager raised in poverty in a slum on the outskirts
of Nowhere, South America so long ago. He either had been
one special teenager or this was a rewrite, a final copy he had
written as an adult.*

As he often did with cases, Sam took an early guess so that
later, when he figured everything out, he could see how astute, or
not, he had been. He made a final note: *Journal is not original,
but author believes the story to be true.*

Sam pulled out the pad where Camille had written the names
of the church employees. He closely compared the writing to
the tight cursive in the manuscript. He was no expert, but the
writing was not even close. He looked hard at the tight cursive.
He felt he had seen that writing before. But then, many people
wrote in similar ways. Sam drained his glass, refilled it again,
and leaned back in his chair to read.

FEBRUARY 21, 1957

I am worried about Paul. I fear that years of Miguel's abuse
has damaged him inside beyond repair. He is a smart kid but so
angry and dark inside. When a black mood strikes him, he acts

crazy. I worry he will be killed or arrested. For years, his fear of Miguel's wrath subdued him. I'm not sure my mere love is up to the task.

Yesterday we stopped at a cantina on the side of a long dirt road. While I spoke to the owner inside about a place to sleep, a group of drunken men left the cantina. I heard the yelling, but by the time I burst out the door, Paul had stabbed two of the men with the small knife he carried. In the confusion of the ruckus, I leapt onto the motorcycle and spun it around, spraying gravel towards the cursing group of men, two of whom lay screaming on the ground. Even in the flurry of seconds between grabbing Paul's hand and pulling him onto the bike, I saw in his eyes—in the hardened and menacingly confident way they looked during a dark spell—that such a mood had struck him. The drunks had been no threat at all. Paul had mistakenly believed we were in danger.

Today, our motorcycle roared and bumped over the dirt road into Buenos Aires. The colored lights of the city emerged from the darkness like those out of a magic kingdom. Paul sat behind me, hands gripping me tightly and head buried in my back.

"Hurray!" I called out over the loud motor. I wanted to be able to see his face, perhaps to see that rare occasion of a smile. His arms relaxed as we slowed. These outskirts were, of course, filled with my people—not Roma, but the shack dwellers without the means to live either inside or far outside the center of commerce. I revved past the shanties.

We entered downtown. I want a new life. Maybe one where we are happy, like the Americans on the comedy shows. Maybe I am not crazy or evil and only worry so because I have seen so little of the world. But I am learning that sometimes fate, pure luck, or some other force lightly pervading this world leads us to a place that makes sense—for better or for worse. As our motorcycle glided on the streets of Buenos Aires that evening I saw, within minutes, just what I was looking for. *Room for rent.*

"How old are you?" the cragged-faced landlord asked me.

"Nineteen, sir." I felt his mind, soft at the edges but firm and circling around that which he knew well: money. He looked skeptical but saw the hundred-peso notes in my hand.

"Two hundred and fifty a month. Paid up front, the first of

each month. One day late, you're out." His huge red nose sniffed. Annoyed. Neither Paul nor I had bathed in days.

I handed over the money and gripped Paul's hand as we carried our backpacks down the hall. Underneath the smell of cooked meat and mopped floors, our new room in the back of the restaurant smelled like Miguel's shed, a decaying animal's cage. I knew by now that sometimes what I experience as a sense of smell is not about scents at all, but little glimpses into the past. The smell of fresh flowers follows a happy woman, a waft of feces surrounds drunks and liars, and a lemony, icy scent marks places of safety and generosity. The monkey-cage smell meant suffering has occurred here. Just now I tucked Paul into our one narrow cot and now watch him drift off as I write. Our slit window looks only upon an alley, but our room, nevertheless, pumps with the noise of the Palermo district and its even louder emotions. I have never been so physically close to so many people. I need to turn it off somehow.

Moments ago I opened the drawer on the small bedside table and found a roughed-up, hand-sized, Spanish-language Bible with red-rimmed pages. I opened it straight to a passage, the exact words of which I have now memorized. To place the Bible's ownership beyond dispute, I wrote both of our names inside the cover on a space labeled *Nombre*, along with the date and *Buenos Aires*. Whenever I read my name in my Bible, I will picture this room and Paul sleeping deeply and so innocently near me. Maybe this Bible can make us happy. Trinity would be twenty-two years old today. Not sure why, with all our magic, I cannot tell whether she is alive or dead.

• • •

Sam turned over the next page, which began with a new entry. So far, each entry had been dated, but it was not clear whether the mystery man was mailing Father Andrada every entry, or just selected ones.

FEBRUARY 23, 1957

I am unwilling to leave Paul alone in our room at the back of the restaurant. Instead, today we walked together through Palermo, scanning the storefronts throughout the barrio in hopes of stumbling upon a job.

I finally found a proper job for both of us. Shoveling shit at a chicken factory was not exactly what I had in mind, but the loose employment rules at such a place made it an easy choice. Though I am older, Paul is already almost as big as me and tremendously strong for his age. We thus appear closer in age than we are, a good thing for ten-year-old Paul in the job market. From all appearances, we will work with teenaged boys and girls, hunchbacked old ladies, and drunks. The manager says I can work next to Paul all day, and I hope the calmness of my mind surrounding his throughout the day will prevent any sudden dark moods.

Tonight I read to Paul in our room, a ritual I plan to continue. I started with the Bible, the only book we have. There are many other religions, but Jesus reigns in Argentina. In my Argentina, anyway. This is the religion I am stuck with for now. Which is nobody's fault, not even Miguel's.

• • •

Sam turned the page. The short entry was over, and the next entry skipped many months. He stood and refilled his glass again, at first only halfway. The bottle was almost empty anyway, so he filled the glass all the way, the last drips of vodka almost overflowing it, like raindrops falling into a pristine lake in the crater of a quiescent volcano.

Again, Sam reached out for a sense of the writer. If this were the Ripper, his sense of self-grandiosity would justify, even sanctify, the killings. But the current random violence didn't quite fit. The boy's killing of Miguel could be seen as self-defense. Paul, on the other hand, who at the age of ten gleefully knifed two innocent men while in a dark mood, might be a better Ripper candidate. With a sudden Etch-A-Sketch shake of the head, Sam erased these reasoned guesses from his mind, for that's all they were. He hadn't truly sensed anything about the journal's author, whose voice was strong but whose spirit was opaque.

Sam turned to the next entry and paced the room while reading, a common practice of his. A bit like being in the courtroom.

JANUARY 2, 1958

Two days ago, New Year's Eve, I sat alone at a table at a Retiro district street café as midnight neared. I was surprised by the emptiness of the square. About ten minutes before the square clock showed midnight, I heard a tremendous bang. Multi-colored balloons raced for the sky from atop a building. Just as suddenly, throngs of dancing citizens of all ages filled the street. Many wore costumes, from devil masks to dragon heads to clowns. As the crowd focused itself around an intense circle of drummers, I marveled at the utter lack of self-consciousness with which the dancers of all ages moved to the magical tune made by nothing more than drums, clapping hands, and a cacophony of joyous voices.

Then I saw her and instantly knew her name. Salome. She danced alone, moving rhythmically but slowly, both aware and uncaring of the others. She wore a heavy mask—a smiling, blue demon head. My hands froze at the first sight of her. When she saw me, Salome went limp and fell to the ground like a bird shot from the sky. Friendly revelers removed her mask, helped her to her feet, and found her a spot to sit on a curb off to the side of the dancing circle. The party continued, with me now by Salome's side. My heart sang. The best way I can describe it is *recognition*. I think she could see the person I really am.

There was no need to speak in words. Salome was a stranger and, to my eyes and senses, not even Roma. But sitting silently on the curb a foot apart, our auras clung together above the crowd in exhaustingly rapid communion.

Our auras joined the street dance, doing precisely in life what the festive devils and dragons mimicked through art. Our bodies clung to each other and moved away from the crowd slowly, making our way down a narrow alley. My heart burned for the first time with the most pleasant of emotions—was it love? How could it be that I had found perhaps the only person on Earth with whom I could share this form of love?

Salome had beautiful, dark skin. She was both spiritually and physically inviting, and her hands began to caress me rapidly—a surprise which guided me back to one of the brick walls of the alley. And I lost all control. What happened next

I can hardly call sex. It was a frenzy of transcendent jubilance reserved only for gods. But I am still very inexperienced with physical matters. Our ecstasy reached higher and higher levels, and Salome and I were light years away as our empty human vessels thrashed together down on Earth. When I glimpsed back into the mundane present, I realized I was holding Salome's limp body. Even as the trajectory of our clinging auras continued up and up, I had accidentally squeezed the life out of her.

As my senses returned, I again heard the music from the street, and Salome's aura had fled. I ran. I threw myself into the corner of our room and wept. Before falling asleep, I decided to turn myself in the next morning.

Before contacting the police, I had to report to work to get our final pay—for Paul. We trudged through the square in Palermo. He was unaware of the previous night's events. It was New Year's Day and, yes, the chicken factory was open for business. Cans, bottles, and confetti still littered the street. I glanced down the alley. Salome's body was gone, no doubt discovered shortly after I had made my escape. Perhaps her family, her aging German father and her African mother, knew by now she was dead.

I stood still and breathed rhythmically. I imagined my mother kneeling beside me, her elegant finger directing me towards a flower or bird. Soft eyes. I saw it then. My thrashing of Salome's body looked like rage, not love. The celebratory shouts, the drums, and the firecrackers made it impossible for me to tell if Salome had even cried out. Paul kicked a beer can down the street towards a sewer. He faked a right-footed shot, and then pushed the can with his left into the corner of the sewer. He raised his arms and ran back to me, laughing. "Goooooooooooooal!" He didn't see my tears.

Forgive me, mother. Miguel, God, Jesus, whoever is out there. I deserve death or imprisonment for what I did to Salome. But to abandon Paul to a city orphanage would be to condemn him. I cannot leave him. If there is a God, he gave Paul to me, and for what purpose could that be but for me to protect him? I grabbed Paul's hand and pulled him away from the mouth of the alley, looking around to see who may have observed my interest in the accursed scene.

Paul shoveled shit while I discussed the matter of our pay

with the assistant manager of the factory. My next move would cost a minimum of ten thousand pesos, far in excess of the pay we had coming. The manager, Jorge Ramos, was a rail-thin man with a sick wife and three children, two of whom were severely mentally retarded. He slaved as we did, barely a full tier above us in the city pecking order.

I could read Jorge like a book. From day one, I had known he fancied me above the other workers, even above the teenage girls whose fresh faces and muscled bodies had not yet begun to fade under the weight of the stress. Paul shoveled, humming to himself from the wide and rather empty factory bay. He scraped the shovel across the floor, creating a grating metal-on-concrete sound that rattled Jorge's thin nerves. The skeleton crew of New Year's Day shift workers meandered about in their own little trances, robotically performing their tasks.

It was then that I made my deal, owning Jorge's mind for a fleeting second, just long enough for him to believe he had thought of the idea. Jorge had a key to the safe, and we both knew the payroll cash was in it. Within minutes of my brief mind invasion, Jorge and I were in the back office. He spun the dial of the bulky metal box that doubled as a table in the corner of the office. I stood behind him, transcending as far out of my body as possible in anticipation for what I was about to endure.

Then he was all over me. My openness to him made his mind soar with the melody of an orchestra that hadn't played in years. Its rusty strings rose in harmony like they never knew they could. He scratched, rubbed, and clawed his way around my clothes. Once we were both naked, he bent me over the cluttered desk and awkwardly, painfully, found his way inside me while I tilted just so. He thrust quickly over the course of about two minutes. His joy reached the stars, a fact that rendered the experience a bit less disgusting to me. He finished and panted loudly as he pulled up his pants. He eyed the cash on the table. I entered his mind one more time, only to implant a critical jab, something that would affect his behavior in a way he would not consciously understand. *I'll kill you if you try to break our deal.*

Once dressed, he looked at the money one more time. He weakly thanked me, without meeting my eyes.

As luck would have it, a ship heading north, with stops at

various points along the coast and ultimately docking in Miami, boarded today.

The massive vessel, aptly named *La Liberación,* towered above the water, its pristine black sides seamlessly reaching the sky. Paul and I boarded across the riveted metal walkway each holding small, nearly empty suitcases. Sharply dressed detectives and uniformed policemen watched us board, but despite their hawk-like stares, their linear minds sought different sorts than us. I smiled right at an old cop as I handed over our tickets at the booth beside the rickety metal ramp onto the ship. His eyes looked past me—in search of a murdering rapist.

Paul marveled at the ship as we ascended. "How do they build it?" At the top of the winding ramp, a ship's mate sat at a small folding table, taking tickets. By the time we reached him, it was plain to me that Paul and I needed to sign our names to a manifest of some sort. When the mate took our tickets and shoved his clipboard towards us, I saw that he required only names and ages. The ruffled papers looked no more official than the handwritten pricelist pinned to a fruit stand on the road to Buenos Aires. Nevertheless, with police scheming about, our real names needed to remain in Argentina, as far as I was concerned. I quickly invented new ones and neatly wrote them for both of us. As for ages, I told the truth for Paul and made myself an adult. We had good, new names, strong ones, reflecting our hopes.

The crew of the *La Liberación,* a cargo ship, was rough looking but jovial enough men with absurdly thick forearms. They bounced around the deck performing hundreds of little tasks. Our fellow passengers appeared mostly lone business types who know the routine. Our room was small, an enclosed booth really, with the orangey aroma of peace and boredom.

Hours ago, Paul and I leaned against the rail on the polished wooden deck, watching Buenos Aires disappear. While our homeland melted away under the cloudless sky, I felt an inexplicable sensation. As my mother said, I am not alone. Salome cannot be the only one. Thus, recognition, even acceptance, is possible. Suddenly I laughed.

"Fucking happiness!" I cried out across the water in English. A crewman, leaning against the rail and smoking a fat cigar, laughed at me in a way that filled his own heart for just a moment.

The pleasure of an adult at the joy of a naïve child, maybe indeed I am good, God's soldier and not the devil's.

Or maybe Paul and I are like magical spies, dodging and weaving just under the gaze of the world.

CHAPTER 9

SAM GUZZLED A BOTTLE of water and then another, tossing the empties onto the passenger side floor of the Escalade as he sweated in the overly cautious suburban traffic. He parked across the street from the Church of the Holy Angels at eight fifteen, lit a cigarette, continued drinking water, and watched for the next half hour.

About eight forty-five, Camille stepped out of the church, flagging him towards her. Her long, thin arm and fingers made the wave sort of otherworldly at that distance, like a painter's abstraction of a pretty woman waving made artistic by its oversimplified exaggeration. Sam pulled the Escalade into the parking lot and could tell that she intended to approach his window in front of the church—or, put another way, she did not plan on having an involved meeting.

"Really sorry, Sam. He came early, seven thirty. And Andrada heard the confession."

"It's okay." *Suspicious.*

"But we may have caught a break." Camille pulled a stapled paper bag from her briefcase and handed it to him. "The guy wanted communion, and Father Andrada obliged. I usually wash the communion chalices. This is it. Clean before today, used by our man. His saliva will be on the rim."

"You get his tag number?"

"I watched him leave from the window but didn't see a car. He disappeared out of view towards Woodburn Road. You didn't ask me to get a tag number."

"You got the phone records?"

In her oxymoronic mix of rough and soft, laid back and elegant, Camille stepped back as if to walk away.

"This *is* a process, counselor."

Sam watched her closely. He noted his own hesitancy to treat her like a regular client—in other words, to take charge of her.

"It is a process, but do you know what an important part of the process is?" She leaned back into the Escalade, her elbows on the window jamb, awaiting the answer. "When I ask you to do things, it's to help you. I really need you to do them."

They watched each other for a moment.

"Well? Let's have it," Sam said.

"Have what?"

"What'd the guy look like?"

"Oh. I guess he just looked like a young guy. Early thirties maybe? Normal build. Brown hair, average length, but hard to tell 'cause he wore a hat. I only saw him from a distance. I'm sure he didn't see me or know that anyone but Andrada was here."

Sam spun the Escalade out of the church parking lot. He pulled out Sherita's file and began to glance through it while driving.

• • •

"She can plead straight up," Chadwick Sparf said. "Distribution of coke. She needs to go away. And forget about bail, she's on probation. You know our policy—two-time drug losers got to go away. By the way, you look like shit."

Chad's small, black eyes looked over Sam's shoulder for the next lawyer to reject. The prosecutor Sam had hoped for, born-again Sally Ann, had been replaced by Chad, the worst possible draw. Chad was a *Revenge of the Nerds*-type prosecutor, still punishing defendants for the fact that he was relentlessly bullied growing up. Sam had unique insight into Chad's rather simplistic psyche, having attended grade school and junior high with him until Chad left for some kind of a special school to escape the abuse by other students. Sam had not been one of the bullies, exactly, but he hadn't been any hero either. Sparf's behavior towards Sam fluctuated between punishing and nervous because Sam knew about his difficult and humiliating past. Sam sympathized with Sparf in a way, but not too much. Sure, he had been abused. But not by the defendants he locked up. Not by Sherita Owings.

Sam had heard that when Sparf once spoke at a prosecutor's conference, his topic had been Never Live a Lie, meaning never let guilty defendants off on lesser charges. Poor Sparf. Even other prosecutors ridiculed his rigidity.

"Seriously, Chad, take a second to look at this case. It's basically entrapment as to distribution. She's a relapsed user. You guys shouldn't be offering triple the street price to a *user*. No junkie can resist. Raise the price you're willing to pay any higher, *I'll* score and sell it to you."

"And I'll lock you up. Now, out of the way, I'm busy."

Sam stood completely still in front of Sparf. Sam's briefcase, a four-thousand-dollar Louis Vuitton, hung as it always did over his shoulder on a leather strap. The briefcase was part of his uniform, his armor. He always wanted his hands free. People in control were not constantly shuffling items around from one hand to the other. Like his thousand-dollar suits, odd for a guy who didn't own a single nice item of casual clothing, the fancy briefcase was part of a simple mental game. There may be tension underneath, but never, ever on the surface.

Sparf juggled his disorganized files in search of the next one he needed. Sherita's returned to the bottom of his stack.

"Think on it, Chad. I have to be in Courtroom C for a plea. Back in ten."

Sam touched Chad gently on the shoulder, a sign of friendship and acceptance. It was something he had begun to do as a new attorney, making physical contact of some sort with those he sought to persuade, hoping he could feel something flowing from him to another through the touch. There was compassion in it, but something else, too. An invitation. A jab, as he sometimes thought of it. A jab towards the right answer, like one might use to silence a snorer. Sam believed it often worked, could sometimes feel it work. In the end, despite the bravado, a guy like Sparf, deep inside, still yearned for affection.

Sam turned and walked down the hall, reflecting on the best way to handle Sparf and spring Sherita.

Norwood Kapalka paced back and forth in the corner near Courtroom C. Amelia stood near him, clearly trying to calm him down. Norwood's confined paces reminded Sam of a confused hamster in a small cage. As Sam approached, he banished Sparf and Sherita, Camille and Andrada, and Torres and Buterab from his mind. He zeroed in on the problem before him. Kapalka, Amelia's client, was a nervous wreck. He was about to plead guilty to smacking his wife. After an anger-management class, the charge would be dismissed and removed from his permanent record. It was a normal but good deal for a guy who admitted to the police that he hit his wife and was really sorry about it. For Amelia, though, Norwood was a difficult client, high maintenance and a whiner who wanted to talk about his marriage more than the case. Sam could tell from a distance that Amelia's plea deal was not the thing worrying Kapalka. He was still hung up on whether his wife was cheating on him, still trying to get his head around the suspicion that was ruining his life.

"Norwood, relax," Sam said. "This is gonna be easy, easy. You'll be out of here in ten minutes."

"I know." Kapalka's eyes were watery and he gripped a sealed envelope tightly. "I need your advice. On whether I should open it." Norwood's hands shook. Amelia, annoyed, looked at Sam, inviting him to step in.

"You didn't," Sam said. But Sam could see that he had. He'd gotten a paternity test done on his six-year-old son. "Norwood—"

"I know, I know, but I told you, I think she had an affair back then. It's been driving me crazy. I can't sleep, I can't—"

"Give me the envelope." Norwood limply raised his hand, and Sam took the crinkled envelope and smoothed it out. Diagnostia, Inc. Private and Confidential Genetic Testing. "Never heard of them, and I've used labs around here lots of times. For cases."

"It's up on twenty-nine, near Falls Church. Very small. Private. So what should I do?"

Deputy Plosky, standing outside Courtroom C called out, "Almost ready, Amelia? Judge is ready to do that plea."

Amelia shuffled her feet. Her nervousness, her stress, scented the air. She simply was not used to it yet, the constant little tensions of the job. Not enough time for anything, but everything must happen. The cases got called; the decisions got made, ready or not. Sam sighed. He softly rubbed the envelope. He touched Kapalka, trying to get a feeling. All he felt was shivering.

"You've been with Davorka for nine years, right?"

"Right."

"You love her."

"Yes."

"You love your son."

"Yes."

"You have no actual evidence she's cheating on you, now or ever."

"I guess not."

"She forgives you and wants to stay with you."

Kapalka looked down. "But I need her to be straight with me."

Sam held up the envelope. "Norwood, all you need is to be straight with yourself. Either stay with her or leave her. But the answer won't come from a DNA test." He balled up the envelope and whipped it in the direction of the trash receptacle. It bounced against the wall and ricocheted into the narrow opening.

Kapalka gritted his teeth. "Okay."

"Nice shot, Young," Plosky said.

Sam's phone buzzed. "This is Young." Amelia and Kapalka entered the courtroom.

"Sam, where are you?" Public Defender Michael Simmons. His boss. "I haven't seen you in days."

"I'm at the courthouse, representing clients. You know, my job."

Simmons was always in a hurry, always speaking as if he were rushing off to an emergency.

"I'm assigning you a new case. Gilbert Hogman. He's in the mental unit, shitting and pissing all over his cell. Go over there and see him today. See if he needs a competency evaluation."

"I'm pretty busy. Can someone else do it?"

"You have a way with nut-job clients. If he needs a mental eval, we can file for it today and get him to a hospital. Every day he's in the jail is a risk he'll rack up more charges. And well . . . never mind. It's gotta be you."

"Shit, Michael. You mean he asked for me by name? Look, I don't know the dude. Send someone else."

Simmons sighed. Sam could almost see him opening his next file over the conversation.

"Listen, Sam, I give you as much deference as I can, but some decisions are above your pay grade. It's gonna be you. And by the way, we got this kid from NYU Law hanging out all day with nothing to do. He came here to work with you this summer, remember? He's kind of pissed off. Bored. Can you do something about that?"

Sam felt a wince of guilt. Marvin, or Marlin, or whatever his name was. Sam had been too busy to give the guy any assignments.

"Got it." He hung up and glanced down the long hallway towards the courtroom, towards Sparf. This job was so funny sometimes. The utter silliness of the law. Just because Hogman smeared shit all over his cell did not, legally, mean that he was unable to comprehend the nature of the charges against him and assist in his defense. The behavior may be a perfectly rational reaction to his situation. His phone buzzed.

"Sam, guess what?" He could hear the excitement in Juliana's voice. "There's been a development."

Sam turned and looked back down the hallway. Sparf stood alone with his stack of files as if he had finished telling all the defense attorneys to screw off and was getting ready to go into the courtroom.

"I have something for you, too, Juliana. Can't talk now. Meet later?"

She hesitated. "Might be working late."

"Can I come over later?"

"Ten. And Sam?"

"Yeah?"

"You have something on the Ripper?"

"Let's talk later."

Sam hung up, his mind balancing the issue of how much of the Andrada issue he should share with Juliana. She was, at the end of the day, sort of a cop. He walked slowly back towards the courtroom, scribbling a note on a legal pad. His lone footsteps echoed in the now-empty marble corridor. The judge was already on the bench, but Sam walked straight down the aisle and into the well, tossed the note on the table in front of Sparf, and casually walked to the back of the courtroom to sit in the far corner by himself. He pulled out a draft of an appeal brief and focused, zooming in on the supporting legal theory. As always, his physical and mental exhaustion gave way to concentration. The people around him, the courtroom, the judge, Chad's arguments against bail for all the locked-up defendants, faded. Hard and clear. His mind sharpened itself on the brief. *Hard and clear.*

Sam broke out of his zone when Chad touched him on the shoulder and nodded towards the door. The courtroom was almost empty now, and a different prosecutor was handling the last bond motions. The last besides Sherita's.

Chad walked and spoke quickly, an intentional display of hardhearted confidence many prosecutors affected while handling routine dockets like arraignments and bond motions. *I don't fall for sob stories. They're all guilty as hell. Next. Next. Next.* When Sparf walked inside the witness room, Sam's certainty that he had read him right jumped from 90 to 100 percent.

"If your knucklehead pleads guilty today, and I mean *right now*, she can plead to possession, thirty days to serve, probation with drug testing. And she'd better not balk on it in court or come back in to withdraw it later. Case closed today."

Chad's tight face and rigid posture didn't exactly reflect the tough-guy image he thought it did. Chad had retreated to a face-saving position of demanding something they both knew was no demand at all. Sherita would be falling all over herself to take the thirty-day plea. Sam fed the beast.

"Today? That might be a hard sell, Chad. She just expects a bond motion. You have no lab results, and—"

"Today. Or no deal, and I argue against bond. I'll win it, too. A distribution charge? With her record? I know you guys all come in here asking me to buy into your bullshit stories because that's your job, but seriously, it gets old from where I stand. 'She made a mistake.' 'She's got a kid.' 'She didn't understand.' 'She didn't know,'" Sparf said in a poorly acted whiny voice. So much like the younger Sparf would have spoken.

"If there's one thing a few years in this business has taught me, it's that people fucking well know what they're doing. They all know. Every one of them. So take it or leave it."

"Okay. You got a deal."

"And you should know, the FBI called today. They wanted to charge Sherita federally. To make her into a snitch. Agent Diggens. Acted like a real jerk, like I had to do whatever he said. I told him to shove it."

"Thanks, Chad. But why do that for her? I thought your boss had a policy to always defer to federal prosecution."

"Who cares why? I did it. It's over."

"Because sometimes I'm just curious."

Sparf looked down, either searching himself for the answer or for whether to tell it to Sam. "Because fuck the feds."

As Sparf turned to leave, his head snapped back in Sam's direction as if to blurt out an afterthought, a forgotten dreg of unimportance.

"By the way, very funny, dude." He tossed the note on the table and left.

Sam picked up his note and read it again. *Plea to possession. 30 days. Drug testing. And by the way, fuck you, Sparf.*

"Fuck the feds," Sam said to himself. So Sparf didn't like being told what to do. Not even by the FBI. And what was more, Sparf held his own boss's authority in less than perfect regard. It made sense. It fit Sparf's psyche. The Bennet County Commonwealth's attorney was, after all, a politician. Just another superficial, popular kid. *Good to know.*

• • •

"Camille, the phone records?" Phone in hand, Sam walked briskly in the thick humidity towards his office.

"Soon. When can we meet? Also, I received another manuscript entry. I need you to see it."

"You did?"

"We did."

Sam scanned his calendar in his head. He had the routine jail first appearances at two. New cases. New public defender clients advised of their rights through a closed-circuit video system, with the judge and the prosecutor at the courthouse and the defense attorney and client at the jail. It could take ten minutes or three hours, depending on the number of new arrests. He also had to deal with the new client, the nut job, Hogman. Then the DNA lab. Then Juliana.

"I should be able to meet. Eleven at the church?"

"Eleven at your place. And Sam?"

"Yes, Camille?"

"Don't forget to eat again today. It's bad for you." Her tone was businesslike, yet mothering. The personal nature of the comment caught Sam off guard. Eleven o'clock meetings? Reminding him to eat? She was getting to know him.

Sam kept walking and dialed Steve Buterab's number. It did not surprise him when Steve knew it was him. Gamblers. They were good like that.

"Samson, Mr. Las Vegas. So, you too good for us now? You haven't been at the game in months." Steve sounded friendly, glad to hear from an old friend. Steve, who had attended a prep school in New York, then Cornell, still spoke like a fast-talking con artist when it suited him. A second-generation grifter and son of the just-short-of-famous Raj Buterab, Steve struck Sam as a decent guy struggling to figure out who he was supposed to be—a gambler, a shady importer-exporter to and from Eastern Europe, a pot dealer, an Ivy Leaguer, or something completely different. Steve had to wonder where he fit.

"Ahh, kidding man. So you in for Thursday? It's bigger now. Almost in your league. Five is the buy in."

Steve's weekly high-dollar poker game took place at his warehouse in South Bennet. Purportedly a moving and storage company, it was a huge space with multiple bays that Sam always envisioned serving as a base for all kinds of local criminality. But on poker nights, the warehouse was empty but for the round table in the middle, where local lowbrow big shots wagered up to five thousand dollars a hand while Steve and his crew served cheap food and drinks.

"You cutthroats can take me any day. But hey, Steve, I got a favor to ask. Not about poker."

"You ask, you got. I know you're busy, bro. Me too. What's

the favor? No need to make small talk with me."

Sam mentioned Dr. Torres and the debt. Silence followed. A long one. Steve finally spoke when Sam turned the corner and his office came into view.

"I'll tell you what, Sam. Since you asked, I'll look into it." The joviality, however, had left Steve's voice.

"Thanks, Steve. Really, thanks."

"No promises. I just said I'd look into it."

Steve hung up. He did not re-extend the invitation to the poker game. Sam should have met with Steve in person about Torres. Experience told him that people's desire to help him went way up when he asked face to face. Especially with Steve, who'd been calculating angles since he was in the crib just to keep up with his old man.

Feet still moving fast towards his office, Sam pocketed his phone. A young Asian man leaned against the wall next to the door of his building, rapidly texting with both thumbs. Sam immediately recognized the moussed-up spiky hair and the skulking demeanor of Nguyen Jones and indulged in the hope that Nguyen wouldn't notice him. Nguyen looked up, eyes alight, as if surprised by an old friend. Sam kept moving forward.

"What are you doing here?" Sam asked when Nguyen stepped into his path and could thus no longer be ignored.

"Looking for you, buddy."

"That scares me. Why?"

"I need your help. To get my record sponged."

Sam shook his head. "I don't like you and the word 'sponge' being used in the same sentence."

"You know, when you get your record erased. I was found not guilty, right?"

"If you want to get your arrest record *expunged*, Nguyen, do it. You don't need me for that. Go to the clerk's office window. They'll tell you what to do."

"Call me Skipper, buddy. You know that."

"I'm not calling you Skipper. We're not friends. I'm really busy."

Nguyen launched into a rapid explanation of how important it was that he get his arrest record expunged. Sam zoned out and pictured Nguyen on the witness stand last year. A computer genius, Nguyen had served, against Sam's advice, as his own expert witness, captivating the jury with his vast knowledge of computer forensics while explaining how he had no clue how his computer had downloaded hundreds of images of prepubescent child pornography. It had been an impressive feat of obfuscation. The frustrated prosecutor hadn't been able to put a dent in Nguyen's story, and the jury had found him not guilty in ten minutes. Of all Sam's cases, the murders and rapes and molestations, Nguyen's horrifying photographs of children being raped and sodomized had rendered him his least-favorite client ever.

"I'm telling you, buddy, I got a chance for a tech contract with Homeland Security, and they're about to do the background check. I need the shit sponged. This job could be serious money."

"Nguyen, if you get a contract with the Department of Homeland Security, there's something seriously wrong with this country."

Nguyen laughed. "No shit, buddy, you can say that again. Anyway, you gonna help me or what? I want *you* to get it sponged. Besides, with this new gig, I'm hooked up. I can afford you. Coins are gonna be shooting out of my ass by October, buddy." Nguyen cranked his arm to mimic a slot machine. "Cha-ching!" He stuck his butt out to facilitate the ejection of imaginary coins.

"I can only handle cases appointed to the public defender's office."

"Stop pretending to be an asshole. Everybody knows you do side cases. What's your problem?"

Sam placed two fingers on his lips, as if to consider a difficult question.

"Ten thousand."

"Whoa. That's a lot for just going to the clerk's window, eh?"

"Take it or leave it."

Nguyen sighed. "Okay, buddy. And call me Skipper."

"I'm not your buddy, and I'm not calling you Skipper. In fact, if I were you, I'd stop going by Skipper." Sam walked around Nguyen. "I'll file the paperwork when I get the check."

"Sam!" Nguyen said it forcefully enough to cause Sam, grudgingly, to turn back around.

"Why do you hate me? What have I ever done to you?"

Sam just stared at him.

"You know, you're supposed to be this great defense attorney, believe in your clients and all that. In my case, you had two choices, both of which were possible. Either I was this pig who had pictures of babies being raped, or I was a normal guy who didn't know those pictures were on my computer. It's always bothered me that you chose the shitty, cynical option instead of believing I'm a decent person. You're worse than the judge. You know what, Sam? Fuck you!" Nguyen raised his middle finger in the air, feigned jamming it into his own ass, and shoved it in Sam's direction. "Get over yourself."

Sam turned and grabbed the door handle, remembering the day of Nguyen's acquittal. Judge Bass had lectured him harshly, right in front of the jury that had just exonerated him.

In my sixteen years on the bench I have never witnessed such a contrivance as you convincing this jury that those pictures magically appeared on your computer. You are a disgusting human being. I hope I get a chance to sentence you someday. But for now, you're free to go, unfortunately.

Sam had looked over at Nguyen as the judge spoke. Suddenly, he saw the moment in vivid, 3D-like detail. He did not see triumph in Nguyen. Nguyen had been a crushed person, delving as far inside himself as he could to escape the public nightmare. Sam shook his head, as if to break out of a trance. Sometimes his little hangovers were an epic journey.

"Skipper!" Sam called out. Nguyen scuttled back towards him. "What if I did your expungement in exchange for some computer work?"

"Now you're speaking my language, buddy. Like what?"

"Investigation. On some people. Deep, deep background checks. And you can't get caught."

"Ah, man. I'm the best. I'm nutty."

Sam laughed. "I believe you on both of those things. But this is really sensitive."

"I'm your man. What's it about?"

"To start with, I want you to find out everything you can, without getting caught, about a nun named Camille Paradisi. Background, job history, education, where and when did she become a nun. *Is* she a nun? I want everything. This may require some legwork. I'll email you what I have on Camille, and the rest of the project, later today."

"You got a birth date, anything like that?"

"Not a birth date. She's about thirty-five. I'll send you what I got. It's not much. Oh and hey, can your computer guys do handwriting analysis, like with a program or something?"

"Huh?"

"Take two writing samples and tell if they were written by the same person?"

Nguyen shrugged. "If computer guys can do it, I can do it, pal. Bring it on. You got the samples?"

"Right now, just one. I'm trying to figure it out."

"No problem, Sam, I got it. Can I ask what these projects are about?"

Sam took a deep breath. "Have you heard of the Rosslyn Ripper?"

Nguyen's eyes grew wide. "This is making me hot."

"Stop saying things like that," Sam said.

• • •

"Sam, when you get a chance, I'd like to talk to you." It was Amelia, speaking from the doorway of his office. Her slouched posture conveyed concern and a tepidness that surprised him, given her huge victory just the day before.

He opened his e-mail and flipped through the stack of phone messages on his desk.

"You worry too much. Relax. Enjoy it for a day."

"I know. It's kind of a personal thing. When you have time? I know you're busy."

"Sure. Tomorrow?" He glanced toward the pile of case files and notes on his desk. "And Amelia, you're doing a great job. You've got to give yourself a break once in a while."

CHAPTER 10

"SALIVA ON THE RIM of a metal cup," Sam said into his office phone. The representative from Diagnostia would not quit asking questions.

"Is that really necessary?" Sam asked. "It's a private matter. I'll drop it off today. How much for the expedited results?"

• • •

The stuffy video room at the jail made Sam sweat through his dark suit. They made these places uncomfortable on purpose. The row of new arrestees, shackled, some in their orange jumpsuits, all speaking and gesturing at once, demanded his attention. Most of them, repeat customers, knew the video appearance was their first chance to be released pending trial and that every second counted to explain to Sam why they so desperately needed bail.

"My job, my kids . . . I'll lose my apartment . . . I didn't do this shit."

Their stories were real, sometimes true, but all too often defeated by the standard prosecutor's argument for high or no bail: the defendant should have thought about his or her job, kids, or apartment before committing the offense. So typical, and such bullshit. But as a former mentor of his often said, "Shit makes the world go round."

Sam always showed up at the jail advisements early, wanting to give each defendant enough time. To meet them. To make sure they did not say something stupid in the video. He brought one defendant at a time to the other side of the room, out of earshot of the others. An earnest but bored deputy leaned against the wall.

The last defendant Sam spoke to was the least likely to be released. Cornelius Pritchard, nicknamed Acorn. While Sam had never personally represented Acorn, he did know some of his story. Domestic battery. Public intoxication. The petty stuff of an angry drunk unable to get it right his whole life. Now about forty years old, it was about time he grew up. This time he was charged with rape. Acorn, a tall, muscular man with intelligent eyes, a shaved head and crisply manicured goatee, did not look at all what his criminal resume would suggest. He always looked together. Now though, he was afraid.

"This doesn't sound like you." Sam searched Cornelius's eyes, wanting to connect with him and perhaps read him. Sam's heart clenched mildly as he saw it. Cornelius had screwed up. Or at least Cornelius believed it to be so.

"Exactly, exactly." Cornelius was clearly relieved to speak to someone official who thought he was innocent. "This is crazy. I got a job now. Nine months. Driving."

Sam noticed Acorn's outfit. While rumpled and jacketless, he sported half a tuxedo, like the morning after a wedding reception gone bad. Sam jotted notes.

"You drive for Burke's?"

"Yeah, they love me there. I got to get out. We got a gig tonight. I'm s'posed to pick up a body at the hospital at three, man."

Acorn did have the job going for him. Burke's Funeral Parlor was a well-known local business that handled the funerals of prominent, and not-so-prominent, Bennet residents, including Sam's mother.

"Relax. If the judge won't let you out today, I'll call Burke's and get some confirmation of your employment. I've dealt with them before. I'll try to schmooze it over for you until we can figure this out. We can file a motion in a few days once we learn more. But we can't put forward your side of this story today. Today we just—"

"Will *you* represent me?" Cornelius had picked up on Sam's *"we."* He employed it with every defendant, and it sometimes spawned the false hope that he would personally handle their cases.

"Not sure. We'll see. You'll get someone good. This is a serious charge."

"Hey, man, you get me out of this, I'll never forget it. I'll repay you somehow, someday. Believe it, Sam."

And then Cornelius leaned forward and whispered in Sam's ear, the practiced words carefully crafted by one who sensed their volatility. He placed one hand on the small of Sam's back to create a secret trust beyond what was available in the crowded video room. Sam felt a minor but perceptible jolt, as if Cornelius had just walked across a static-laced carpet. But there was no carpet, and Sam suddenly had an odd clarity—Cornelius had screwed up, but he was not guilty of rape.

"The bitch slapped me in the side of the head right when I was about to come."

"Do me a favor, Cornelius."

"Anything to get out of here, bro."

"Don't ever, ever, say that again."

The video screen went black after forty-five minutes of back and forth between Sam, the prosecutor, and the judge. Out of eight new arrestees, the judge had granted bail to six of them, Acorn not among them.

"You got one more," Deputy Wilson said, as Sam stood and picked up his briefcase.

"Oh yeah, Hogman."

"Sorry. He's down in the mental ward. Listen, Sam, he's—"

"I heard."

Sam followed the deputy to the elevator and down to the mental ward, a row of four cells with metal doors.

"You want me in there with you? He's a whack job."

Sam put his hand on the deputy's shoulder and winked. "I got it."

Wilson opened the cell with a flat metal key. "I'll be right out here." He shut the door behind Sam, but not so far as to click it locked.

The cell reeked of disinfectant. Hogman, a pale white guy with thinning, blondish-gray hair, looked about fifty. He sat cross-legged on the metal bench. He was short but wiry, the strong kind of thin. A fighter. A grappler. The only other thing immediately apparent about Hogman was his albino-pink eyes. *Shit, no wonder they think he's crazy.*

Sam approached him, extending his hand.

"My name is Sam Young, I'm going to—"

"I know who you are, Young."

Sam slowly pulled his hand away and scanned Hogman's jail intake sheet, the only document he had about the case.

"You're charged with destruction of property, but it looks like you have no record. If you straighten up your act a little, you can probably get out on bail. What's your deal?"

"It's a sad day when the only way I can get the lawyer I want is to crap and piss on the floor, but there you have it."

"You know something about me?"

Hogman nodded. The corners of his eyes wrinkled, reflecting a thoughtful emotion of one kind or another. Perhaps a sad secret. Or maybe he was just crazy. Sam had long since learned that reading crazy people was a dodgy business. The very centers of Hogman's eyeballs were pink. Hogman looked, or seemed, like a scrappy little mouse.

"I'll behave from here on out. And don't worry about the confounded bail. Just find out about my case and come see me in a few days. I'll be out of the crazy unit by then. Just tell them I was coming down from PCP or some shit. Whatever you can think of. I'm a decent guy, believe me. Odd perhaps, but decent."

Nothing like a low-maintenance client.

"Okay then, I'll get discovery on your case and see you later this week. Call me if you change your mind about bail."

"You can be sure I won't." He held out his pale hand to Sam, who gripped it. Hogman's limp hand was cool and dry. Calm. Upon touching Hogman's hand, Sam's eyes jumped to Hogman's again, as if the handshake was meant to be a hint that Sam had missed something. But Hogman just looked at him with the same even expression.

"You all right?" Sam said.

"Are you?" Hogman met Sam's gaze silently until Sam buzzed the door.

•••

Sam whipped the Escalade out of the sprawling suburban strip mall that housed Diagnostia. His fist gripped his balled-up copy of the confidentiality agreement he had just signed. Twenty-four hours. Confidential DNA typing results. Unless— the crumpled paper declared in bold writing—it came to the attention of the management that the results were relevant to a serious criminal investigation.

As with most legal waivers, no one had any idea what it meant. It wouldn't matter. Sam had fidgeted nervously as he informed the salesperson at Diagnostia that he wanted to find out if his wife had had a weekend guest who just may have sipped from the metal chalice Sam had found on his night table. The clerk's caring smile said exactly one thing—the mantra of all private investigators in spousal cheating cases: *In your heart, you already know. Perfect.*

Sam started the Escalade and looked at the time on his phone while his mind checked off things on his never-ending to-do list, always wondering if he could fit in one more thing. Juliana was likely waiting. The letter from the storage company and the odd new connection to his mother's home away from home—Holy Angels—both arriving at the same time seemed, like so many things in his frantic life, fortuitous. Like a force from somewhere else trying to give him a hint. Or, as he often thought when he noticed what appeared as a notably serendipitous series of events, maybe it was just his hungover brain clawing for a special meaning, utterly unsubstantiated by the facts. Magic, clairvoyance, depression, or craziness: there was no way to tell the difference. He eased the Escalade out of the parking lot, his phone buzzing untouched on the seat beside him.

As far as Sam could tell, You Keep the Key Storage had not changed in sixteen years—beyond a new paint job. He had rented the space about a week before he drove his mother's Toyota down to college. It had taken him mere minutes to load the six boxes into the stuffy little storage area. Twelve ninety-nine per month. In the years since, the price had tripled for the tiny square room. Sitting in the Escalade, Sam held his key ring and fingered the small, flat padlock key he had never used.

"Hey, man," the uniformed attendant said. "So you're the guy, huh? The guy who hasn't been back since the nineties?" Sam stood in front of his storage unit, examining the new padlock. "Can't wait to tell Otto I saw you. Anyway, we change the padlocks every five years or so. Never look inside, just change 'em, you know. Here you go."

The guy stepped in front of Sam and opened the shiny new lock with what must have been a master key. He gently opened the door to reveal Marcela Young's six unmarked, neatly packed cardboard boxes.

Sam carefully began to remove one box at a time and carry them to his car. When he finished, he slammed the hatch.

"Good luck, Mr. Young. If it matters to ya, you had the record." Sam drove away slowly, watching the kid wave at him through the rearview mirror.

CHAPTER 11

"YOU CAN'T FOLD ME into attorney-client privilege. I work for the state."

Juliana sat naked in the center of the carpet on her living room floor. As usual, one leg was folded under her and the other bent to prop up her smoking hand, the cigarette like a pointer at a lecture.

Sam lay on his side next to her, holding a glass of wine and looking at the floor.

"I'm not saying it's like a formal attorney-client privilege. I'm just saying that we can help each other."

"I could get shit-canned for this." But her eyes said she did not care. They gleamed—dark orbs, deep in complex thought.

She stood and walked towards the kitchen, where she stood, flatfooted and naked in the bright light, slowly pouring a glass of wine. She then walked back towards Sam, staring him directly in the eyes, her playful smile dodging the serious issue on the table. Sam sat up just as Juliana softly dropped to her knees, set her wine glass on the carpet, and put her mouth on him as he lay back. Minutes later she sat before him again. Her lighter flashed in the dim light, and she continued the conversation as if nothing had happened. Sam looked at the ceiling as he let out a heavy breath.

"Your client thinks he has information on the Rosslyn Ripper, maybe even his DNA profile. He can't go to the cops for some bizarre reason, and you may want me to check out the DNA result. Am I hearing this right?"

"It's probably all BS. I'm not asking you to compromise a bit of what you're doing. Just lay my result up against what you're working on. If it's worth pursuing, we'll figure out together how to manage it."

"Hmmmmm."

"So, you got anything new?" Sam asked.

Juliana pulled her legs under herself and sat erect. Testifying once again.

"I ran Powerplex 16 on swabs from the necks and undersides of the chins of all three victims. I got a very partial profile from Joni West's face. One faint allele on TPOX."

"TPOX?"

"A locus. The same allele appeared at it as the bra snapper showed at TPOX. Just fainter. This is a very weak result. No one would ever bother to run tests on it."

"So does it add anything?"

"For the court, not really. But it does for me. It means it's the profile of the same guy. The guy who touched Joni's bra also touched her neck or the underside of her chin. Now I'm convinced the bra snapper is the killer."

"Odds?"

"Not worth doing. It's weak. A one-allele match could never, ever, be used in court."

"So let's say I have a complete DNA profile from saliva. Can the lab get the Powerplex 16 typing?"

"Sure, but you have no chain of custody. It wouldn't even be admissible."

"This would just be for me. To know if it's anything at all."

"Why didn't you bring this straight to me? Why a private lab?"

Sam stood, put on his underwear, and stepped into his pants. Juliana lay on her back on the floor, one leg over the other, smoking and looking at the ceiling.

"You better know what you're doing, smart guy." She blew smoke into the air.

• • •

Sam pulled into his parking space in front of his building a couple minutes before eleven. Camille was already there, leaning against her car, her leather briefcase slung over her shoulder. She wore sneakers, long shorts, a loose, gym-appropriate T-shirt, and a baseball cap with a Holy Angels softball logo. Before he reached her, she had the brown envelope out.

"That couldn't wait, huh?" he said.

"Actually, maybe I was bored. But really, Sam, you have to read this. I want your take on it." She said it like a teacher telling a student he would agree with her calculation of a math problem by the next day.

"Why me? You really think this thing was written by the killer or has something to do with the case?"

Sam watched Camille carefully for any clue of deception, but saw nothing, just a relaxed young woman in a softball uniform leaning against her beat-up old Toyota Camry.

"I know it has something to do with something." She opened her car door and got in, but the window came down as she started the engine.

"Don't drink too much tonight," she said.

• • •

Sam shifted the journal from one hand to the other. Then back. He stood still for a few moments. Not smoking. Not looking at his phone. Not thinking of a client. Just breathing. He looked up along the side of his building. The red bricks. The fire escape. His second-floor window that watched the busy street. No cars, no people; nothing moved anywhere around him. The quiet moment ended soon enough, and Sam moved quickly upstairs to his apartment and its makeshift bar.

Sam's phone buzzed. "This is Young."

"Samson," Steve Buterab's mellow voice said.

"Hey, Steve." Sam braced himself for a possible brush back.

"I got a question about your doctor friend. You see here's the problem. He's no good. If you'd come to me before, maybe, but I'm sorry, he's too far gone. There can't be an extension at this point, and you're even asking for a reduction."

Sam did not answer. He was accustomed, possibly too accustomed, to hearing affirmative replies to his requests for small favors. Spoiled, maybe. He had taken it too far with the Buterabs.

"Unless—" Steve said.

Sam's spirits buoyed. He sensed a chink in Steve's armor through the phone.

"Unless?"

"I wouldn't wish it on you, but if *you* wanna guarantee it, we go a ways back and all, and I think you're a standup guy. If you wanna get involved, I can look into a price. To settle. To save the trouble, you know. For everybody."

Sam swallowed. He thought of Torres, the clueless idiot, with his daughter waiting by the mailbox for her acceptance letter to MIT. He took a deep breath while climbing the stairs to his apartment. He poured himself a drink while he considered Steve's offer. It would save Torres if he forked over the bulk of his new fee from Barnabus to the Buterabs. On the other hand, he needed the cash. Why did he so often get into these situations?

"Can I think about it?"

"Okay, pal, but don't just think, you gotta know. I'll tell you what, no guarantees, no promises yet. Let's say you're provisionally interested. I'll get back to you. I gotta say though, Samson, you're one fuck of a friend. This guy save your life or somethin'? Or you just a goddamned do-gooder?"

Sam smiled but said nothing.

"I sure hope it's the first thing, counselor," Steve said. "I sure fucking hope so. Anyway, back at you soon."

Sam set the phone on the table and took a sip of his drink, a long enough sip to generate a need for a new trip to the kitchen. Good old Steve. Always there to help out a friend. Yeah, right. And, of course, Steve would give a cut to his old man. And why not? The wheels of commerce turned for saints and sinners alike.

Sometimes, people—witnesses, prosecutors, clients, even judges—seem momentarily befuddled over why they acceded to one of Sam's suggestions or requests. He had always believed that his little mental jabs and punches had an impact their targets never noticed.

So was he working Buterab over, or was it just the opposite?

Sam sat in the chair in the center of his living room, vodka in hand. The long, bar-sized mirror on the wall behind his couch allowed him a view of the bright digital clock on the kitchen counter. Almost eleven forty.

Sam thought about Juliana while the first half of the drink worked its magic on his nerves, his stomach, and his entire body. He knew he was taking a risk on several levels by sharing information with her. And while he could not see the endgame of doing so, she was his only way, at least his only potentially private way, to find out how Camille's mystery man's DNA compared against evidence from the actual Ripper crime scenes. If there was a match of some kind, they'd have to deal with it, which was, of course, why Camille had hired him.

In the end, while Juliana's duty to science certainly trumped any loyalty she had developed to Sam over the last few months, he sensed that she would work within his constraints, at least within the bounds of reason. He pictured Juliana's excited face, her animated gestures while she held forth on her subject of expertise. Sure, like cops and prosecutors, she wanted to catch bad guys, but Sam trusted her anyway. Juliana Kim was, as much as could be said of any person, devoid of guile or artifice—a heart-on-her-sleeve scientist. Sam finished the drink and stood to get another.

He pulled the next section of Camille's manuscript from the brown envelope and again studied the neat script of a person careful to perform each quirk and angle of his block letters correctly. Sam repeated his Q-tip swabbing, this time covering the entire back of each of the top three pages. Plainly, the papers would contain more than one person's DNA, including, probably, Camille's. When to actually test the swabs was not the point. The point was that he had them—he might have the Ripper's DNA on swabs in plastic bags in a drawer in his kitchen. And what was the point of that? To know more than the police? To help Camille or an old priest who realistically faced very little legal peril? No. The point was that there was no point at all beyond that he wanted to work, to solve the puzzle, to outsmart the person on the other side of the aisle, to keep his mind chewing through problems instead of merely swimming through liquor. On this point, he and Juliana were just alike. Soul mates, even. He sipped his second vodka and pulled out his notes and phone.

Chicken Industry, Argentina—Argentina is currently the eighth largest chicken producer in the world. But in the 1950s?

Sam found worldpoultry.com and then Buenos Aires Chicken Factory. Indeed, chicken production in and around Buenos Aires appeared to be a booming business. Sam found an article distinguishing indoor from outdoor chicken facilities, noting that because of the USDA American chicken-rearing methods are the safest and, for lack of a better phrase, less cruel than those of developing countries. He satisfied himself that it was at least possible that an indoor chicken factory existed in the '50s in Buenos Aires.

Sam recognized that his methods, historical websites and the like, were not exactly foolproof. But half the time the cops did no better. The mystery man's story, up until this point, was possible, grandiose, to be sure, but possible. Sam found it very unlikely that police records could be obtained for the death of a tourist in 1957, but because the mystery man had confessed to a murder and named the victim, he needed to follow it up.

Retiro, Clock Tower, Buenos Aires—this was an easy one. The British clock tower stands a bit over seventy-five meters high in the center of the square in the Retiro neighborhood of Buenos Aires. Of course, easy to prove meant easy to fabricate.

Information about shipping from Buenos Aires to Cuba in 1958 was scant. Of course, ships sailed from Argentina to Cuba in the 1950s. Ships were the primary method of world travel until the 1970s but all in all, not much for Sam to go on.

Sam refilled his glass in the kitchen. One more. One hour. One drink. One chapter. One. He sat down and pulled out the journal and realized what had been on his mind all day. Sure, he was tired. Sure, he was working and drinking too much. Still, he was almost sure he had seen this writing before.

• • •

JANUARY 7, 1958

After a meager lunch, Paul and I stood on the deck. My gaze remained fixed on the coast, which had been reduced to a thin, green line as we proceeded north. I gripped his hand, and as was my habit, massaged his thoughts as if to gently hold clay without imprinting upon it.

"Shoot for the sky. If you miss, at least you'll land on the mountaintop."

Startled, I faced the speaker, ready for anything.

"First time away from home?" The man had one of those complexions common in Bariloche. The ruddy face, crafted by years of sun, drink, hard work, or some combination of the three, made young men old and pretty women plain. He stood near us, one hand on the rail. He wore a round, white hat, white pants, and a fancy, blue jacket, like the clothes of a businessman or a landowner. But his rough demeanor and accent said different. He was one of us, or at least used to be.

I forced a childlike blush. "Is it so obvious?"

"Oh no, no. Not to most eyes, at least. But to mine, yes. First time away, I would say. And not planning a swift return, eh?"

I swallowed. I had a gift for seeing thoughts and the twisted meanings in things, but the impression put forward by the man caused me pause for a convincing false show of confidence.

"It's okay." The man stepped closer. He lowered his voice as he leaned in. His whisper was like air, like a soft wind with no sound behind it. His skin smelled like cologne, perhaps overdone, much like his clothes, so as to cover his true nature. Something pulsated in the man, though, a familiar, attractive force I could not place.

"Your secret is safe with me, friend. But be wary of the mate—Aguilar, they call him on the ship. But his name is Ramon Ortiz. He works with the police and has been asked to watch the two of you. Specifically"—the man turned to look around, then met my eyes again—"you."

Again I hesitated, and then flinched as the man touched my arm.

"No need to say a word, friend. I'm someone you can trust, and you need to listen to me. You've always wondered if you're special. Stop worrying about it. You are. But you're no demon or devil. Just keep to your roles, two young people abroad for a short holiday. Maybe to visit relatives in Florida, no?"

"They aren't roles. Who are you, sir?" I gripped Paul's hand and could feel the heat of his nerves coming alive at the man's proximity, though he knew of neither of the murders from which we fled.

The man winked. I looked him up and down and then pried into his eyes, perhaps a bit too hard. My heart unclenched.

"Are you . . . ?" I hoped for an interruption, since I did not know how to phrase my question.

"A kindred spirit? One like you? No, I'm certainly not like all the rest. You could say I'm the sort of person who recognizes your kind when I see them. I've taken a special interest since I was very young. But no, I'm not your brother. Not your kindred spirit you might say. Cousin maybe. Johannes Van Zyl."

The man extended his hand to me. It was dry and calloused, which confirmed my suspicion about his humble origins.

"You're always bothering yourself with the origins of things," Van Zyl said, though I had not said a word. "Like you, I'm no Argentine, just a misplaced foreigner from a race of no-good castabouts."

I laughed. Indeed, I had seen his heritage beneath his leathery tan. Afrikaner, Dutch from Africa. Pretending to be somebody else. Same as us. I don't know why I felt such a level of comfort with a man who claimed the knowledge to expose me.

"Remember what I said," Van Zyl said. "Watch Aguilar. He's a fool but powerful, with the authority to arrest you." His face went grim, his next words froze my heart, and they might have been his last were we not standing in public view of a dozen fellow passengers.

"Miguel's death means nothing, but Salome was a foreigner, with money and a family and a life. Be careful." Van Zyl's whisper whipped through me like a long, cold breeze through trees.

"Your gifts can't bust prison walls. I suggest you leave this ship in Cuba. If they look for you, it will be in Miami. Wait in Cuba before making for America. They have too many problems there now for the authorities to worry about some fugitives. Stay alive, and keep moving north."

Van Zyl strolled away towards the main cabin. He turned back quickly and half saluted from the brim of his hat.

"Shoot for the sky. If you miss, at least you'll wind up on the mountaintop!"

Paul stared at me quizzically. "Diablo?"

I shrugged. "And what would that say about us?"

Before we came to our room tonight, I saw the man called Aguilar. Perhaps Van Zyl has my mind overworked, or is a devil of some sort either for or against us, but the fat Aguilar is watching us. His mind is spinning with thoughts not of justice, but reward. He carries a little notepad on which he pretends to scribble shit about the ship.

• • •

JANUARY 10, 1958

For days I have not been able to get Aguilar out of my head. Even Paul made note of the man's movements. For someone presumably trained as a spy, he was mentally sloppy, always forgetting to keep his mind on the task he was pretending to do while he actually watched us. This morning I resolved to solve the matter if the opportunity arose.

Tonight, Paul and I stood together on the cold upper deck. He shivered while I smoked cigarettes, a habit I picked up just today from a fellow traveler. It makes me feel older somehow. We were all alone and watched the horizon as we passed the very northernmost point of South America. From the far-away lights, I envisioned a town, a small one perhaps, a peaceful one without the craziness of Buenos Aires or the ominous unknowns of the north. I thought about how I might never again be so far south on the planet. I even surprised myself by feeling nostalgic for my hometown. There was no particular reason to blame little Bariloche and its sad wooden cross and stinking dogs for my life thus far. It was just itself, as I suppose all places are.

"One more." I pulled another cigarette from the crumpled, red Pall Mall pack. But Paul's eyes focused past me with alarm. I turned around and saw that someone was watching us from about thirty meters away, at the end of the darkened deck. The man leaned forward, hand above his eyes to block the glare from the dull electric lamps lining the edge of the cabin roof. It was

Aguilar with his little notebook flipped open, pencil in hand. I closed the distance in seconds and was upon him. Instinctively knowing that no other human eyes pierced the darkness this late at night, I quickly snapped his neck and launched him over the side into the noisy ocean. It was a bit overdone. He spun, as I once heard a Venezuelan say, ass over ankles into the darkness. Before his notebook followed him overboard, I learned from it that his real name was indeed Ramon Ortiz, and he was an undercover policeman.

So odd, the interplay of luck and fate—are they the same thing? The answer is, of course, that it does not matter. Ramon was on to the next world, and we were on to Cuba. One second he was just doing his job, the next he was heading toward the great mystery beyond, whatever that held for him. For some reason, this death of Ramon Ortiz makes me think of Trinity. Where she may be, and, if dead, would Ortiz see her in heaven? In hell? Would they talk about what I have done? My mother once said the magic was stronger in me than in Trinity, but I never actually believed that. Her dancing and laughing and her thoughts, which floated above our Bariloche shit pile, proved differently to me. Why are we not drawn together, instead of this empty silence? Surely, she would know what to do.

I had to kill him. It was a question of odds, I suppose—he presented a chance of apprehension and punishment, even death. I can't believe Paul and I are evil. And what about my mother? Or Trinity? Or Salome? Or Van Zyl? Did he suggest this murder to me? Maybe the myths of the human culture— witches, wolves, and demons dancing around fires in the thick and brambly medieval forest—touch the truth. Could it be I am one of these very creatures? Why are spirits, demons, and angels (call them whatever you wish) any more evil than puppies, locusts, or sharks?

Paul now sleeps while I read our Bible, wondering if the ship's crew will come knocking when Aguilar fails to turn up wherever he is supposed to be.

Exodus 20:2-5 says the following:

I am the Lord your God, who brought you up out of the land of Egypt, out of the house of slavery. Do not have any other gods before me. You shall not make for yourself an idol, whether in the form of anything that is in Heaven above, or that is on the Earth beneath, or that is in the water under the Earth. You shall not bow down to them or worship them; for I am the Lord your God and I am a jealous God, punishing children for the iniquity of parents to the third and fourth generation of those who reject me.

This is the beginning of the Ten Commandments. Certainly the Great One is a jealous God. But not even he claims to be alone. I find it noteworthy that the Decalogue, these Ten Commandments, appear twice in the Bible. I cannot discern why they have been selected above the Bible's other prohibitions. But many of the Ten Commandments, to my eyes, were penned by a chest-pounding Bariloche bully so sure, yet so wrong, that his personal ego means anything in this world.

Another passage that caught my attention was Revelation 12:9:

And the great dragon was cast out, that old serpent, called the Devil, and Satan, which deceiveth the whole world: he was cast out into the earth, and his angels were cast out with him.

It is obvious to me that exposure of my identity, and not only my crimes, would mean death for me at the hands of humans. Like what happens to witches. But even the Great God seems to tolerate only a solitary special one. All the rest must be the same. Or be cast out. I wonder how many others are like my mother, or indeed if I am even like her. Able to see the meaning in all things and live after death. Another passage strikes my attention, in part as it relates to some inconsistencies in the passages above. Psalms 19:7:

The law of the Lord is perfect, refreshing the soul. The statutes of the Lord are trustworthy, making wise the simple.

Is that so? And yet the Great God punishes traitors' children to the fourth generation? And the castaway angels for how long?

Forever? And he created me this way yet casts me into the world alone to figure it out?

I shut my eyes but felt no urge to sleep, suddenly alive inside, if perhaps a little afraid, with the desire to learn more of this Bible and its nonsensical power.

I flipped to the book of Job, the man who sued God. Again, the Great One's Bible provides just enough for curiosity but not much more. Such a sad story, and I see my mother's point though I wonder what it has to do with me. So the Great God ruins his faithful servant's life on a dare from Satan? And, what's worse, rejects Job's demand for an explanation and merely boasts back at him like a mean landlord? And why did my mother call Job's plea a suit? *Shoot for the sky, if you miss, at least you will land on the mountaintop?* It seems to me Job landed nowhere good.

The Bible talks about miracles but says nothing about kids who can read minds, toss fat men three meters into the air, and kill without hesitation. Am I part of the covenant so often described in the Great God's Bible, or am I, and perhaps Trinity, Salome, and my mother and the like, more like Job? All alone, fools if we believe in the Great One's promises?

I listen to Paul's breathing as I try to sleep. I wrap my arms around myself. Surely my duty is to protect us, to give Paul a chance for a life. And not to worry about Job, mysterious old writings, or strangers who mean us harm. But as I had launched Aguilar over the rail, I had seen too much. A wife who loyally awaited him at home. She planned to use his extra pay to fix the family car. I shuddered and eventually must have fallen asleep, because Paul woke this morning complaining about his late breakfast.

CHAPTER 12

SAM AWOKE TO A buzzing phone. He looked at the time—
1:01 p.m., August 1. Thank God it was Saturday. But the number
coming in was his boss.

Suck it up. Take the call now.

Taking difficult calls as they came in usually turned out to be
worth it. Otherwise, they swelled, like a wave cresting to crash.
Sam spoke aloud before answering to clear the phlegm and
hungover edge from his voice.

"This is Young," he said cheerily, as if jumping from one call
to another.

"Seen the news?" Simmons said.

"What's up?"

"Bennet PD arrested a guy last night for assaulting Chief
O'Malley. Punched him in the face at a fundraiser at the Ballston
Mall."

Sam didn't see where this was headed. The office had a dozen
assault-on-police-officer cases at any given time. Sure, punching
the chief was interesting, but a call from his boss?

"The guy is Jerome Johnson, the father of Carole Kingsley,
the second Rosslyn Ripper victim. Seems he was upset with

O'Malley campaigning instead of working on solving the case. After he sucker punched the chief, he got a beat down from half a dozen cops and spent the night at Bennet County General. Overnight, the cops searched his apartment in the projects. They're saying they found a pound of pot and three automatic weapons. The press has the police station surrounded, and it looks like Johnson is being transported from the hospital to the police station any minute. Johnson's a former client of ours. He suffers from PTSD from his time in Iraq."

"So why—"

"Here's the problem. If Johnson confesses to the automatic weapons and the pot, the case will go federal, with twenty-five years of mandatory minimums at play. Without a confession, they may not have enough evidence to convict him of anything but assault. Two other unemployed vets stay at the apartment, and people are always in and out of the place. You should go down there and try to stop the interrogation. You'll have to move pretty fast. I'd say get there within an hour."

"But there's no case. No appointment. We actually don't represent him. The statute says we can't act until appointment. I could get sanctioned, don't you think?"

"Ah, the rules," Simmons said. "That always stops you, doesn't it?"

Five minutes later, as Sam pulled the Escalade out of his parking lot, his phone buzzed. A blocked number, which he usually did not answer. Telemarketers or, potentially worse, someone he knew deliberately blocking his or her number, to whom he was not prepared to speak. The phone buzzed and buzzed in his hand. It could be somebody from the Bennet County jail calling about Johnson.

"This is Young."

"Samson Young." A soothing, slightly accented voice. "Long time no see."

"Raj?"

"How are you, Samson?" Ouch. If Raj was calling personally, it probably meant he had really crossed the line with Steve. "Hey. Let's get a coffee, you and me. I need a favor. Nothing big, you know, but something you can help me with."

"Now?"

"Sure. I'm at the coffee place, you know the one." The place they first met, when Raj approached him about Steve's drunk-driving case.

Sam looked at the time. Still only ten minutes since Simmons's call. He thought of Torres, all the clients Raj had referred to him over the years, and, well, that it was Raj Buterab.

"See you in five."

• • •

Just like the first time Sam had met Raj years before, Raj was strikingly out of place in the bland atmosphere of a suburban Virginia Starbucks. He sat alone at a table, his large hand covering almost the entire white cup from which he sipped. He appeared huge at the small table, but it was his formal manner, pressed dress shirt and slacks and genteel calmness that made him stand out from the yuppie parents and the sandal-wearing twenty-somethings. Sam sat down.

"Hi, Raj."

"You know, it's funny. You're one of the only people other than my family to call me Raj. They say Mr. Buterab. I say, hey, call me Raj. They say, okay, Mr. Buterab. Go figure. I'm glad you call me Raj. It's not a problem . . . Really."

Sam managed a hesitant nod.

"I'm sure you're in a hurry, Samson. I'll get to the point. You're a smart guy, that's what I like about you. I've always thought of you like a son. Kinda like a son that's more responsible than my other son—if you follow me. I think you know a little about my business, my reputation, anyway. I've sold things. I've bought things. If people needed some help, some extra cash, that's never been a problem. But I've been done with all that business for years."

Raj's well-manicured hand extended towards Sam, offering him a business card. *Buterab Enterprises.*

"This is what I do now. For fifteen years I've worked on it. In 2013 we raised four and a half million dollars for scholarships for poor kids from Hungary and Romania to attend college in the US. We donate to politicians who wanna actually do something to eliminate poverty. Naïve, I know, but that's my life now. I like you, and it's important to me that you see. Sure, I cut some corners to get where I am, but I haven't broken a law in ten years. I know you hear this all the time from all your clients. But the church is my life now. I got no reason to lie about that. Ask anybody. Hey, Samson, did you know that the Catholic Church is the largest charity on Earth? That it does more work to eliminate poverty than anybody, even the US fuckin' government?"

Sam nodded solemnly.

"Now my son, Steve. He's a different story. This is what we need to talk about. Obviously, people are gonna gamble, and people are gonna smoke pot. Me, I never gamble. I don't even drink. I've never understood it. But whatever people wanna do, I got no problem with it."

Raj held Sam's eyes but softly, like the pseudo-politician he was. Small talk. *Here comes the kicker.*

"Except I do have a problem when people are stupid. God bless him, but my son and his friends, I can't help it. I love him. But you know, I spoiled him, maybe. But people act dumb. They gotta pay the cost. That's just how it is. I wish it were some other way. You see the news today?"

"News? No. Not yet."

"Well, check it out. You know the news, they make a big deal out of things that aren't a big deal, but look it up. This guy, this veteran from the hood, clocked what's his face, that police chief of yours."

Whoa. "I know about that. Jerome Johnson. He's a former client of my office."

"I figured. You handle cases for poor people. That's great. Everybody needs a lawyer like you. So anyway, I don't want the police questioning that guy Johnson."

Sam looked down at the time on his phone then back up at Raj. Twenty-five minutes since Simmons's call. Raj had one of those old faces without wrinkles. He picked up his coffee, and they regarded each other while Raj took a long, slow sip.

"You know how it is, Samson. A guy gets in trouble. The cops put the scare on him. Punching out the chief, what's that worth these days? Some jail time maybe? But these guns and the pot. Nothing wrong with some pot, and don't get me wrong, I don't like guns, but to each his own with the guns as far as I care. But you know the cops, and this guy from the hood who's dumb enough to punch out a cop, so they'll be comin' heavy at this guy. And here's where my worry comes in."

Sam checked the time on his phone again.

"I'm almost finished, I know, you gotta go. So here it is; they come heavy at this guy. Like, he's going *under* the jail unless he tells 'em where he got the drugs and the guns. And he's scared. And this guy, he's not all there in the first place, that's my take on it. You know how it works. So the guy may say some things. All of it could be wrong, doesn't matter. And my son and his friends, with their parties and women and drugs and what do I know? My son's a good guy. He doesn't know one gun from another, but the pot? I just don't know. What I care about is people being stupid, and I'm very unhappy. But my son's friends shouldn't be selling pot to a guy like that. So, whatever Johnson says, yeah, these guys sell pot. And then the next guy says, *no, not me,* and then somebody says, *you know this guy Steve, he's got money, weed, the card games.* And his old man's a big shot in town that made his money gambling and donates to candidates like he's some kind of do-gooder. This guy Johnson. He can't be talking to the cops about drugs. You go down there and help him. You got twenty large today. And Samson, there's always more where that came from. I've referred you what, two-dozen good-paying clients over the years? And don't get me wrong. I do it 'cause you're good, not 'cause I want somethin' back. But still, we got a relationship, right?"

Sam took a deep breath. "Raj, there's something you gotta know." Raj nodded slightly. "If Johnson's my client, I act in his best interest, no one else's. Not yours. Not Steve's. That's how it has to be."

Raj stood to leave. "You're an interesting guy, Samson. I like that. So you gotta see what's good for me is good for Johnson in the long run. Those two things are one and the same. You get them to release this guy, and I'll pay for his stay at the mental unit up at Bennet. I'll be his friend. If he needs to do some time, he'll do some time. But I'll take care of him. Financially. In the long run. And twenty large to you. Don't forget that part."

Raj paused. "I'm sorry about Steve and this silly business with the doctor. You help me, or you don't, doesn't matter. Problem solved. Tell that doc to pay when he can. You don't gotta threaten people to make money in America. You just don't. I don't know what that boy's problem is, I really don't."

Sam narrowed his eyes at Raj.

Raj laughed. "You're right, I do know what his problem is. He's trying to be like me. A dumb move, Samson. A real dumb move."

Sam stood, shook Raj's hand, and turned towards the door.

"Hey, Samson!" Raj called out. Sam turned back. Raj, with all his huge exuberance, was oblivious to the suburban Starbucks crowd, all of whose heads turned towards his booming voice.

"Slow down once in a while. The simple things in life are the best."

• • •

Sam approached the glass information booth at the police station. Sally, the police department's civilian receptionist, greeted him with a huge smile. He had represented her nephew on a DUI and gotten him off.

To Sam's left, outside, at the other end of the long lobby, he saw the television trucks. Whichever cop tipped off the reporters had screwed up, because without the press's attention, Simmons, and Raj for that matter, would never have known to call Sam.

Some people just can't see the angles.

"Detectives are about to question my client, Jerome Johnson," Sam told Sally. "I formally invoke his Fifth Amendment right to remain silent. I am recording this conversation, and I need you to inform the detectives of all of this now. It's eleven thirteen, according to the clock on your wall."

Sam pulled out his iPhone and took a photograph of the clock and Sally with her mouth wide open. Without speaking, she picked up a phone. After a hushed conversation, she winked at Sam. "Have a seat, Mr. Young. Someone will be with you shortly." Her tone was crisp and professional.

Sam raised his eyebrows at her. "The recorder's off now."

"What the fuck is going on?" she mouthed in barely a whisper.

"That's what I'm trying to find out."

Sam took a seat in the lobby and breathed. He noted the time and opened a notebook. Exactly eleven minutes and twenty-two seconds later, Chief Edwin O'Malley himself emerged from the end of the lobby and walked slowly towards Sam. Rumor had it that O'Malley, after his thirty years on the force, was about to retire and run for city council.

O'Malley took a seat right next to Sam in the row of plastic lobby chairs. He folded one leg over the other and placed his hands over his knee.

"Mr. Young." O'Malley spoke with the blue-collar accent he grew up with. His present objective was obvious. . His only hope to get Johnson to confess to owning the guns was to muscle Sam out of the way. O'Malley glanced down the empty hall to the station entrance, where reporters plastered themselves against the glass doors. Sam mimicked O'Malley's sitting position. O'Malley sported his black eye gracefully, like the unsuperficial tough guy he wanted to be.

"I'd sure like to know what the hell you think you're doing," O'Malley said. "Your man tried to knock my block off this morning, and he's living in an empty apartment with enough weaponry to take on my SWAT team. We're gonna question the guy. Period." *Period,* a signature O'Malley comment Sam had heard so often during televised press conferences.

"I'm making sure you don't screw this up, Chief." Sam looked straight ahead, as if speaking to an annoying fellow airline traveler. O'Malley flinched and cleared his throat.

"If Johnson is under arrest," Sam said, "he invokes his Miranda rights. If he's not under arrest, I'm driving him home. You've seized the weapons."

O'Malley, arms folded, rolled his eyes. "You're not even appointed to his case, Sam. There is no case. This is an investigation, my friend. That's it. Period."

"Listen to me, Edwin. Johnson invoked his rights through me, and if you guys asked him a single question, it's worth nothing to you. You got a problem with me representing him right now? Take it up with the state bar. But if I don't see Johnson in the next five minutes, I'm taking it up with the people down at the end of the hall. And you know what I'm going to say? That Edwin O'Malley should be trying to help this guy, this war hero with mental health problems whose daughter was recently murdered. But instead, O'Malley is trying to prosecute him because his feelings got hurt when the guy punched him out. What you *should* do is release Johnson to me right now. Give a gracious speech about it. I'll check him into the psych ward at Bennet for a voluntary thirty-day stay. Once he gets on his meds he'll plead guilty to hitting you, and you can come to court and ask the judge to give him a suspended sentence. Now which way is going to look better come election time?"

O'Malley straightened his uniform by tugging at the bottom of his shirt. Sitting this close to O'Malley, Sam realized the rumors were indeed true about O'Malley's wanting to run.

But O'Malley ignored the election comment. "The guy's dangerous, Sam. He knows how to get his hands on firearms. And the feds are gonna want some answers about those guns."

"Fuck the feds. This guy needs help, not twenty-five years."

O'Malley glanced down the hall at the reporters pressing up against the glass wall, shook his head, and looked back at Sam.

"I'll deliver your man to you by the back entrance. And I'll have a cruiser follow you to Bennet psych. But Sam, if this sucker bolts or hurts anyone, you're through. You know I could make that happen. You and your fancy car and extra cash. Yeah, we know about that."

"You got a deal, Chief. With one caveat."

O'Malley raised his eyebrows, as if being challenged by an insolent child.

"It's a misdemeanor assault," Sam said.

"Man, you've got an overly bold-ass attitude. I'm pretty sure it's gonna get you into some trouble right soon." He stood and began to turn his back on Sam.

Sam stood as well, and extended his hand to O'Malley. "That's what my therapist keeps telling me."

O'Malley started chuckling, eventually rolling into a full-throated laugh.

"One question, Chief. Why'd you call the press down here?"

O'Malley flinched, but decided not to deny it. "I have my reasons. You don't know what it's like in my world." O'Malley turned towards the elevators, ignoring the muffled calls of the reporters.

•••

"Mr. Young? Your results are ready," the Diagnostia clerk announced cheerfully.

Sam reached into his briefcase as he approached the counter. "I need these swabs typed, too. Expedited result." He held out a large plastic bin containing smaller bags, each with a Q-tip from his manuscript swabbing. The clerk frowned sympathetically. She handed Sam a thin, white envelope, the chalice DNA results, and a plastic bag holding the chalice.

"You know, these results do nothing for you unless you, well, have your own DNA type for making an exclusion. Or, I guess, the type of the, uh, the person you think it might be. Are you sure—"

Sam slumped and gave her a sad smile. "Let me worry about that." She nodded and gently accepted the sealed bags.

In your heart, you already know.

CHAPTER 13

JULIANA SAT UP AND placed her hand on Sam's back. She always touched him—a lot.

Sam turned towards her. "Let's talk DNA." He opened the Diagnostia envelope. "I have a DNA result here from saliva on the rim of a chalice. I haven't even looked at it. You don't have to tell me anything more about your investigation. Just look at this result and react. I've got the chalice right here."

Sam reached into his briefcase and handed Juliana the neatly labeled plastic bag holding the chalice, then the two-page document. Sam recognized the standard DNA typing chart on page one, the loci and their corresponding alleles on the Powerplex 16 graph.

Juliana's eyes rested on the paper for long enough to make the point that she was seeing something odd. She then stood and walked across the room, hips weaving her around her dining room table. She knelt, reached underneath a large wooden bureau, and stood with a thick manila file in her hands. Her worry had given way to the strongest emotional current she possessed—a love of the hunt, the game, the puzzle, the race.

Juliana walked to the kitchen and poured each of them a full glass of red wine before returning to the couch with the file tucked under her arm. Her eyes darted quickly around each of Sam's documents for several seconds.

"How fresh a sample was this?"

"Yesterday."

Juliana took a deep breath. "There are a few things I can tell you. One, this is a corrupted sample. Not a full profile."

"It was fresh saliva!"

"So you *think*. That's the problem with lacking the chain of custody. You don't know shit. But either way, not everyone leaves enough saliva on the rim of a cup to get a full profile. He could have just sipped it. Dry mouth, I don't know. It happens. Evaporation."

Sam reached for the results, but Juliana pulled the thin folder away.

"I'm not done. Incomplete or not, presuming this result is accurate, there's a pretty good chance this is the profile of the Joni West bra snapper, and, to a far lesser degree of certainty, the profile of her neck squeezer as well. Your mystery man's saliva profile has ten alleles at four loci, all also possessed by Joni West's bra snapper. There are no eliminating alleles."

Juliana breathed deeply and tossed the sheet next to her on the couch. She picked up her glass of wine.

Sam frowned. "I thought you said the bra snapper profile was too weak to mean anything but exclusion."

"For the court. I'm telling you how it *really* is. The ten alleles mean a lot to me. To any logical person. Add to that the fact that you, for some reason, wanted the comparison made, and I can deduce you're in possession of some volatile and dangerous information. You're putting me in a weird position, my friend. We've gotta do something with this. Ten alleles aren't enough to calculate odds, but I can tell you from experience, a ten-allele match, unlike a one-allele match, means something. Even if the odds that the chalice sipper and the bra snapper are different people are as low as one in ten that means a lot when combined with whatever you're not telling me. Basically, we both now suspect that you know who the Rosslyn Ripper is, or at least someone who touched West's bra near the time of her death."

She was right. Weak profile or not, it meant something.

"I don't know whose profile it is," Sam said, "and I can't find out without doing some legal wrangling. Forty-eight hours. Then you can do whatever you want with the chalice. My client wants the guy caught, too. But it's complicated."

Juliana drained her glass. "No shit?"

• • •

Sam sat alone again in his living room. Eight o'clock at night. The sole light in the room, a lamp on a corner table behind him, barely provided enough light to read. Yet the black script on the white pages seemed to reflect the fuzzy blue light coming in from the street, from the faraway lamps, themselves out of view. He looked at the two stacks of old white boxes on his coffee table. He pulled the lid off one and looked in. Papers. Used books, including a stack of religious textbooks. He went to the next box, which mostly had more of the same and a stack of medical records. Sam flipped through the records. Some of them related to a fact he knew well—he had been delivered early by C-section. At the bottom of the stack was his own birth certificate. He did not recall ever having seen it before. As he did know though, no father was listed. Then he saw something interesting. A manila folder holding a stack of old photos. He flipped through them. Most appeared to be from before his time. He had plenty of pictures of himself with his mother, the normal growing-up shots taped into neat photo albums that every eighties mother made. But he had hardly any photos of his mother as she was before him. Even so, all the old photos fit his constructed memories. Her with a small group of hippie-seeming friends. Her grad school group, the ones he enjoyed eavesdropping on from his room down the hall.

The men and women in the photos sported that distinctive seventies look—standing by old cars with their arms around each other. Some of the shots were from the American University campus. One photo showed a dancing woman. His mother stood near her, applauding, smiling broadly while watching the dancer along with four or five other happy friends. Some held glasses of wine, some gyrated to music, but all of them seemed full of the excitement of young students who cared about each other.

The dancer's leg kicked high, and daringly, into the center of the group. Sam wondered when his mother had become the serious, often melancholy, lady he knew, or if she had always been that way, with this photo a rare exception. Like when Sam himself would occasionally forget everything he was stressed about and laugh at something for the pure pleasure of it. Rare moments. Usually when drunk.

Sam held the photo of the dancing woman and the happy friends for a long time, thinking about the remaining boxes and what they may hold. He flipped through more of the photos until he got to some of himself as a boy, and even a few depicting him in high school. He stopped at the last one in the stack. His mother had both arms around him. He wore a dirty soccer uniform. It was senior year of high school after a St. Ambrose game. She looked barely older than he did then, and far younger than he did now—what with all the smoking and drinking from college to the present. He tried to see into her eyes for some kind of idea about what she was thinking. Nothing but happiness for her son. She would die six months later when her flight to Frankfurt crashed into the Atlantic Ocean, just weeks before Sam headed to college. For all Sam knew, it was the last photo of her ever taken.

Sam put the photographs back in the envelope, stood, and placed it on top of a row of books on his bookshelf. He then picked up the manuscript, shifting gears like he did when a judge called the next case. The mystery man had upped the ante during Sam's last reading by admitting to murdering a sailor, apparently based on a paranoid delusion. He also claimed he might be inherently evil, like a demon or something.

Sam had once hired a psychologist, Dr. Thomas, a fair-minded man, for a sentencing hearing to evaluate his client's hostility. Millie Turnbull had been convicted of threatening to bomb city hall, a felony, despite the fact that she was a bi-polar homeless woman who never would have actually done anything. The point Sam tried to make through Dr. Thomas was that Millie's threats, many of which were not only outlandish but also impossible, did not support that she was actually dangerous. Millie had variously declared her intentions to bomb the Pentagon, assassinate the president, and rent a boat to rescue the terrorists from Guantanamo Bay.

While the jury had failed to acquit her by reason of insanity, Sam had still hoped Judge Bass would see that the more bizarre the claims, the less danger Millie actually posed. The prosecutor—Sparf, as a matter of fact—made the opposite point and made it well in his bratty, nasal, hall monitor sort of way. Sam could still see the argument in his head. Judge Bass's eyes had focused softly on Sam's while Sparf spoke. A compassionate and wise look, an *I want to help you but you know why I can't* sort of look. Sparf had gone on and on.

"With all due respect to Dr. Thomas, I can't imagine you will bet lives in this community on his opinion, Judge. And it is just an opinion. Do I believe Millicent Turnbull is a serious threat to rescue the prisoners in Cuba? No. But let's not be silly here. The fact that she wishes to do so makes her extraordinarily dangerous to the men, women, and children of Bennet. Kill the president? No. Shove a commuter in front of a Metro train? Maybe. Blow up the Pentagon? Ridiculous. Stab some poor sleeping homeless person? Definitely. You won't bet lives on Dr. Thomas, Your Honor. You won't bet lives on Mr. Young's compassion for this woman. We'll all be safer with her in prison, including her."

Bass still held Sam's eyes when Sparf finished. Sam had known then it was over. Sitting rigidly, awaiting Bass's decision, Sparf brushed his right shoulder as if flicking an annoying piece of lint from one's coat. Bass sentenced Millie to the recommended five years in prison. He had not wanted to do it. But he'd had to.

So once again Sam pondered the relation between crazy talk and dangerous actions. Did his mystery man's extreme claims of special powers suggest that he was not the serial killer, or that he was?

Sam dialed Camille, who answered on the first ring.

"Hey, boss," she said.

"Major development."

"Is it him?"

"Yes."

"How sure are you?"

Sam hesitated before answering. The science itself was obviously not conclusive enough for court. But the confessions. The ten matching alleles. The coincidence was too great.

"I'm sure. My friend gave me two days to decide what to do,

but she never would have if she knew about the confessions. I'm thinking we may have to report this sooner. Like maybe tonight. The police have way more tools than us to find the guy."

"I know, I know. There can be no more victims. But give me the two days to discuss it with Andrada, to figure some things out. I won't let any harm come to him. We'll end the murders and protect—"

"Camille—"

"Two days, Sam. Please."

They hung on the phone in silence for a moment as Sam searched for the right words to tell her it was too risky to wait two full days during which another murder could happen.

"Okay. Two days."

CHAPTER 14

SAM LEANED BACK INTO the chair on his balcony holding the unread pages of the journal. Two days? Easy enough. But he had been here before. In the position of having made an agreement that sounded, even seemed, wise and decisive at the time—but was, indeed, foolish. A dodge of the primary issue. Which, in this instance, was the need to control the client and do some damage control. By giving Camille two days before reporting what they knew, he had, in a sense, sold her out. No one would understand that decision later. And if someone else was killed. *Well never mind.*

JANUARY 15, 1958

Our ship chugs along, sometimes with the coast in sight, sometimes not. Paul and I, for the first time in his life, have begun to spend substantial time apart, exploring the ship and its inhabitants in our own ways. Paul is enamored with the vast upper deck, where the sailors jump about. For me, below deck, with its twisting passageways and odd personas, is the way of it.

For I am learning that my real interest lies not in interpreting the mysteries of the outer world but the less-charted universe inside human souls.

Di Giorgio is a middle-aged art dealer who has quit his life in Buenos Aires to devote himself to the class struggle that will liberate South America. He is Italian by birth, Latin American by passion. Yesterday was the first I heard the term *Latin American*. Di Giorgio, who goes by no other name, has begun to educate me about the class struggle and the political identity of South and Central America versus that of the imperialists to our north. I drink with him as he lectures. He becomes increasingly passionate as he drinks, and I am thus able to prod and pry my way through his mind quite freely. He believes what he believes, or wants to believe it so badly the result is the same.

It is quite educational. My personal conflicts have thus far been small—like myself versus Miguel or Aguilar. The type of struggle that dominates Di Giorgio's thinking—politics—strikes me as terribly mundane. To my natural way of thinking, a political battle is much like a war between opposing ant colonies as a flood approaches to wash them all away.

We discussed colonialism. England, Spain, France, Portugal, Italy, Germany, the Belgian Congo, slavery, the American Civil War, and the Monroe Doctrine. Di Giorgio is no professor. He simplifies the topics to an almost moronic level. Di Giorgio's central truth is that the evil, white capitalists from Europe and America oppress the valiant, earthy, brown-skinned southerners—a conflict which will culminate in a worldwide war that will set things right. His personal concept of right involves extensive brutal retaliation against the soon-to-be-defeated white capitalists.

Di Giorgio has served time in prison for a crime he says he did not commit (a lie). He suffered greatly there, though he did put his artistic abilities to good use by becoming a skilled tattooist. His flabby forearms tell the tale of his boredom over the course of his seven-year sentence. He tattooed my thigh with a graceful brown doe, looking at her observer just so—just enough for one to know she understands. It is the deer I feel Salome could have been—quick, bounding, untouched among the trees, outrunning the demons in a dark German forest.

Di Giorgio has fallen madly in love with me, and I have no problem with allowing him his needs. The depth of his passion whenever he touches me is interesting and, indeed, sad. Such loneliness. I don't mind the attention, but the truth of it is, I feel a deep longing for appreciation, not of me as I appear, but as I really am.

Di Giorgio plans to disembark in Cuba and join a band of fighters in the southern mountains to take part in the revolution against the capitalist government. He speaks of the Sierra Maestra, the 26th of July Movement, and of our countryman Ernesto "Che" Guevara. When he speaks of Che, his drunken eyes fill with water and his hands shake, both tightly gripping his glass as he leans forward in his seat. I find it interesting, this worship of one human by another.

• • •

JANUARY 21, 1958

The port at Santiago de Cuba hums with a busier but somehow less dramatic form of commerce than Buenos Aires. The town is the second biggest collection of people I have ever seen, and it has its own unique screech of humanity, unlike that which bounced through the streets of Palermo. I shut out the noise and gripped Paul's hand tightly as we disembarked with our mostly empty suitcases.

Di Giorgio followed close behind me, not likely to touch me openly, but keeping me well within his sight. As we approached the port, I had cut a deal with the man. An odd decision, no doubt, but Paul and I have very little money and no plan to get to America. Being foreigners in Cuba, our prospects are even dimmer than they were the day we rolled into Buenos Aires on our motorbike. We simply need a benefactor. In exchange for some money, provisions, and some clothes, Di Giorgio asks only my companionship—and that I accompany him on his sojourn into the Sierra Maestra Mountains to join the revolution. The idea is revoltingly silly, bereft of even an answer as to why the revolutionaries would want a middle-aged foreigner to join them. But seeing no direct path to America before me, I agreed. Plainly, if Di Giorgio lives, I may eventually gain what fortune he has. If he dies, well, he dies.

Di Giorgio huffed impatiently while I watched all of *La Liberación's* passengers leave the ship. As I suspected, Van Zyl was not among them. Perhaps he got off quickly, before we did. Or maybe he hid onboard. As in Buenos Aires, the police scanned the departing passengers for clues about a murder and found none.

We followed behind Di Giorgio while he made his secret arrangements in Santiago de Cuba. It is obvious that Fidel Castro's revolution is a unique human event. Anyone in Santiago who whispers his name betrays a deep inner belief that he and his fighters in the mountains will succeed. I must admit, I find this a bit exciting.

Di Giorgio bought backpacks and rifles for Paul and me. At my request, he also bought me a long, shiny, leather-handled knife with a sheath. He tried to teach us to hold and aim the guns in our motel room the night before our adventure began, and we tried to appear interested in his lesson. The guns are easy to understand, and they bore me. I did, however, after Paul and Di Giorgio fell asleep in our small room, practice jabs and various twists with my new knife. There is something about the knife that captures my imagination. It's like an elegant extension to my fist. I also practiced jabs and punches without the knife, dodging and weaving about the room like a prizefighter with a dangerous secret weapon.

We hiked through the humidity for an entire day, higher and higher into the mountains with each sweaty hour. Di Giorgio breathed hard, talked little, and stopped often. Paul and I, both strong for our ages at eleven and sixteen, breathed easily as we glided through the thinning jungle. By now I can read Di Giorgio like a newspaper, so I knew that the extent of his plan to rendezvous with the revolutionaries was simply to keep walking until they found us.

We were thus captured by a group of three young bearded men. Their lack of skepticism of us, their casual manner, and their bold maneuvers through the jungle bespoke an easy confidence. A sense, one might say, of inevitable victory. Impressive people, but not kindred spirits of mine. Their minds spin political mantras, not the answers to my greater mystery.

But victory is far from inevitable for these fighters, a fact that became apparent when we marched into the rebels' ramshackle basecamp in time to see a young captain scolding a group of quivering revolutionaries. He screamed in their ears and smacked them across their faces. He brought one to the ground with a sudden kick to the groin. I glanced at Paul. *No matter what happens, just do what I do.*

Our guides, faces down, showed no reaction to the captain's tantrum and marched us past the incident to a clearing in the jungle that would serve as our sleeping quarters. This evening we ate in a big circle with a group of other recruits and Di Giorgio. Di Giorgio, too excited to eat or even go looking for liquor, told me that the screaming comandante was Che Guevara.

I have never felt this sense of excitement, of humans bonding themselves together for a dangerous but important cause. I cannot say I care about the politics of it. It's the complexity of the intertwining souls that has captured my attention. They are going to have to kill to pursue their cause, and yet none of them seems cruel or evil. I feel I will be able to sleep tonight without hours of that horrid cringe I feel inside when I think of Salome or Ortiz. Ortiz's wife remains in my mind, but somehow I can hope that she would understand if she knew the truth. The Great One's religions promise redemption and forgiveness. Maybe if I live right, that covenant will extend to me.

• • •

Sam awoke in his chair with the manuscript on his lap. The first thing his eyes registered was the empty vodka bottle on the coffee table. His head throbbed. He did a double take on his phone. Three in the afternoon? Was that even possible? No calls answered or made since the one with Camille. Why, then, did he feel like he had spoken to her since then? Maybe it was a dream. He felt a sick level of stress. The hangover. The Ripper issue. And to top it all off, Cornelius Pritchard's preliminary hearing the next day. Acorn, a client he was supposed to be representing, deserved his best efforts. He breathed deeply. For today, screw the Ripper, Church of the Holy Angels, and even Camille. Today, he would do his job. He stood up and headed for the shower. The jail. Then the office. No side work.

That evening, police reports and witness statements memorized, Sam struggled with how he would end his cross-examination of Tamika Bradshaw, the woman accusing Acorn of rape. The known facts of the case unfortunately carried several standard indicia of reliability that tended to support Tamika's story that Acorn had raped her.

One, she reported the alleged crime to the police relatively quickly. Two, an examination conducted hours afterwards established that Tamika had fresh vaginal abrasions consistent with rough sex. Three, at the time of his arrest, about an hour after the alleged offense, Acorn had a hand-shaped bruise on the side of his face consistent with Tamika's statement that she had slapped Acorn while he was raping her. Four, Acorn was drunk at the time of his arrest, which corroborated Tamika's statement that he was drunk when he assaulted her. And, perhaps most troubling to Sam, he could not discern a plausible motive for her to fabricate the offense.

She had known Acorn from the neighborhood for years, and even Acorn agreed she had never shown any animosity towards him. The standard reasons women make up rape allegations also did not seem to apply. Acorn had no money to extort through a bogus lawsuit. By his own account, he had not scorned her in any discernible way. Acorn's version of events, communicated privately only to Sam, was that he had been sleeping with Tamika for months. Her sudden decision to make up such a monstrous, life-altering lie made no sense.

Sam stood, arms folded, on his fire escape. Ten o'clock at night. Acorn's hearing was at nine the next day. He needed something else. Tomorrow would be the only chance to have Tamika on the stand before the trial, the main opportunity to persuade the prosecutor not to go forward with the case.

Sam quickly descended his apartment stairs, jumped into the Escalade, and took off towards the projects. Canal Street. Tamika's address. He wasn't sure why he was going there. She had already twice refused to speak with his office investigator, and banging on her door after ten o'clock the night before court would be viewed as blatant intimidation. Nevertheless, Sam eased the Escalade into a spot in front of her apartment. He lit a cigarette and watched. His phone showed that Juliana had called six times in the last few hours. He thought about calling her back, but he didn't want to hear it just then, her worries about the forty-eight hours. He needed to focus on Acorn.

There had to be something else.

CHAPTER 15

SAM'S THOUGHTS WERE CLEAR on the way to court Monday morning. He had prepared his cross-examination of Cornelius's accuser long into the night without one drink. He picked up his phone and saw that Juliana had called twice already that morning. Instead of calling her back right away, he hit a different preprogrammed number.

"Hello." Dr. Thomas answered his cell in his usual manner, sounding as if he had been disturbed from some sort of intense psychological treatise.

"Hey, Mike; Sam Young."

"Sam! Hey there." Thomas's voice became friendly. Sam knew he was one of Thomas's favorite lawyers. He always had the nuttiest cases and kept Thomas in the courtroom just enough to feel that he was part of the action.

"I got something for you," Sam said. "Call it an evaluation, but no court."

"Tell me about it."

Sam walked quickly towards the garage elevator. It was almost nine.

"No time. I'll e-mail some journal entries over later and we can talk. Bottom line though: I want you to read what I send you and tell me if they could have been written by the Rosslyn Ripper."

Thomas paused. "Sure, Sam." A subdued chuckle. "Your cases are never boring."

"And, Mike, this is serious attorney-client privilege. E-mail me your confidentiality pledge. With three unsolved murders, the lid on this has to be very, very tight."

"Whatever you need. But you said three. Haven't you seen the news?"

Sam did a quick Google search on his phone. *Rosslyn Ripper Strikes Again.*

Forty-one-year-old website developer Zebulon Lucas. Worked in the tech section at the United States Postal Service. Cause of death was a broken neck, but unlike the other victims, his face and head had not been mutilated. He had been found on the grass in a park in a residential neighborhood early yesterday evening, across the street from the D-Day Memorial. Sam knew the neighborhood well and could picture the towering mansion-like row houses. Very close to where the other victims had been found, but not on federal property. But a man? It broke a distinct pattern, to be sure. A copycat? The police would have thought of that. A quote from Chief O'Malley's early-morning press conference closed out the article.

"We are aggressively pursuing DNA testing as we vet suspects. But based on the location of the body, the injuries sustained, and information we are choosing not to release, we believe the same perpetrator who killed the three women committed this murder. We're quite sure of it. Period."

Sam stepped into the courtroom just in time.

"All rise," the deputy called out just as Sam opened the heavy wooden door and walked a straight path down the long aisle between the two sides to the gallery, never slowing as the Honorable Rebecca Smith took the bench and the spectators sat down.

"Commonwealth versus Cornelius Pritchard," the clerk announced. Sam passed into the well of the courtroom, and the lockup deputy led Acorn to the defense table.

"The Commonwealth is ready for a preliminary hearing, Your Honor," Amy Marshall said confidently. Sam nodded to the judge, indicating his readiness, then sat down and whispered to Acorn.

"Not one word."

"The Commonwealth calls Tamika Bradshaw as its first and only witness," Amy said. This was just a preliminary hearing. All Amy needed to prove was probable cause to believe Acorn had committed rape. She would do so by briefly questioning the alleged victim of the rape. As long as Tamika said Cornelius had forced sex on her, Judge Marshall would have to find probable cause to bind the case over for trial.

Tamika walked towards the witness stand, a bone-thin woman with tightly braided hair. Mid-thirties. She glanced up into the gallery at a fifty-something man. A brother? A boyfriend? She wore no wedding ring. She did, however, sport the false swagger of one who was very nervous.

"State your name for the record, please."

"Tamika Jessica Bradshaw."

"Where do you live, Ms. Bradshaw?"

"Fourteen-sixteen Canal Street, Apartment one-B, in Bennet, Virginia."

The projects: a good quarter of his cases originated there. The red brick row houses and black metal gates had grown more and more decrepit since their construction back in the 1960s. The short, ugly buildings were cookie-cutter models of each other, two windows across on top, one window and a door on the bottom. The one Sam had staked out the night before had seemed a bit better kept than most of the others.

"Do you know the defendant, Cornelius Pritchard?"

"I know Acorn. Everybody knows Acorn."

A few chuckles from the courtroom. Everyone from the projects did know Acorn, but not as a rapist.

"Did you interact with Acorn on July 21 of this year?"

"Against my will, yes, I did." Tamika glared at Acorn, then again glanced quickly at her friend in the gallery. Sam had seen this man the night before. He'd stopped outside Tamika's house, peered in the front window, and then knocked on her door. Someone let him in, but the angle was such that Sam couldn't see who.

"What I mean is, did you see him? Talk to him?"

"Yes."

"Please briefly tell the judge what happened." Amy would have prepared Tamika to give a very succinct description of the so-called rape. At trial, she would expand on it.

"I was at home, alone, watching TV. I know it was about eight thirty because I was watching *American Idol*, and it was about half over, and Acorn knocked on the door." Prosecutors loved little details like that because jurors loved them. What a great witness, right? Innocently watching *American Idol*, not knowing the show would provide the critical detail of exactly when Acorn had arrived. So typical. Such bullshit.

"How do you know the defendant?"

"From the neighborhood. We went to school together. Now I know him as being a guy who just hangs around."

"What was your relationship to him?"

"Ain't no relationship."

"Have you ever dated?"

Tamika scowled, but took a couple seconds to answer the question.

"We never dated."

Acorn kicked Sam gently under the table then whispered loudly. Too loudly.

"Can't you tell she's lyin'?" A few more quiet laughs in the courtroom.

"What happened next?"

"Acorn made like he was being friendly, then asked if he could use the phone. He said he needed to call his job or something. Like about his schedule. He was all into this job of his. The funeral parlor. Talked about it all the time."

Acorn scoffed, again too loudly, then whispered, quietly this time, to Sam, "Everybody knows I got a cell phone." He scrawled a phone number on his pad and pushed it in front of Sam. "Ask her if she knows my number. Ask her!"

"What did you say when Acorn asked to use the phone?" Amy said.

"I said, sure. I let him in and shut the door."

"Did you notice anything unusual about him?"

"No—well, he was wearing his tuxedo, so it seemed to me like maybe he was on his way to work and was late or something."

"What I mean is, did you notice whether or not he had been drinking?"

Tamika's face lit up in an almost cute sort of way as she recognized the meaning of the precious question.

"Oh, sure, he'd been drinking. But that ain't nothin' unusual."

The whole courtroom laughed. Even Acorn.

What happened next?"

"He sort of tried to grab me and kiss me. I pushed him away, and the next thing I knew he was on top of me on the couch. I was freaking out. I started fighting. Then he hit me."

"Hit you where?"

"On the side of the face."

Amy approached Tamika and had her identify pictures of her facial injury, taken by police later that night.

"What happened next?"

"I kind of stopped resisting. I was scared. The next thing I knew all my clothes were off and so were his. He was on top of me. All over me."

"What exactly did he do?"

Tamika hesitated. "He put his penis in my vagina and started to have sex with me."

Amy had over trained Tamika on this point. She needed to prove that intercourse occurred, but she did not have to make it sound so canned. No doubt Amy would improve the script by the time of the trial.

"How long did it last?"

"A few minutes, I guess. I was just lying there. Afraid. Then, in a last-ditch effort, I smacked him. Then he stopped. Put on his clothes and left."

"Did he say anything?"

"No, not really. He just left."

"What did you do next?"

"I was upset. I was crying. I thought about it for a few minutes, and I drank a glass of vodka to calm down. I hadn't been drinking before, only after. To gather my thoughts. Then I called the police."

Nice one, Amy. No drinking until after. Beautiful, really.

"Did you tell the police what happened?"

"Yes."

"Did they take you to the hospital for an examination to determine if you'd been raped?"

"Yes."

"When had you last had intercourse, aside from when you were raped by Acorn?"

Tamika paused and tilted her head as if to ponder.

"I don't know. It had been a while."

"Do you see the man in the courtroom who raped you?"

She pointed a shaky and angry finger towards Acorn. "He's right there."

"That's all the questions I have, Your Honor."

"Mr. Young," Judge Marshall said. "Your witness . . . Mr. Young? Mr. Young?"

Sam was somewhere else. His hand rested softly on Acorn's back, as if about to lean towards him to whisper a quick question. He felt a soft pumping energy through the physical connection. An oversimplification to be sure, but like Morse code. His mind bounced from Tamika to Acorn and behind him to Tamika's friend in the gallery. Then to her, to Acorn, to the friend, and back. And again. He could not see every detail. But he did see that Tamika was lying, and had a reason to do so. The man in the gallery, whoever he was, had seen Acorn with Tamika. *Through the window?* Either way, Acorn did not know the man had been at the window or had any idea why his on-again, off-again fuck partner cried rape. He just knew it wasn't true.

"Mr. Young! Mr. Young!" yelled Judge Marshall.

Sam stood. "I'm sorry, Your Honor."

Sam looked down at his notes, and then at Tamika, and then at the clock, unsure of how much time had lapsed. But guessing from the clock and the curious look of the court clerk, his journey into Tamika's living room had probably lasted seconds, not minutes.

"No questions."

Sam stood and rubbed the sides of his head as the judge left the bench. He closed his eyes, aware that the courtroom deputies were watching him, wondering why he had failed to defend his client at the hearing. Before opening his eyes, Sam asked himself the question he had been dodging for days. What was happening to him?

Sam turned his phone on as he stepped out of the elevator and into the parking garage. He sighed. Nine missed calls, including Camille, Juliana, Diagnostia, and a city number, O'Malley maybe? He could have, and probably should have, dismantled Tamika in a cross-examination. But Amy, not privy to Sam's new information, if one could call it that, would have indicted the case anyway. He needed some time to figure out what to do about Acorn.

He pulled the Escalade out of the parking garage towards the office. His mind raced. His office. Then Diagnostia.

CHAPTER 16

"IS NOW A GOOD TIME?" Amelia asked. She leaned against the doorjamb of Sam's office, earnest eyes begging for his attention. Sam looked up, his hands still moving rapidly over the keyboard. He was great at divided attention.

"Good time for what?" He was careful to keep a kind, carefree tinge to his voice, a subtle cover up for his racing heart. He locked eyes with Amelia.

"For what I wanted to talk to you about." She stepped into Sam's office, shut the door, and looked expectantly at the chairs in front of Sam's desk. He nodded, and she sat, eyes on the floor. Sam stopped typing.

"Two things. They're asking me to get involved with a death-penalty case."

"Ugh. Who's asking?"

"Simmons, and the people in Richmond. They're putting a team of people together to represent Carter Muldoon, the guy accused of killing the prison guard, and he—"

"I know who he is; I've represented him three times. Don't do it. I'll get you out of it. Carter Muldoon has no defense. He confessed, and the stabbing is on video. He's already in for murder. You know what this is going to be like, right? A year and a half of investigation into his childhood and all that shit? Interviewing his third cousin five times removed to see if he was picked on or if he sniffed glue and stuff? It's all about mitigation. All that touchy-feely crap. And in the end, you'll watch him get executed. I've been through this, Amelia. You don't want it. You're a trial lawyer, not a social worker. Seriously, let some do-gooder in Richmond do it." His hands were shaking. He put them in his lap, out of Amelia's view.

"Stop pretending to be an asshole," she said. "I've already decided I want to do it. That's not my problem. My problem is, well, Simmons was going to ask you to help me with it. I think maybe Burt should help me instead. I don't think you're up for it. Especially if you're saying things like that."

"Like what?"

"Sam, this is really hard, but I'm worried about you."

Sweat sprung down his back, mixing with the air conditioning. He shivered and masked a dry heave with a muffled cough. *Control. Control.* Hard and clear. He maintained eye contact with Amelia, leaned back in his chair, and delved inside for his professorial tone.

"Go on."

"Well, for one thing, it's your drinking. I think it's kind of like, going up. And I know you can handle it, but I guess I'm not sure it's making you happy. You have a law student who's supposed to be working for you. He's really good, and you haven't even talked to him. He surfs the Internet all day. Melvin Collins, remember? He came here because he wanted to work for you. But more to the point, some of your clients have been complaining. At the jail. Frankly, Scarfrowe has been over there sticking up for you. And then, I guess, there was today."

Sam raised his eyebrows, burrowing them softly into Amelia's mind. She reacted with a perceptible flinch.

"Tamika. You should have cross-examined her. Even the deputies were talking about it. I feel like since Scarfrowe you've been falling apart. I know it's only been a few days, but still. Can I ask, have you been sleeping? Eating? What's wrong?"

Sam tried to focus on the only critical piece of information Amelia had delivered.

"Tell Scarfrowe thanks. Tell him I owe him one."

He went back to his computer. Amelia stood, lamely probing him with her eyes, until the silence softly beat her away.

• • •

"This is Young." Sam turned into the Diagnostia parking lot.

"Where the fuck are you?" Juliana demanded.

"I know, I know, the new murder."

"I've been calling you all morning. I'm freaking out. Something crazy is going on. I'm home."

"Why?" Sam pulled the Escalade into a spot in front of Diagnostia.

"The FBI showed up today. Not scientists; agents from DC. And, well, I guess you could say they shut down the lab."

Juliana sounded both excited and worried, not an abnormal condition for her, but being rattled was.

"You're telling me that the Federal Bureau of Investigation has shut down the Northern Virginia Department of Forensic Science, thereby preventing forensic investigations of thousands of cases in one of the biggest criminal jurisdictions on the East Coast?"

"Shut down, maybe not. But they sent almost everyone home. All of us. Over three hundred people. And in the biology section, they—get this—searched us on the way out. They literally watched me—specifically me—shut down my computer and my lab station to make sure I didn't print or copy anything . . . It's freaking me out."

"And this has to do with what? The Ripper?"

"The new victim, Lucas. I went in late last night and worked the samples from his case. I ran Powerplex 16 on his baseball cap, because, well, because the detectives suspected it had been placed back on his head after the attack. I swabbed the brim and got a strong touch DNA profile on all fifteen loci, but it was weird. Impossible, really. And then, well I hadn't told you this yet, but the day before, I had swabbed the stem of your chalice, you know, thinking maybe the guy left sweat or skin cells on it and maybe I could get a fuller profile than the Diagnostia result. I mean, I told you I would keep the chalice private for forty-eight hours, but that didn't mean *I* couldn't work on it, and—"

Sam stepped out of his car and into the heat. It had to be pushing one hundred degrees. Sweat burst from his skin and beaded on his temples. He started across the parking lot towards Diagnostia.

"Juliana, stop. I need to hear all this, but I'm running into Diagnostia right now, then I've got a quick meeting."

"Hurry, Sam, I have to tell you what happened."

• • •

Sam now stood in Diagnostia's frigid lobby. He glanced at the two young women waiting. He knew instantly they were there for the same reason the vast majority of Americans seek private DNA testing: *Who is my baby's father?* The clerk beckoned him forward. He covered the phone to engage the clerk.

"Mr. Young, I'm sorry, but the scientist on duty is on her break. I can't release your result to you until she signs the cover sheet." The clerk was a kind, rule-following lady with a high-pitched, singsong voice. "She'll be back in half an hour."

"I'll wait." He modulated his voice to reflect a calm understanding, but his mind told her something else. Just a little jab to hurry her up. *Just go get the result. You can do it.* He retreated to one of the plastic lobby chairs to continue his talk with Juliana. She still spoke rapidly into the phone.

"I'm sorry, Sam, I—"

"Stop talking, Juliana. I'll be over in two hours."

He pocketed his phone and took a deep breath. So, Juliana told the FBI she had been speaking with him about the Ripper case. About the chalice. Sam Young—a defense attorney now representing an actual, though innocent, suspect and secretly investigating a legitimate, real suspect—who might know the identity of the real Rosslyn Ripper.

"Your results are ready, Mr. Young."

Sam signed for the envelope and headed back towards his car, half expecting to see agents charging across the parking lot to arrest him. *Slow time. Observe.* He was a lawyer. He had every right to keep his client's secrets.

• • •

Back at the 1416 Canal public housing apartment complex it felt like a week since he had parked here, but it was just last night.

Before getting out of the car, Sam opened the Diagnostia envelope. If the FBI were after him, they certainly were taking their time. *Fuck the feds, anyway.* Sam focused on the lab sheet for the swab he had run over the corners of the manuscript. A weak profile with five alleles, one each at five different loci. *TPOX*: 9, *FGA*: 10, *DS18*: 11.5, *D3*: 9, *CSF*: 8. He could still see the partial chalice-sipper profile in his mind. None of the alleles matched, which, he supposed, meant little, since both profiles were so incomplete. On the other hand, by Juliana's real-world analysis, it meant that the chalice sipper and the manuscript handler were probably different people. He tossed the results on the seat next to him.

• • •

Sam knocked on the door of apartment 1B.

"Oh," Tamika said. Not friendly, not unfriendly, just matter of fact. She seemed neither surprised nor scared.

Sam glanced behind Tamika. *Public housing. Seen one, seen them all.* Inside there was ratty Berber carpet, a large flat-screen television dominating the small living room, two teenagers playing Xbox on the couch, grandma's knickknacks adorning most of the available space on cloth-covered end tables, and stale cigarette smoke.

Sam stepped inside. Tamika turned, yielding the issue of invitation, and walked in front of the teenagers, who dodged around to continue their video game. Sam, as Tamika appeared to wish, followed her, quickly stepping past the television to avoid interrupting the game.

Tamika sat calmly at a wooden dining room table, gesturing with her eyes for Sam to sit. Her shaking hand gripped a plastic bottle of Diet Coke.

"Mind if I smoke?"

"Your house." Sam pulled out his own pack and lit a cigarette himself. Tamika slid the plastic ashtray to the middle of the table, her eyes skittishly dodging away from Sam's as his mind delved into hers. He briefly wondered how much Tamika could perceive about what was occurring between them.

"Tamika, you seem like a nice person, so I didn't want to bring this up in court in front of everyone."

Tamika stared blankly at Sam. Nothing. And nothing.

"I know why you lied about Acorn, Tamika. I know why and I understand. Tell the truth, and I'll make sure your friend keeps thinking you were raped. I promise. But you gotta come clean, or he's eventually going to find out about you and Acorn. It's your only play, Tamika."

Tamika sighed. "I'm gonna get locked up, ain't I?"

"I can stop 'em from charging you with perjury. But you gotta act now and drop the charges."

Tamika blew smoke out of the side of her mouth.

"Fuck it. If it's not one fuckin' thing, it's another. Will you represent me?"

• • •

Juliana lay on her couch in the dark. Drawn shades blocked the blazing summer sun.

"It might not be that big a deal." Sam spoke with confidence and delivered Juliana a soft mental massage. He felt her frantic brain loosen just a bit under the weight of his warmth.

"We're friends, so what? Friends talk about work, right?" He said it, but he was not sure he believed it.

"I was the lead scientist on the biggest case in the United States. They talk about it on cable news every night. It's on the news in fucking China. I blew it. The FBI just took over the case. DFS has been—"

"You don't know why they shut down the lab today. It can't be because you brainstormed a hardly secret DNA investigation with a public defender. What, exactly, did you tell this guy?"

Juliana took a deep breath. "You cut me off earlier. Before the Lucas murder, I ran a swab from the stem of your chalice. Just in case the guy had left sweat on it when he took the sip. I got a strong profile across fifteen loci, but something wasn't right. The optical density was strong across the board, but the profile was homozygotic at all fifteen."

"English, Juliana."

"*Homozygotic* means that at certain loci, a person will appear to have only one genetic marker instead of two. It means the person got the *same* genetic marker from both parents at those loci. If one of the killer's markers at one of the nine loci is a homozygote, it means we actually know *both* of his markers at that location."

"Okay, so whoever touched the chalice got the same alleles from each parent. I get it."

"It can't happen," Juliana said. "The odds are just too high. Lots of people are homozygotic at one or two loci, but all fifteen? I've never seen it. I did odds on it. Inbreeding can account for some extra matchup among one's parents' genetic markers, but the odds of somebody being homozygotic at all loci are probably one in ten to a power greater than fifty. That's one with fifty zeroes after it, the threshold at which physicists are willing to call an event impossible."

"How can anything with odds be impossible?"

"I tend to agree. Statistics play games on the mind. Many events that actually happen carry ridiculous odds *before* they happen."

"Like the lottery, right?"

"Not like the lottery, smart guy. With the lottery, they keep playing the same exact game until someone wins. Under that scenario, an eventual winner is guaranteed. The high odds on the lottery are not that the numbers will eventually hit, but that *you* will have those numbers. Anyway, last night, Detective Massey delivered Zebulon Lucas's hat to the lab. Massey was sitting right there while I ran preliminary results. The hat swab contained a DNA mixture. One contributor was Zeb himself, who I typed for elimination purposes. The foreign DNA in the mixture matched the chalice grabber at ten loci. Again, all homozygotic. At this point, it's like ten o'clock, the very day of the murder, and I'm realizing that I have this chalice that probably has the saliva of the Joni West bra snapper on the rim and the skin cells of the Zebulon murderer on the stem—and they are *different* profiles. And of course, I promised you forty-eight hours, but Massey is standing right there, and I'm freaking out.

"Massey's telling me that Zebulon is definitely a Ripper victim. The location and all. The manner of death. And the chief's already been on TV saying Lucas was offed by the Ripper. But Lucas's elimination profile kind of rang a bell and Jesus, I almost shit—it matches what we have on the bra snapper. And I'm like, holy fuck, Zebulon touched West's bra. I gotta do something, like now. And you weren't answering your phone . . ."

Juliana was sitting up now, gesturing wildly. Sam walked to the kitchen and poured two glasses of wine, draining the half-empty bottle Juliana had already begun.

"Keep going," he said. But his mind was racing. *Slow time. Observe.*

"So I leave the lab and go to Harpoon Hannah's, thinking maybe you would show up, and I start drinking vodka tonics. Slowly at first, then I guess I kicked into overdrive."

Sam watched her carefully.

"It's a little fuzzy from there on. But next thing I know I'm standing outside, talking on my cell phone with my *Main Justice* counterpart, a lab guy from DC, and I'm going on and on, and he's trying to slow me down." Juliana took a large gulp of wine. "I'm sorry, Sam."

"What did you tell him?"

"How the fuck should I know? But I do remember saying *chalice*, saying *it's a fucking chalice*! I was yelling it into the phone. And I think, I mean, I'm almost 100 percent sure, I didn't say your name. So I get to work today and the place is swarming with agents. They sent us all home. They wouldn't let us take any lab documents out of the building or our laptops. Dr. Agress told us he would be in touch. Then I came home and called you."

Sam put his hands on Juliana's knees and met her eyes.

"It's okay. Really. Everything you did came from a good place."

Juliana sighed deeply. "You just need to know, I couldn't bring *anything* out of the building. *Anything.* The Diagnostia cert is in a folder on my desk, and the chalice is in a bag next to my computer."

Sam squeezed Juliana's shoulders. "You've done nothing wrong. Shit, when they find me, which could be a day or more, I'll tell him I brought the chalice to you and you insisted, against my wishes, to bring it to them, which you then did. You're fine."

"What about you?"

"Attorney-client privilege; I can't divulge anything. And I haven't revealed my client's name. Not even to you. When you get questioned, tell the truth. You've done nothing but your job."

And in a moment of mutual need, they let it go at that, in effect pretending that something as murky as a legal privilege would cover Sam for having failed to report information that could have saved a life. Not in a case this big. Not with a new murder after Sam saw the chalice result.

Sam pulled his new Diagnostia result from his briefcase, slipped the manuscript lab sheet out of the folder, and handed it to Juliana.

"Yes or no?"

Juliana studied it carefully. "Without the chalice grabber or Zebulon lab sheets in front of me, I can't say for sure, but my memory is usually pretty good on these charts. Obviously, it's partial. All homozygotic. And as far as I recall, all the alleles match. So yes, it looks like this profile could come from the chalice grabber and could not come from the chalice sipper."

"And according to you that means it's also the same profile as the guy who planted Zeb's hat back on his head after offing him, right?"

Juliana sighed. "It appears so."

"Same guy—the manuscript, the chalice stem, and the hat?"

"That's what I'm telling you."

Sam stood to leave. "Hang in there. You're a great scientist, Juliana. They need you."

"Great or not, I'll be labeled a nut case after the unscientific theory I floated last night. Jesus, I *feel* like a nut case." She looked scared.

"What's the nutty theory?"

Juliana did not respond right away, but looked down, shaking her head quickly from side to side, like a cringe of sorts.

"Never mind."

• • •

Sam sat behind the wheel of the Escalade, counting his breaths. He released the emergency brake, cranked the motor, and gunned it up over the steep hill, briefly noting the view of the county spread out below him. He descended rapidly, his engine softly humming through the quiet night. He looked at the manuscript on the seat beside him. Just before Sam entered his own neighborhood, he pulled into the lot of an empty 7-Eleven, with its rows of cold beers and shelves of cheap wine, his soldiers, waiting to be ordered into battle. He figured he had at least a day before they showed up. They would get his cell phone records first. Track his movements with cell-site data, match up his calls with his locations, which of course would initially only show them that he was all over the place all the time, making dozens of calls to dozens of people a day. Hah, they would get excited when they saw Steve Buterab's number all over his records. They would initially focus on a few false leads. They were good, but investigations took time. It would be at least a day before they showed up at his door, and even longer before they got agents out to the Church of the Holy Angels. By then he would figure out what to do.

Back at home, Sam poured a full glass of wine, snapped on some fresh latex gloves, raised the glass to his lips, leaned back on the couch, and flipped opened the journal.

CHAPTER 17

APRIL 3, 1958

Guevara is a disappointment. A spoiled baby. Childish. Not particularly smart. And mean like a hungry Bariloche dog—not hungry for food but for righteousness. His primary talent, which appears to be training men in guerrilla warfare, stems from a relentlessness I liken to the ability of a rat that chews its way through a tin can to get to some meat.

Guevara has trained us along with the other recruits. More arrive regularly. For whatever reason—age, I suppose—our training has consisted of recycling shell casings by filling them with powder and inserting them into the cartridge belts worn across the chests of the men. We also haul jugs of water in sacks for hours to practice delivering them to the men during combat. Mainly, though, we serve as helpers to the group of women who cook for the men. There are two female soldiers. Both are gritty and beautiful in their sweaty camouflage, and both, to my great interest, appear to have Che's ear and even the respect of Raul Castro, whom I finally saw today. Today I also approached Che and asked why it was that I should not be allowed to fight. He placed his hand on my shoulder. "You have the heart of a panther, comrade. All roles in our struggle are equally important. Play yours." Those were his exact words and lovely ones in his educated Argentine accent (so different than the Bariloche trash). But then Che traipsed off, his tumultuous mind grappling with one communistic truism or another. As I write, I can feel Che's mind at war with itself from the other side of camp. Such tumult is not a great quality in a leader, but it does make for an interesting little scuffle. Rather endearing, like the bravado of young boys on a playground.

• • •

AUGUST 10, 1958

The war is on. Bands of men leave our camp in groups of several dozen, usually returning after small skirmishes in the fringes of the mountains. And without casualties. Today was the first time a soldier with substantial wounds returned to camp, and it was Di Giorgio. Che (while a comandante, leader, and fighter) is the only medical doctor in the camp. He scrambled to examine Di Giorgio's chest wound while barking orders. I ran to Di Giorgio, knelt beside him, and held his hand. Che applied pressure to the wound while screaming towards one soldier or another to boil water and retrieve clean bandages. Sweat streamed down Che's face and, during a moment when only the two of us surrounded Di Giorgio, Che's eyes met mine. "Place your hands like so. I'll be back." He quickly glanced behind him and then dashed away in the direction of his tent, leaving me with both palms pressing down on the deep wound on the right side of Di Giorgio's chest.

Di Giorgio's eyes, while open, were half vacant. What an end for him, bleeding in the mountains while Guevara tries to save him. He could not have planned it any better. I truly felt sadness for Di Giorgio, and as I do from one time to another, I said a brief word under my breath, directed at all that was around and above. Che returned and slid in next to me holding a thick, tan compression bandage, bound up with some sort of belt. When Che's hands replaced mine on the wound, his face froze. He looked around, then at me. He shrugged.

"I must be losing my mind out here. I thought he was a dead man. It only grazed him." Che, his exuberance regained, laughed with joy and clenched his fists over his head. He playfully patted Di Giorgio on the cheeks. "You will live, comrade!" Che sprang to his feet and strutted away, yelling his usual orders. "Stop that bleeding! All comrades in formation in one hour. We're moving out! We're moving out!"

I bandaged Di Giorgio's superficial wound and then joined Paul, who was sitting quietly against the base of a thick tree. He had watched the whole thing. We did not speak, but in merry symbiosis, we laughed together. I looked at my hands, bloody yet normal. So human. Today was the first day since Salome that I did not think about how I deserved to be dead and in hell or, like Job, suffering a punishing slavery at the hand of the Great One. Until just now, I suppose, but only by noticing the absence of such thoughts.

• • •

SEPTEMBER 1, 1958

Some of the men are getting scared as they sense the imminence of our departure from the safe havens of our mountain hideouts. So often at quieter times they sit in circles and discuss their philosophies. Or sometimes they read political books with flashlights before they sleep. A teenage soldier, a white Mexican named Cecil, gave me a book he finished today. Indeed, I have seen him reading it for days though it is a thin book one could read in an hour. Cecil always has a smile, but these last few days his cheeriness has become a dark gloom. When he handed me the book he made a self-indulgent statement such as, *all men must die* or some other nonsense. This new fatalism of his plainly comes from Cecil's fear. He likely loved the political books he studied at university but this business about getting shot at has gotten him all trembly. The book, though, was not communist propaganda but a book with Jesus in it called *The Grand Inquisitor*. It is apparently a segment of a larger book by a well-known Russian writer named Dostoyevsky. The book fascinates me and indeed echoes some of my less-developed thoughts about the Great God and Jesus.

In the book an old Spanish man, the Inquisitor, whose business it has been to burn non-believers at the stake, encounters Jesus in his very prison camp. Instead of falling to his knees to praise his God, he essentially curses him for setting up such ridiculous expectations of humanity while at the same time declining to prove to them that he and his Father even exist. The Inquisitor, as I have, questions Jesus's refusal to prove his power to Satan in the desert. So silly, that the Great One's son won't provide us proof, yet his father destroyed Job on what amounts to no more than a gentleman's bet with Satan. And the two things are the same in this way—neither the Great One nor his son will help their creatures when it counts. At the end of the Inquisitor's rant, instead of consoling or explaining, Jesus merely kisses the Inquisitor, thus providing no information to a man who has devoted his life to saving souls who have no hope to navigate human freedom and save themselves. Jesus kisses him on his "bloodless" lips. Why bloodless? He is old I suppose. But the writer must have meant more than that. I sympathize with the points made by this Inquisitor. His words remind me of my mother's words about Job and me. One must be strong inside, and not expect any help from above, now or ever. I shut the book and took a deep breath. The Inquisitor tried to sue God. And like always with the Great One and his son—nothing.

I have this small book practically memorized after two readings this evening. I gave it to Di Giorgio, who flipped through it and tossed it aside.

• • •

SEPTEMBER 9, 1958

Paul and I share a donkey. Often we follow along a grassy road behind a column of hundreds of raggedy revolutionaries. This is war. No more running around in the trees. Our column marches east, out of the mountains and straight towards Havana. For mile after mile, marching soldiers block our view in front while tall sugar cane looms along both sides like a menacing maze. It is said we will meet Batista's soldiers in open battle. The baskets adorning the sides of our donkey carry bullets, some old pistols, and, tied tightly in a blanket, a half-dozen of American grenades.

Today I awoke as the sun rose and caught sight of Che angrily lecturing a circle of young lieutenants (I call them lieutenants; they bear no sign of rank). He met my eyes from far away and dwelt on them longer than he ever had before. He had no real idea about why he took such an interest, unable to see even a fragment of my nature. Hours later, I learned from one of the crusty old maids who does the cooking that Paul and I would be attached, out of the three possible choices, to Che's column.

• • •

NOVEMBER 11, 1958

Today Paul and I wielded rifles and fired at the tan-coated soldiers during a skirmish near San Martin. After the battle, I saw Che order the execution of fifteen Batista soldiers. His sloppy firing squad killed less than half the men on the first round. Che, fiery satisfaction plastered on his face, dispatched them one after another with his pistol. When it jammed after four of these murders, he threw it across the field, where it stuck in a mud puddle. Then he screeched at a lieutenant to give him another gun. The men in our column exchanged nervous glances. Many just stared at the ground. That's how it is, a few Che Guevaras and a thousand cowards. Che thinks it's politics. At least I know better.

After the murders, I heard Che say to the rest of the men, "An army of sheep led by a lion is better than an army of lions led by a sheep." He said it was a quote from Alexander the Great. I assume Alexander the Great is a soldier, or a warrior from some time in the past, but I doubt a great warrior would say that. I think Che has a talent for finding reasons to believe in the righteousness of his own evil acts. A gift, I suppose. Indeed, maybe I can learn to do the same.

• • •

DECEMBER 19, 1958

I saw Fidel today. He stood in a group of captains at the end of a gravel road that ran next to a wealthy sympathizer's farm. The others argued, passion bristling through their gestures and wide eyes. By contrast, Fidel stood still. His bearing suggested if anything, an earnest (or amused?) annoyance at the conversation, as one might feel about an important but mundane topic, such as the cost of a roof repair. Fidel Castro's aura simply shined. Fidel gazed past the huddled group of captains, straining to see his fighters milling about as darkness fell. I hustled across his view as if upon an important task, not able to resist testing him. Certainly what Che so easily missed, this man would see. But Fidel's manner did not shift as the strategy session continued. Hours later, I heard Fidel had left camp. It will be Che's column that will march towards Santa Clara and Che's column that will secure the final victory before the march to Havana. When, so the story goes, Fidel will supplant Batista, and the people will rule Cuba at last.

Moments ago, I sat outside my tent. The camp was devoid of human noise, but in that very silence, the symphony of crickets and frogs made it difficult to hear Fidel approach. Oddest of all was that I did not even sense him. Suddenly, he stood above me, relaxed, that same annoyed look on his face. But now, aside from annoyance, I saw something else. Puzzlement. Suspicion, even. His hooded eyes sized me up.

"Where are you from, young one?"

"From Bariloche, Argentina, Comandante." I looked down, purposefully shy. One did not, I knew, rise to this man. Not at my age, maybe not at any age.

"One of Che's recruits then?"

"No, Comandante. My brother and I were recruited by a man named Di Giorgio, a Comandante Guevara recruit to be sure."

Fidel slit his eyes a bit more. He saw! I knew it. But what a human sees, he cannot believe.

"Since when do children travel to Cuba alone, only to fight a war for others? And peasants at that? Che's recruits are always the fancy ones, the professors and the lawyers. Why are you here? What are you doing with us? Tell me quickly!"

Fidel leaned forward, his eyes ripping into mine, and then relaxed once again. What a person. His expressive aura would have intimidated the meanest crime boss in Buenos Aires.

"My brother and I ran from the law. I killed someone in Buenos Aires. We're poor. We have nothing. We're two people the world has tossed away like trash. Where, Comandante, would you suggest we belong, if not with you?"

Fidel burst into a rich laugh and pulled out a cigar. I smelled whiskey, a scent which, coming from Fidel, conjured strength, trust, and protection as strongly as Miguel's booze-filled panting had stood for fear and hate.

Fidel stood. "You don't lie. But there's something not quite right about you and that funny brother of yours." Fidel winked. A wink that said *I know how it is, comrade.* And now I saw that Fidel's standard facial expression, which I previously read as annoyance, was more like loneliness. An amused loneliness, perhaps, like one who found it oddly funny that he was being screwed over and may as well play the advantages he has. A man like Fidel is always alone.

Fidel dragged hard on his cigar, raised his eyes to the stars for just a moment, and then disappeared into the darkness, like the way I imagine a stage actor fades away without moving under dimming lights.

Camp lore has informed me that while Che is a doctor, Fidel is a lawyer. A soldier and a lawyer at once? Or do the roles match? Maybe Fidel could lend some meaning to God's allegedly trustworthy rules and statutes or let me know how I could go about enforcing them. Fidel seeks equality for the people of this island, but what of my equality in the eyes of God with the others born on Earth?

Something not quite right about you! If Fidel only knew what a quote for the ages that was. He makes me feel I deserve to be alive. He cannot understand it, but he sees me. A cousin maybe, Van Zyl would say. Being around such people makes all the difference.

• • •

DECEMBER 29, 1958

An epic day! We were nearing the end of our march to Santa Clara for the battle, which Che believed would be the final one in the war against Batista's army. As always, Paul and I trudged near the end of Che's column, which now numbered about three hundred men (and a dozen women). All we could see during much of the marching were the men before us, and the tall fields of sugar cane along our sides. This method of travel petrified our comrades of similar rank, as one's imagination arrayed a battalion of tan coats hidden in the cane ready to mow us down at any moment.

I knew no tan coats hid in the cane. Indeed, I have come to understand that Batista's army lacked not only the skill, but also the will to counter Fidel. We also knew that Che's guerillas scout from inside the cane, ready to alert him to ambushes. In such a way, Che's eyes and ears covered miles of our flanks. Today, though, Che suffered a lapse in his brilliance as a guerilla leader. First, I heard his voice, shrill, passionate, and proud, calling desperately from the front for the column to get down. Then the machine gun fire began.

As I had done during previous such (albeit false) alarms, instead of merely hitting the grass like the men all around us, I yanked Paul into the cane. Enveloped within its prickly protection, we knelt beside each other, gripping our rifles. I saw Che's dilemma in my head, even though it was occurring football pitches away and out of human sight. Che and another soldier tore through the cane after a small group of tan coats. And then I was off, flattening a path through the cane, knife in hand, rifle cast away. I burst out of the thicket into a clearing to see five tan coats training their weapons on a kneeling Che's back while a pock-faced captain held a pistol to the back of his head. Suddenly I was among them, and the captain's head tore in half, his face flying away and flopping onto the ground at the feet of a horrified tan coat. None of them had long to be afraid. Not one of the tan coats presented a defense while I ravaged them, so shocked were they to see someone my age mowing through their comrades so quickly. After a combination of guttings, maulings, and even one near-decapitation, I placed my foot atop the body of the captain. I looked at Che. Still on his knees, he had turned, calmly watching the carnage as if it were nothing more than one of his communist propaganda films. It seemed he was in a trance brought on by an experience one sees but lacks the capacity to believe. I shrugged and strode purposefully back into the cane. When I reached the back of the column, Paul standing quietly with some other soldiers, waiting for me.

• • •

Sam stood and paced the room. He held his phone in one hand, his drink in the other. He hit a number.

"Hello, Sam." Camille sounded alert. Like someone picking up a prearranged phone call. Like maybe she knew he would be calling.

"How do you know Andrada was born in Spain?"

Camille hesitated. "I guess because he told me so."

"I need you to get me a DNA swab."

"From whom?" she said.

"You know who. By tomorrow, Camille. Make it happen."

Camille breathed heavily. Her voice felt tired now. "Okay, boss."

Sam refilled his glass and resumed reading.

DECEMBER 30, 1958

Today, Che, arm in a sling from the bullet wound that should have taken his life, led us into Santa Clara. We routed Batista's remaining army, and by late evening Santa Clara was not a bloody battle zone, but a party. Men and women danced in the streets, and peasants surrounded us with crude signs proclaiming, *Viva Fidel!*

Two minutes before midnight I sat on a dirt pile, rifle by my side, just outside the main city square, watching the celebration. Women held babies in the air, and everyone danced in the streets. The revelry reminded me of one year ago, the day I killed Salome. I cried on the dirt pile for her and for the dancing peasants and city workers who believed their lives were about to improve. I also cried for Che, not because I care for his politics, but maybe because I know I have no business sharing in such things.

It is time for Paul and me to go.

• • •

JANUARY 1, 1959

Today—New Year's Day, 1959—Paul and I made it to Havana with Che's column. Batistas and his soldiers are gone. The war is over. From this day on, Paul and I are no longer revolutionaries, at least not of Che's kind. A highly impaired Di Giorgio hugged the breath out of me. It was interesting to me how strongly he believes we will be together—happy revolutionaries in an illicit love affair, right? So strong is the power of human want and so weak the ability to gain its objects.

By late afternoon, Paul and I, transformed from revolutionaries to escaping young Batistists, watched from a dock outside Havana while Americans and a smattering of well-dressed Cubans scrambled to load boats with everything from fine china to furniture. (Furniture? So funny!) Every moment counted, or so they believed. It was as if Fidel and Che would come tearing out of the woods at any moment to take their fancy sofas.

I pried around for a Di Giorgio-type, someone both sexually drawn to me and willing to act upon it. I found one soon enough. Jacob Rubenstein is a nice enough man, no dumber than most. More importantly, he has a boat. He and his captain loaded it with two huge, metal safes and cartons of random junk, which I learned were the expensive trappings from a casino.

Jacob is a soft man who smokes cigars. He has nice eyes and a simple thought pattern. His mind concerns itself primarily with the trifling financial profits one can earn by engaging in little scams and gambits. So much time on math, he bothers with little else. His old, white boat travels fast and has a cabin with plenty of space for Jacob, his captain, Paul, and myself.

At the beginning of our voyage, Paul stayed above with the captain while Jacob took me from behind as we stood in front of the mirror in the cabin's bathroom. His rough-skinned hands were nevertheless gentle, and I actually stayed present for the speedy encounter.

•••

JANUARY 9, 1959

Today I watched Fidel on TV riding his donkey into Havana. Fidel is just a man, not a kindred spirit, yet he sees far and wide—a skill that has begun to strengthen in him upon his short interaction with me. As his donkey lurched slowly to and fro through the adoring crowd, Fidel wore the same facial expression I had noticed when I met him. Then he saw me in his mind. A fleeting look of puzzlement crossed his face. He was confused because I was not cheering from the Havana Street but watching him from a Miami restaurant. He wasn't sure why the kid from Bariloche would not leave his head.

CHAPTER 18

SAM AND HIS COLLEGE friends strongly believed one could drink oneself sober. Somehow, especially several days into a streak of binge partying, the sloppy feeling of inebriation that kicked in after polishing off a twelve pack would transform into a clear-headed, sentimentally melancholy plateau. One more beer just did not matter. Ten more didn't matter.

But that was then.

• • •

Sam stood on his fire escape, filling his lungs with the early morning air. He had read the entire journal twice before delving into an all-night Internet research session spurred on by not one, not two, but three bottles of wine. The mystery man had a basic knowledge of the Cuban Revolution, but nothing a high school kid couldn't learn online in three or four hours. The key was the personalities. Their guy was trying to convey a distinction between Che, the human side of some kind of cosmic equation, and Fidel, possibly the divine side. Or maybe the evil side? In all his grandiosity, the mystery man identified with Fidel and almost paternalistically pitied Che.

Fidel is to Che as what is to what? As the mystery man is to his victims?

Sam remembered something about a historical conspiracy theory. About Fidel having orchestrated Che's murder in Bolivia, betraying him somehow. But this theory was roundly considered bogus, and if the mystery man believed that theory, he showed no sign of it, despite his professed ability to read Fidel and Che.

Sam sipped from a plastic cup of iced coffee, his day stretching before him across the expanse beyond the fire escape. A field marshal surveying the battlefield. The Cuban digression meant something, whether it was true or false. Was it possible that Leo Andrada was born in Argentina in 1942, fought in the Cuban Revolution, and wound up a priest in the DC suburbs? His age fit. And sure, he could be Roma. His tough yet wise bearing did suggest an unusual level of life experience for a priest.

But perhaps it was not the truth of the manuscript that provided clues but its falsity. Maybe all of it was just a story. And fiction, unlike fact, has meaning. Regardless, Andrada had less than a day before Sam went to the police, unless something broke the other way.

Sam stepped back over the windowsill, walked to the coffee table, and picked up his notes. It was almost eight. He would go into the office early this morning.

• • •

"This project may be a wild goose chase, but what the hell, have some fun with it, Marvin," Sam said. The intern held Sam's investigative memorandum in his hand, a two-page description of a research assignment. Sam leaned back in his squeaky swivel chair, feet on his desk. The young man was clearly pissed off at him. Sam hadn't been around to supervise him or to give him any interesting assignments. Basically, Sam had not lived up to his end of the bargain—free summer work in exchange for an interesting learning experience.

Sam's intern was a stocky, African-American Princeton grad at the very top of his NYU law class. He had gone to law school after three years as a successful investment banker on

Wall Street. He spoke fluent Spanish and rudimentary Russian. The lad was indeed the rare law student who could command a decent salary as a summer associate at a big New York firm, even amidst the financial devastation that had left many lawyers unemployed. His decision to help society instead by working for free at a Virginia public defender's office had likely turned out to be a major disappointment.

The intern wore an expensive gray suit and a red power tie. A shiny leather briefcase rested by his chair. His presentation made a clear contrast with Sam's T-shirt, jeans, boots, and hung-over eyes. He sat politely in front of Sam, jotting on a pad, the very picture of professionalism. But his furrowed brow and barely disguised smirk told a different story. The kid was over it, over Sam, over a boring summer of neither paychecks nor excitement, over his crappy cubicle, and over working for a guy who, good rep or not, did not appreciate his sacrifice. He was over the whole bullshit package. He looked forward to getting back to school and applying for some real jobs.

"My name's Melvin, Mr. Young." Melvin looked Sam in the eye, and his voice carried an edge. Kind of like a cop who realizes he has spent the last hour talking to an eyewitness who, in the end, had not seen anything. "Do you mind if I ask what this case is about?"

Sam looked at the ceiling, hands behind his head. He probed in and around Melvin's mind. He leaned forward and motioned Melvin to do the same.

"Not one word of this, Melvin. Not to your friends, not to the other students, not to anyone."

Melvin held Sam's gaze. He shrugged, almost mockingly.

"Mum's the word."

"This project has to do with the Rosslyn Ripper."

Melvin swallowed. He scanned the investigative memo again, picking up on the details of the actual assignment for the first time. Melvin stood.

"The office will never pay for this, will it?"

"Don't worry about it. You'll have a firm credit card."

"The Public Defender's Office has firm credit cards?"

"No." Sam calmly watched Melvin. "I said don't worry about it. But you'd better hurry. All your other projects are on hold until you get this done. I'd like something within a few days."

Melvin picked up his briefcase. "I don't have any other projects. But I can handle this one. I won't let you down."

"I know you won't, Melvin." Sam held his eyes for a second. "It wouldn't be your way to let somebody down." Sam pivoted back to his computer, politely dismissing Melvin from his office. As Melvin left, his parting thought was apparent to Sam.

Maybe this bullshit summer will be worth something after all.

• • •

Sam shut the door of the Escalade and looked at his phone—almost eleven thirty. The lights from Camille's carriage house illuminated the walkway in front of him. His steps echoed across the empty hall between the rectory and Camille's room. Sam glanced towards the church on the other side of the parking lot, a sole light shining from a narrow side window. Andrada's office.

"Crazy day?" Camille stood in the open door and remained leaning against the jamb for several moments, as if to make an assessment of some kind.

"We need to talk." Sam stepped inside and followed her to the couch.

"Vodka with ice?" she called over her shoulder.

Sam sank onto the couch without answering, waiting for Camille to place the cool drink in his hand. When she did, he moved it slowly across his forehead, the cold glass almost painful on his hot skin. He shut his eyes while he brought the glass to his lips.

Camille settled in on the other side of the long segmented couch. She folded her legs under herself, and her eyes rested on Sam's. He had come with an agenda, but a different thought shot out of him.

"Do you know Raj Buterab?"

"Of course," Camille said without hesitation. "He's the biggest donor to this church. Great guy."

Sam watched her closely and, for the first time, caught her.

"I don't know why, but you're lying about something."

"Everything I just said was true."

Sam kept watching her closely after that non-denial.

"Have it your way. Look, I told you already, your guy is the Ripper. The DNA from the chalice proves it. But that's not all."

Camille waited.

"We got a second profile from the chalice. From the stem. It looks like the DNA from the stem is consistent with a profile found on the new victim's hat."

Camille almost frowned for a moment. "Okay."

"I also tested the manuscript itself. It seems to have a similar pattern; nothing conclusive, but it certainly can't be ruled out that the person who touched the manuscript also touched the chalice stem and the hat. If I'm right, that means one thing and one thing only, and you know it. I've dealt straight with you. It's time for you to tell me what the hell is going on. Did you get a DNA swab from Andrada?"

Camille watched him carefully. "No."

"Why not?"

"Because he isn't the Rosslyn Ripper."

Sam stood and paced away from Camille, then approached her.

"That's not how I'm seeing it, Camille. His anger. The rages. The DNA. I have to deal with the fact that there's a pretty good chance you know a lot more about these murders than you're telling me. I have a duty now. Have for a while. In a matter of days, if not today, the police will learn about our investigation anyway. I'll protect you, but I gotta know more."

Camille stretched her legs in front of her and massaged the back of her neck. A strained look crossed her face; one Sam attributed more to an internal pain, like the sudden onset of a hernia or the sharp pierce of a bleeding ulcer. She stood, turned her back to Sam, and walked towards the window. She looked out the window and across the parking lot. When she turned back she was crying, uncontrollable sobs so at odds with her normally placid demeanor.

Sam stood, approached her, and grabbed her shoulders as she shook.

"Camille, you've gotta tell me what's going on."

"There's something I've been wanting to tell you for a very long time. I'm truly sorry I've waited for so long. But some of it you have to come to on your own. Trust me on this—there won't be another murder."

Sam flopped onto the couch and covered his face with his hands. He was suddenly so tired.

"How can you possibly know that?"

Camille just watched him.

• • •

Sam awoke to his buzzing phone on the couch in his apartment. Six o'clock in the morning. Juliana. He declined the call and sat up just as another call came in. Camille.

"Hello?"

"Did you get some rest?"

Sam took a deep breath.

"Did you ever care about stopping the Rosslyn Ripper?"

"Very much. But you remember from the beginning, I told you I had more than one reason for wanting to meet you. Look, I promise, Andrada won't leave the church grounds. If he does, I'll call you, even call the cops if you tell me to. But bear with me. Give it another night. Before you left last night, I didn't have the chance to tell you we received another portion of the journal. I scanned it in and emailed it to you just now. Figure out the relation, if any, between the manuscript and our present situation. Trust me. Just give it a try. Call me later. And I swear to you, Sam. Andrada is not the Rosslyn Ripper. And there will be no more murders.

"There's a lot of biblical stuff in those journal entries," she said. "You're great at the legal analysis, but do you even own a bible?"

Sam shrugged. "I'm pretty sure I have one lying around."

• • •

Sam sat in a plastic chair on the fire escape with a coffee in one hand and the new section of the journal pulled up on his computer. His phone buzzed. A text from Dr. Thomas: *Call me.* Sam picked up the phone, but before he could call Thomas, it rang.

"Dude," a gravelly voice greeted him.

"Barnabus? What are you doing up?"

"Me? I'm a hard worker, my friend. You're the one who sounds tired. Hey, I got a letter."

"What kind of letter?'

"You know, one of those things that says you gotta go to court. Some cop slapped it on my door last night. Used fuckin' tape, too, the prick."

Sam sighed. "Barnabus, you know what a subpoena is. What's it say?"

Sam heard some papers rustling as Barnabus pretended to be too dopey to understand his legal predicament. Just a nice guy fumbling through life. "United States District Court for the Eastern District of Virginia. Grand Jury Summons, you are commanded to appear—"

"Got it. They're summonsing you to the grand jury to ask you about the cigarettes. Don't worry about it. You're not going. I'll call later. E-mail me the summons."

"Thanks, dude, you're the best. Hey, you get my check?"

"I don't know. I'll check the mail later. I'm kinda busy."

"No sweat, dude. But remember, I'm on your side. You rub my back, I'll rub yours, or whatever."

"Wonderful, Barnabus."

"Hey, Sam, one more thing."

"What?"

"You sound kinda stressed out. Don't worry; you'll get through it. I believe in you, man. And I've been through some shit."

"Barnabus, that means a lot coming from you. It really does."

"Oh, I know. Believe me, I know. See you, dude."

Sam climbed in the window and sorted through the mail on his coffee table, quickly finding Barnabus's small, sloppily written envelope. He tore it open. Back on the balcony, he laughed to himself. Only Barnabus. A cashier's check for twenty grand. Double the requested fee and almost a third of Sam's public defender salary.

Sam set the check on the coffee table next to his mother's boxes. The lid of one of the two boxes he had dug through the other day sat off kilter. He sat on the couch, lit a cigarette, and opened the third box. Maps. Travel itineraries from her job. Sam's old report cards and some art he had done as a kid. The fourth box had framed photos from her office and more books.

The fifth box had papers. He dug through them and found bank information, school schedules, bills, and the contents of a disorganized desk drawer for the most part. And amid the clutter a small bible. He pulled it out, flipped through it with his thumb, and placed it on the couch.

The sixth box had her nicely matted American University Diploma from 1975, her framed 1985 award from the Peace Corps for work on a development project in Eastern Europe, and then, nearer the bottom, some old greeting cards. Sam flipped through them. Congratulations cards from professors for her PhD. *John Horne. William. Steven Colter.* He opened a few more cards. One was a card from his mother to him. He opened it and saw that it contained a small paragraph to him on his seventeenth birthday, but shut it quickly. He placed it in his briefcase. And then at the very bottom was a thick, black, hardbound book. *Doctoral Dissertation of Marcela F. Young.* Sam put the dissertation and the small bible on top of the manila envelope on his bookshelf. He would look through all the items more carefully soon enough. Finally, he leaned back on the couch, breathing hard. Mission accomplished with the fucking boxes. After sixteen years.

Back to the mystery man.

• • •

APRIL 16, 1959

The four seasons—the cycle of living and dying appropriate to this world—are muted in the sunny paradise of Miami. I have come to realize Paul and I will never secure legitimate employment here. We have no citizenship, no green cards, and no rubber-stamped visas from the anti-Castro camps. We are smuggled aliens, illegal, and it has taken some months for me to formulate our next move.

A few days ago, the Sunray Motel became our home. It sits at the shit end of the beach strip but busies itself more with druggies and hookers than tourists, though the white American tourists from up north visit often enough. Funny they are, pasty and fat, with their fancy shirts and neat leather wallets and crisp, green cash. Their auras are so plain, so bereft of the basic understandings possessed by the simplest Bariloche peasant. But they do have the wallets.

Paul sticks to drugs. He is so athletically impressive now that it seems as though he has always been a natural American thug of sorts. He certainly has no cause to fear the addicts and nervous travelers to whom we ply our trades. Today, a herky-jerky Cuban homosexual grabbed a bag of cocaine from Paul's hand and ran. I'll never forget the boy's jagged run and his torn jeans pathetically slapping the sidewalk in pace with his rough grunts. Even from across the street I could smell the horror upon him, the years of malice and hate and greed he had seen since he was a very young boy. Indeed, I even sympathized with the thief, having myself (depending on how one looks at it) suffered the same kind of abuse that had defined his youth, sadly, as it is the human way to pass misery on to the innocent. The hophead is surely destined to return the favor on down the human line to any person dumb enough to depend on him. Paul shrugged at me from across the street. I love our moments of connection—the stark, mutual recognition that he sees my abilities and still loves me. And so the hophead remained in the human stream.

• • •

FEBRUARY 8, 1960

Late this afternoon I sat in a plastic chair on our balcony, watching Paul from above as he served his customers. Police are not much of a problem here. They mostly can't be bothered to intervene in the sad commercial enterprises lining our strip. To the extent a diligent policeman occasionally decides to endeavor upon a futile attempt to curtail the suffering by making some kind of an arrest, Paul and I are safe. I can read them in their slow-rolling, black-and-white cruisers. Oh, the drama. Where to have lunch? How much overtime this month? Will the wife actually believe I am working tonight? Or will she drive by the station looking for my car? Before any police get near our block, I have the blueprint for their next twenty-four hours right down to their preferred pit stop for a shit. Until today.

I suppose there are those like Fidel who seem at first glance insightful enough to be kindred spirits but are merely human all the same. Not siblings, but special nevertheless. I believe they are capable of seeing the truth of things, albeit only in brief glimmers. Another way to put it would be to say that some humans can see far and wide but lack the ability to understand what they see. I think these people form an extreme minority of the human population.

I stood on the Sunray balcony, casting a subtle, protective radar round and about Paul while he finished unloading his little handfuls of cocaine. I then suffered a mental slipup. A man caught me by surprise. I saw him two blocks away, a pedestrian walking casually towards Paul. A tall, bearded black man with a fine leather jacket and some fancy red boots. Not poor. Not a hophead. I narrowed my eyes at him. Seemed strong enough, just a man looking to score for a night out with his friends, a normal man with a real job, a perfect customer, in fact. Not dangerous. Pocket full of cash and no worries.

But then he got up near Paul, and as soon as they began to speak, I saw it. Before I could shoot out a warning, the man spun Paul around and shoved him against the wall, professionally frisking Paul's legs and waistband. Paul, in that unique way of his, looked up at me, waiting, I suppose, for approval. Permission.

I knew the arrest itself was not worth the cost of violence against the policeman, which would provoke a reaction beyond my ability to manage. I also did not fear the legal punishment Paul would face if arrested. I feared the question of identity. I have little knowledge of the police identification tools about which I have heard. Fingerprints. Blood tests. But my worry was that if the police arrested me, they could figure out the one thing that could truly harm us. And so I did what I had to do.

The policeman was simply not a proper subject of immediate mind control. His studied undercover methods, his living the role as I could sense he called it—his acting—had fooled me. In his mind, he pretended to be what he pretended to be with his body. I scanned the strip, easily finding what I needed: a weak-minded hophead. I had never tried this before—prodding another with my mind to take physical action. But with the slightest of thrusts from me, he charged. He ran full speed across the street, where he dove, jaws open like a rabid dog, into a group of young men who gathered on the corner one block down from ours. He made full contact with one of them, flattening the man to the ground, his teeth digging for the neck. The melee was loud and furious and (I did not intend this) gunshots banged and echoed loudly over the block. Everybody ran. The detective looked only once from Paul to the fight and then broke into a run towards the danger. I jumped into his mind briefly as he passed under the balcony. Brave and smart, a truly impressive human. A cousin. Were he not so focused on his job, he would have sensed me above him. Instead, he desperately performed CPR, banging on the hophead's chest again and again.

The tawdry scene once again brought into focus a question that has been weighing on me more and more heavily and demands an answer. Why am I this way? What did I ever do to warrant being sentenced to this solitary exile? While I may not be totally alone, it is beyond question that I am among an extreme minority of creatures different from, and perhaps less protected than, the Great One's humans. Are those like me barred from the reward promised by the Great One? Are we, indeed, the descendants of those cast out of heaven and forbidden to return? Of Satan himself. The victims of our ancestors' decisions? Would that not make God crueler than the most arbitrarily abusive parent? Worse than Miguel, who at least suffered from some kind of disease? Where can I find someone to teach me the answers to these questions?

• • •

NOVEMBER 17, 1963

The best drug dealer on the strip this year is Marcus Fowler, a black man from New York who poses as a Jamaican, with his dreadlocks and phony lilt. He also pimps as it suits my needs, and this mutual endeavor allows me to own his mind. Drugs, on the other hand, are a way to earn real money.

Marcus is a talented drug dealer, having lived it since his youth. He has a decent heart by the standards he knows. But his mind yearns so badly for guidance that I can move around his cluttered brain like a shopkeeper stocking my shelves, swapping one item for another to suit my daily fancy.

Last night I asked Marcus to take me to a hotel downtown.

To relax, I said. For fun. I would make him feel good. I still remember the view from our window at dusk. The Trinity Episcopal Cathedral. Soft light shone from the windows, illuminating the old stone.

I let Marcus pump his load into me one last time. In his frenzy, he could not possibly notice my vacant eyes and dead touch as I soared along the beautiful Florida coastline like a dragon. When he finished, I decided to spin his neck. He would be gone. No further need to concern myself with his pursuit. Paul and I would have our earnings free and clear. I placed my hands on either side of his face. His eyes shut and he crumpled onto a pillow next to me—tired from the drinks and the pot and the sex. My palms adjusted themselves on each side of his jaw, ready to twist.

Moments later I stood by the door, breathing deeply, rhyming my breaths with Marcus's, who now slept soundly with his drunken little snores. "Thank you," I said aloud. As for whether I was thanking Marcus, the universe, or even the Great One, I had no idea. Leaving Marcus alive puts us in danger. He'll wish to chase us, for the money and for me. Then why the inner sense of levity as I softly shut the door on his snoring? I took the stairs, popped out on an alley, and purposefully crossed the street and entered the cathedral. It was near midnight. An old woman knelt in a pew near the front, sobbing about who knows what. I strolled straight down the center aisle, leaning back on my spine. Slow time. Observe. Christ on the cross looked sad. His depiction mirrored his reality by remaining still, unmoved by earthly events. I could feel the tears on my face. I whispered to him a short message. Part of me wanted to tell the Great One's son I was sorry for everything, for Salome and Ortiz and Miguel and the tan-coat soldiers and the hophead and the drug dealing and for selling my body and for all my other sins. But all my life I have only acted consistently with my nature. I may as well be what the universe says. I am anyway. And yet, why did I leave Marcus alive? I wanted to ask Jesus. But instead, I said something more important.

"He made me this way. You get that part, right?"

I stood in silence for what must have been many minutes, listening to Jesus ignore my question.

"Repent, you said, and enter the kingdom of heaven. That means me too, right?"

I looked deep into Jesus' eyes. I know the eyes were crafted to be kind. To me they were cold.

"We're alike you and I. Surely not equal but alike. You went through this, did you not?"

I would have kissed him on his bloodless lips had he not been suspended so far above me. But that would not have made any difference. Like always with the Great One and his Son—nothing.

Trinity was waiting for me outside the cathedral on the empty sidewalk, wearing a blue beret and a black business suit. Both hands were in her pockets. She smiled at me. Tears ran down my face and onto her neck. Where have you been? Where have you been? I tried to ask her through sobs.

"Don't bother with Jesus. He doesn't welcome us," she said.

My heart burned like a fire inside a forge with love for Trinity, but I felt terror all the same. Terror because the emphasis she placed within her sentence conveyed what I have feared all my life about myself. Not "*He* doesn't welcome us." Not "He *doesn't* welcome us." Not "He doesn't *welcome* us." Trinity's sentence meant I had been right all along. That we were, but for so few, alone. "He doesn't welcome *us*."

"I know you wish it were some other way," she said.

Trinity and I stood, clasping each other's hands for many minutes without speaking. In her eyes I could see the pain she had both endured and, yes, caused others, on her journey, many, many others. I feel for her, but I must say this insight grants me some relief. That my sister has more blood on her hands than I do. That she believes she is also, by birth and acts, destined for hell.

"I think there's a way out of this," Trinity said. "But people have tried it before, and it's not going to be easy."

"Are we people though?" I smiled at her.

"My point exactly."

CHAPTER 19

THE PHONE BUZZED. "THIS is Young."

"Sam, I've been calling you all morning." Dr. Thomas's nasally voice was friendly, but, what? Concerned?

"Sorry. Working."

"Your journal. You wanted my opinion. About whether this guy could be the Rosslyn Ripper."

"Well?"

"Of course there's no way to be sure of anything when it comes to profiling, but off the record, I'm almost certain that your mystery author is not the Rosslyn Ripper."

"Anything else?"

"This is a bit superficial, but I'll let you have it." Sam could hear Thomas leafing through some notes. "First, this all presupposes that the writer is attempting a serious, factual narrative, and isn't just having you on with a story. But I'd say the writer is elderly, has probably been quietly suffering from mental illness for many years, is likely nonviolent, and has been living the same false narrative for a very long time. The grandiosity, while perhaps real, has not been acted upon in any *real* way. This type of person has probably held one simple job for decades, probably reliable, like a ticket taker at Amtrak or a custodian, stays quiet, and pays laser-like attention to everything, eventually twisting and turning all the details into his narrative. These are the people our writer encounters every day—the train passengers, the busy bees and their meaningless lives. The writer is superior to them all, but silently so. Graciously so, even. Probably a solo binge drinker or maybe a pot smoker, and a voracious reader and writer."

"But he talks about killing. His stepfather. The sailor."

"Hyperbole, I'd say. Probably hasn't killed anybody. My guess is someday, in some shabby apartment complex, the police will find a body, dead of natural causes, surrounded by decades of dusty notebooks. It's sad, really. Something medication could cure."

Sam rubbed his head. "Thanks, Doc."

"Sam, are you ever going to find this person?"

• • •

Sam's lungs burned as he walked from his car to the jail through the one-hundred-degree heat. He was exhausted. He knew he was pretty well running over his forty-eight hour deal with Juliana. Nevertheless, he was on his way to do what he always did when he had no idea what else to do—his job. His phone buzzed.

"Mr. Young?"

"Yes."

"This is Elizabeth Vertolli from Bennet Mental Health. We spoke the other day, and—"

"Yeah, yeah, Jerome Johnson."

"Yes, well, because you brought him in, it's our policy to notify you that he walked off the property this morning."

"Walked off? They can do that?"

"Yes, sir, this is not a secure facility. It was a voluntary admission, technically. No court order or anything."

"So that's it?"

"That's it, have a good day, sir."

Sam hung up. There was no end to it. Now he had to call the chief.

• • •

"Hey, buddy!" Nguyen scurried across the jail parking lot. "Man, it's hard to get you on the phone. I just followed you here. You want my report or what?"

Sam lit a cigarette and watched Nguyen thoughtfully. "Nice haircut." He had shaved his signature spiked, glistening hair. He also wore slacks and a collared shirt.

"Thanks, buddy. Like my new look?"

"Well, for one thing, you don't look like a child molester."

"Tough world." Nguyen shrugged. "Anyway, I got the goods on your bodies. You want it?"

"The basics."

"Mary Beth Schneider. A straitlaced babe. Chemistry major. Clean as a whistle. A real tragedy. Her Google account and Facebook pages are devoted to nerdy science stuff. No boyfriend. No nothing. She went to work, went home, watched TV, and went to movies and shit. I didn't know there were people like this still out there."

"Next."

"Carole Kingsley. A chick from the hood. Smoked a lot of weed. Got fired from Starbucks last fall. Her mother basically cared for her two year old. Her father, well, I think you know some of this, racked up a petty rap sheet after getting back from a tour of duty in Iraq. He's on disability and smoked crack regularly until you, I believe, checked him into the Bennet County psych ward. You want more on this?"

"Maybe later." Sam made a mental note to call O'Malley about Johnson leaving the psych ward.

"Joni West was depressed. Spent most of her online time on mental health websites and yoga-guru kinds of shit. I think she tried to kill herself last year, but that's a little murky. She disappeared from the web for nine days and got a bunch of cryptic get-well-soon shit from friends on her social sites. Bunch of nude pics of her, too. She chatted with random men on hook-up sites and met one or two of 'em for a quick bang. Wanna see the pics?"

"No. Let's get to it."

"Ahh, yes. Zebulon Lucas. This dude was effed up. He put up hundreds—no, thousands of psychotic posts on crazy websites.

Some of them are terrorist rants, like about bringing down the US government, stuff like that. One of his screen handles was— get this—the Angel of Death. On a recent diatribe he blogged that he was the spawn of Satan. So anyway, Zebulon was committed to a mental hospital for ninety days about three years ago. Since then he's been living in a group house in southwest DC. A real dump. His roommates were basically a bunch of potheads. I got shit on them, too. You want it?"

"No. Anything else?"

"He's a sexual freak, if that matters. I got lots of his Internet chats. Photos too. Not pretty. He's half a fag, for real." Nguyen held a stack of computer-printed photographs towards Sam.

"Watch your syntax, Skipper. Bitch this, fag that. At least be selective." He took the photos and tucked them neatly into his briefcase.

"What's it matter? I get good stuff, right?"

"It matters if you're gonna work as an investigator for me."

Nguyen shuffled his feet and looked down. "Thanks, Sam."

"Let me ask you something, Skipper. Why do you think the Ripper would kill three attractive women and then a guy like Zebulon?"

Nguyen masked a smile, obviously pleased that Sam had asked his opinion.

"I gotta say, I know people are gonna talk copycat, but that makes no sense. A copycat would kill a woman."

"What else?"

"It can't be a coincidence, not with the location and manner of death. The odds against that would be pretty high, anyway. It's related somehow."

After a quick thought, Sam added, "Great work."

"Oh, and your nun. Sorry about this, but I couldn't come up with anything much. A Camille Paradisi did attend American University in the seventies. But I can't even access what she studied or whether she got a degree. Couldn't find anything on her anywhere else, and I checked birth records in all fifty states. But, you know, you can't trust that; every state is different. And as far as the Catholic Church, it's a weird organization. Not like a company you can hack into or anything. Shit, a lot of their records are on paper. Searching nuns doesn't get you far."

"Anything else?"

Nguyen scrolled through his phone.

"Big city convents do have some records that can be accessed. I checked the ten largest American cities and every big city on the East Coast. I got one name, not Camille, and not your girl."

Sam waited.

"Paradisi, took vows in Miami, Florida. No first name listed. I even called down there and got a guy to dig around to see if there was any more info. Don't worry though. He thinks I'm an historian from Portland."

"So how do you know she's not my girl?"

"Because she took final vows in 1964. Fifty-one years ago."

• • •

The deputy buzzed the door to the 4CF unit, one of the large general population units where the inmates were free to mill about, watch television, lift weights, and talk on the phone. Sam immediately saw Hogman sitting at a small, round table by himself, newspaper opened wide in front of him. Sam joined him.

Hogman hesitated before putting down the newspaper, as if he truly felt interrupted.

"So, what did you find out?"

"Basically, they say you threw a rock through a window at city hall. Officer Grundy's report says an eyewitness described you. A cop found you two blocks away sitting on a bench, and then the witness picked you out of a photo spread. That's pretty much it. That and the fact that you have, well, kind of a distinctive look."

"What was the description?" Hogman asked, a gruff, indignant edge in his voice.

Sam glanced down at the report.

"A Mrs. Jennifer Arnold told the cops, 'Heck, yes, I'd remember him. He was an albino.'"

Hogman nodded his head softly, considering the new information.

"Do they have the rock?"

Sam opened his thin file.

"Strangely enough, they do. It's in police property. I've only seen a picture of it so far. It's just a gray rock, about the right size for throwing, you know. Not too big, not too small." He showed a picture of the rock to Hogman. The rock was neatly labeled with an evidence sticker.

"That Officer Grundy is a veritable Sherlock Holmes," Hogman said.

"Indeed."

"Well, their case is horseshit. I was sitting on the bench minding my own business, and they came up and arrested me. Am I the only albino you've ever seen around here?"

"Yes."

"My point exactly. Who else was in the photo spread? Of course she picked me. All you have to do is get the rock tested."

"Tested how?"

"For my DNA. It won't be on it. The DNA of some other albino will be on it. Case closed."

"They don't do DNA testing in small cases like this. Besides, it's not clear your DNA would even be on the rock."

"So what? It's worth a try, isn't it? If it pans out, the jury'll take a crap all over their case and wipe their asses with that rock to boot."

"Funny." But Hogman did not appear to be joking.

While boy-like in stature, he was also older than Sam had originally believed. His wrinkly fingers bespoke a life of working with his hands. His eyes and voice were serious, but somehow a little off. Like a comic playing a straight role.

"I'll think about it, but your plan has some holes in it."

"It ain't the only thing," Hogman said.

"Fair enough. But maybe we should think of something else."

"Like what?"

"Like maybe you should plead guilty, do a little time, and get out of here. It's not exactly the crime of the century. Maybe you were drunk. Maybe you could take some alcohol awareness classes or something."

"Don't worry about any of that shit, Young. I'm not pleading guilty. Let's just say I have my reasons. And my reasons aren't about doing time. I just don't need the, shall we say, additional scrutiny that could come with such an arrangement."

Some people managed to get booked into the jail under phony names. But if convicted, their prints would go to the national records exchange, thereby exposing the ruse. It happened most often with illegal immigrants who didn't want to be deported, but it happened to another type of person as well—people who lived off the grid, people without credit or bank accounts. Sam searched Hogman's eyes. People who didn't want to be found.

"I hear you," Sam said. "So we go to trial."

"Maybe. But I got one other idea."

"The suspense is killing me."

"I know who the Rosslyn Ripper is."

Sam frowned.

"What's wrong?" Hogman asked.

"That's the second time this week I've heard that one. I don't care what he's been saying, but Morris Talberton is not the Rosslyn Ripper."

"I never said he was."

Sam sighed. "Okay, how do you know who the Rosslyn Ripper is?"

"Because he told me. I spoke to him at Sargent's restaurant the day before my arrest. A few days before that final victim's body was found."

Sargent's, an old, cash-only bar right outside the city projects; Sam had had a dozen cases, fights and thefts, originate from Sargent's.

"And?"

"He was drunk off his ass. He told me, not in so many words, that he was responsible for the murders and that, *in* so many words, he was 'born to kill.' That it's in his genes. I know what the guy looks like, and I can prove that conversation happened."

"How?"

"Because he was also talking to a lady that night. A pretty young one—I'd know her if I saw her, kind of Spanish or somethin', long hair. Way out of place for Sargent's. They were arguing, actually. Like she was pleading with him about something. You should have seen the anger in his eyes. I mean this guy was really dangerous. While he was ordering another drink, I warned her. I told her he was a freak who'd just told me he murdered women. After that, I left. But if you find that woman, she'll tell you. She'll corroborate my story that I was there, that I warned her. Which proves the guy really said it to me."

Sam contemplated Hogman's words, trying to spin past

some of the defenses in Hogman's suspicious mind. But Hogman's mind felt like a maze, like a series of twists and turns and combination locks. Sam was not sure if he had ever tried to read someone with just such a mental pattern.

"So let me get this straight. You're afraid to plead guilty to a petty crime because of the additional scrutiny, but you want to be a witness in the biggest case in America?"

"Let me worry about that. Besides, there ain't gonna be no trial."

"Oh really? How's that? It's death-penalty-eligible murder. No one pleads guilty to it." Sam stood up, prepared to leave.

"Because there won't."

Sam paused. "You said *final*. You said *three nights before the final body was found*. Why'd you say *final*? How would you know it's the final body?"

Hogman smirked. "If you're half the sleuth as our esteemed Officer Grundy is, you'll figure that out before the next time you wipe your ass, Young. All you have to do is open your eyes. The Ripper murders are over. Now are you gonna bring 'em my fuckin' offer, or not?'

"Let me think about it."

"You do that."

• • •

Sam sat in his car in front of the office. He felt wired and exhausted, excited and overwhelmed. He was used to the feeling and solved it, quite often, with a drink. He laid his head back on the seat and breathed deeply through his nose, thinking about what to do next. He hit Nguyen's number on his phone.

"Sam?"

"Hey, I got a project for you. And you gotta hurry."

"On it boss."

"Ever heard of Sargent's restaurant?"

"Unfortunately, I know it well."

• • •

Sam leaned back in his seat and shut his eyes. As he fell into half sleep, he felt like he was softly falling—down and down—to a place from which it would be very, very hard to emerge.

Sam stood alone next to his friend Andrew's running pick-up truck. He was in front of Holy Angels—not the fancy new church, but the old one, the one from the mid-90s, before the renovation. Andrew sat behind the wheel, patiently awaiting whatever it was that Sam felt he had to do, which, at the moment, was to wait for the priest to reach him. The priest walked slowly, lips pursed in solemn grimness. There had not been a formal funeral. Sam had decided on a simple memorial service and had been surprised to see that Andrada had returned from wherever he had gone to officiate the small ceremony. All of the other attendees had driven away at least ten minutes before, but Andrada was in no rush. He maintained the same facial expression until he reached Sam, and then he smiled. He placed his hands on Sam's shoulder. "She was one of a kind," he said. Sam did not reply. He looked into the man's eyes. One brown. One green.

"There's a lot you don't know, Sam, about the faith, about some of your mother's beliefs. Some of it, she was saving for you until you grew up. Which you've now done."

"Okay," Sam said.

"Let's talk soon. We'd really like to keep in touch."

"We?"

"The church. Your mother's friends."

"I'm heading to college in a few weeks. I'll call you."

"Good."

Andrada gripped his hand tightly with both of his before turning to walk away.

● ● ●

Sam suddenly snapped awake. He was sweating in the hot car as the August sun beamed through the windshield. He thought about the day he learned his mother had died, along with every other passenger and the crew of American Airlines flight 1420 to Frankfurt. She had been on her way to Indonesia. He remembered watching the search and rescue efforts on CNN. Many of the bodies, including Marcela Young's, were never recovered. When the commentators stated the obvious, that after several hours it was clear no one had survived the crash into the Atlantic, Sam still kept watching.

Bang! Bang! Bang!

Sam sprang out of his daze, taking a moment to focus on Amelia's knuckles rapping on his window. Her muffled voice seemed desperate.

"Sam, wake up!"

Sam opened the car door and turned in his seat to face her. A rush of cool air caught him by surprise, and he inhaled deeply.

"Are you fucking crazy? Passed out in a closed car? In this heat? You could die! Are you drunk, too?"

"I'm not drunk." And he wasn't. Just exhausted. He peered at her again. "Why are you crying? If you're that pissed off, why—"

"I'm not angry." Amelia grinned through her tears and wiped some strands of wig hair out of her face. "I'm happy."

Sam got out of the car. His head pounded.

"I'm cured, Sam. I went to the doctor yesterday. It's completely gone. My bloodwork shows a complete, totally complete, remission. I've been trying to find you to tell you." Amelia pulled Sam's arm, forcing him to either resist or step closer. She hugged him tightly.

"But we need to talk." Back to all-business Amelia. "If you don't straighten your shit out I'm going to do one of those intervention things."

Sam's phone buzzed. "This is Young."

"Sam? Sam, can you hear me?"

"Melvin?"

"I'm at the hotel in Buenos Aires. Can you hear me?"

Sam kissed Amelia on the cheek, got back into the car, and drove away. He could see through the rear view mirror that she watched him with her hands on her hips as he drove away.

"I can hear you now."

"Thought you'd want an update. This has been a lot easier than I thought. You were right I didn't even have to bribe anybody. They think I'm a history student from NYU. The police chief himself came downstairs to meet me. Gave me a tour of the station in Palermo. It was cool." Melvin chuckled. He was having fun.

Sam pulled onto the highway, headed, he guessed, towards home, or perhaps to Juliana's.

"So?"

"She's real. It happened. Salome Becker." He pronounced it SAH-loh-may. "A German national killed in an alley on New Year's, 1958. I'm holding an autopsy report in my hand right now, can you believe it?"

"Does the report have photos?"

"Black and white, pretty gruesome, really. Sad."

"Okay, what else?"

"Her ribs were crushed. Cause of death is listed as—it's different in Spanish—basically, asphyxiation. Next of kin notified by phone. Body shipped to Germany."

"What about the investigation?"

"It doesn't seem there was much of one. She was travelling with a student group. The members were ruled out as suspects right away for various reasons. I've got their names and the reasons. You need that?"

"No."

"Some detective, deceased now, according to Captain Maniero, wrote that the murderer was likely a strong young male, possibly drunk."

"That's some cutting-edge profiling."

"But here's something else, a notation from January 2, 1958, from a different detective. Two lieutenants and five officers were assigned to survey the passengers embarking on the ocean liner *La Liberación*. All those meeting the age and gender requirements were to be questioned and all IDs checked. I've got a passenger manifest. You want that?"

"Can you scan and e-mail it to my phone?" Sam's heart was beating fast again when he pulled into his own parking space at the apartment. He had, for whatever reason, not taken the exit to Juliana's while speaking to Melvin.

"I'm sure the hotel can handle that. Case was closed as unsolved in March 1958. Hardly a notation in it after January, except some dead-end canvassing of the neighborhood. Nobody heard or saw anything. It was New Year's Eve and all."

"Press?"

"One clipping in the police file from *La Capital*. Mentions Salome Becker by name, but almost no details. *La Capital* is still around, and according to their receptionist they have no computerized archives before 2004. She said it would take weeks to order copies of issues from the '50s. You want that?"

"No. What about access to the police records?"

"Captain Maniero says none of the files from before 2000 are computerized. You wouldn't believe the size of the dusty-ass warehouse where we went to pull the Becker file. I don't think anyone in America could even find out about this crime without knowing what to look for. Maybe in Germany there's more—a family, a history of some kind. But there's almost no evidence of it here, unless the person spoke to someone who took part in the investigation. Or, of course, which I think you're trying to figure out, if the person was involved in the crime."

"Nice job, Melvin. What about *La Liberación*?"

"I knew you'd ask. I spent all morning at the port. First, there was a ship called *La Liberación*, and, you're not going to believe this, but I met an old guy who boarded the sucker on January 2, 1958."

"That can't be."

"It can be. I got the manifest, remember? I checked his identification and everything. I got his photo and even a photo of him with me. The manifest lists names and ages. And who was travelling together. This dude's for real. He boarded alone."

"Okay, okay, so what'd he have to say?"

"He said he really only remembered one thing about it. I doubt it matters at all, but here it is. He says he remembers that a crewmember went missing during the trip. Like, disappeared, mysteriously or whatever. There was some sort of investigation, he thinks. That mean anything to you?"

"Maybe. What else?"

"That's all I got. Sorry, Sam."

"You did great, Melvin, really." Sam opened the door to his apartment, walked to the kitchen, and poured a three-finger whiskey with a steady hand.

"You want all this stuff by scanner?"

"No. Just bring it back with you. I only want the manifest and the autopsy report."

"Mind if I ask you something?"

"Please do."

"Presuming Salome's murderer was at least a teenager in '58, isn't that a little old to be the Rosslyn Ripper? I mean, he'd be old as heck by now."

"That, Melvin, is a very good point."

They both remained silent for a moment. Sam played with a cigarette, watching it roll gently between his thumb and finger.

"One more thing, Melvin."

"Anything you want, boss."

"The guy who boarded *La Liberación*? How'd you find him?"

"It's funny. I wish I could claim some sort of great investigatory powers, but he actually approached me down at the docks. Said he heard I'd been asking about the ship. It was weird. Almost like he was waiting for me. He was leaning up against a pole like he knew I was comin'."

"Hmmm. Anything else important?"

Sam could hear Melvin ruffling some papers.

"Doubt it's important, but the last piece of paper in the police file is a letter from a lawyer from Germany. Apparently, the tanker that was supposed to be carrying Salome's body either lost it or never had it. The lawyer is asking the department to follow up on it. No response that I can see."

"Okay, now one more thing, can you check the passenger manifest for a young pair of brothers? Close to fifteen and ten years old or so, maybe the same last name?"

Melvin remained silent for a full minute or so.

"Nope, nothing like young brothers. A few kids, what looks like a sister-brother pair, but no pair of brothers."

Sam paused.

"Everything okay, Sam?"

"Thanks Melvin. I got it from here."

"Okay, umm, Sam, I've still got two nights booked at the hotel, and my flight isn't until Monday. I haven't even spent half your cash, but this trip is adding up. Should I advance the flight? What do you want me to do?"

Sam sucked on a cigarette, stared at the ceiling, and blew a crisp stream of smoke.

"I suggest a steakhouse, a nice Malbec, and then maybe some tango."

Melvin was laughing as Sam hung up the phone.

Sam showered and shaved. Four twenty in the afternoon. He did not know what he was dressing for. He had nowhere to be. He put on a clean pair of jeans and a plain blue T-shirt. He tightly laced his tan Timberland boots. Somewhere in the city, not near, not far, and apropos of nothing personal, police sirens wailed. He pulled on his old Washington Redskins hat and looked at himself in the mirror. His eyes, for the first time in days, looked clear and healthy. He breathed in deeply, his lungs accepting the hot air in the bathroom without hindrance from the day's chain-smoking. He felt, well, like he used to feel when he was ready for a trial. Healthy. Smart. Hard and clear.

Sam's phone buzzed. Melvin's e-mail with two attachments and then another buzz with another e-mail. Sam hit the e-mail concerning the autopsy first and scrolled to what he was looking for. The scan came in sketchy on his phone, but he could see the dead girl's face. A light-skinned black woman with long hair and dead eyes. Her specialness, if it had been there, had long since fled. He then clicked the passenger manifest for *La Liberación*. The journal was silent on the mystery man's and his brother's names, other than his brother's first name, or the fake names they supposedly used to board *La Liberación*. Sam opened Melvin's last e-mail and studied the photograph of a broadly smiling Melvin with his arm around a deeply tanned, stooping old man in a white summer suit and a fancy white hat.

He jumped back an e-mail and began scrolling through the manifest. It had not only names but also ages. He scrolled quickly—so quickly that at first he passed too many entries. He slowly scrolled back, and his heart jumped. *J. Van Zyl, 43*. He flipped back to Melvin's selfie of him and the old man on the dock.

His phone buzzed. "This is Young."

"Boss, I got the goods," Nguyen said. "It cost me seventy-five dollars to get 'em to pull it right away."

"And?"

"I think it shows what you want it to show. I converted the video to a digital file and just e-mailed it to you. It's keyed up the moment I think you're looking for."

"You're good."

"I told you so."

Sam hung up and checked his e-mail. He clicked Nguyen's digital video.

• • •

Sargent's bar area, which, as everyone at the courthouse knew, had been video monitored by the owners for years, came into focus. Sam had seen several of Sargent's videos before. The cops always pulled them when investigating the fights that happened there regularly. The quality was poor, but by posture alone Sam could tell it was her. Camille was standing in front of a man whose back faced the video. He could not discern her facial expression, but her gestures, compared with her normal silly smoothness, did seem harsh. Edgy. Even panicky. Sam looked closely at the man but could tell nothing from the back of his head. At the bottom corner of the video Sam noticed the date and running time clock. *7-28-2015. 10:57 p.m.* That was about five hours after Camille had first met him in front of the courthouse.

Sam looked back at the video. Camille was still gesturing and speaking to the man. Finally, the man turned his head to the side briefly. The quality was just too poor to be sure of anything, but by now Sam at least knew what he was looking for. Based on the photos he had seen in the newspaper, it was entirely possible that the man in the video was Zebulon Lucas.

His phone buzzed again. "This is Young."

"Sam?" *Juliana?* Her voice cracked, as if she was or recently had been crying.

"What's wrong?"

"Federal agents came to my apartment. They just left. They know a lot. I had to tell them about where I got the chalice. They know about the DNA results. They say you've been running some kind of a scam on me. I don't know. I'm really sorry, Sam. There was nothing I—"

"Juliana, calm down—"

"Sam, I think they may be coming to question you. Maybe even arrest you, I don't know. They were really intense—"

"Juliana, relax. I'm gonna be fine. Listen, maybe we shouldn't talk for a while, until I can figure this out. But hey, I've got a question for you."

Juliana hesitated, breathing heavily.

"Relax, just one question. You're not gonna be in trouble. You're not."

"Okay."

"You said the same guy touched the chalice stem, Zeb's hat, and the journal, right?"

"Yeah, I mean, like I said, maybe not good enough for court, but that's how it looks to me. What about it?"

"Juliana, my question is really important. Think. Are you sure whoever touched the chalice stem, the hat, and the manuscript, was a guy?"

Sam could feel her thinking. That was when he heard the sirens again, and they were coming closer.

"The amelogenin on the hat shows only an X-chro. Right at this moment I don't remember checking that on the other two samples, but I probably would have noticed a Y on either one of them. So presumably, no, but you can never be sure with calls like this."

"Why not?"

"Because with touch DNA samples, skin cells and that kind of thing, *anybody's* DNA could get mixed in. The X chromosome on the hat could be from Zeb. The chalice and the journal have been touched by more than one person—including you."

"So you can't say it was a man? It could be a woman?"

"Correct."

The sirens were close now.

"You did the right thing, Juliana. You really did. I'll call you when I can."

Sam hung up, grabbed his wallet from the coffee table, and swept the DNA file and Camille's manuscript into his briefcase before climbing out the window. He moved towards the window and then turned back, looking across the room at the file containing his mother's old photos and doctoral dissertation. He raced over and stuffed that too into his briefcase. He looked at the shelf one last time and then grabbed the small bible.

But why? Why not? Because fuck the police pawing through his mother's stuff.

Briefcase strap over his shoulder, he dangled from the bottom ladder rung of the fire escape, fell to the street, and ran, his legs cranking.

He tore down an alley as sirens approached on both cross streets. He hit the wall and crouched against the bricks behind a small dumpster. If a single police car cruised down the alley, he was done for. What cop wouldn't look behind the sole hiding place? He glanced at his briefcase. Would disposing of the DNA certificates do him any good? Any good against what? As his breathing calmed, he began to focus on the fact that he had done nothing wrong at all. He was a lawyer working on a case. Sure, Juliana might get in trouble at work, but what crimes had they committed? *Fuck the fuzz.* He would simply go back.

Just as he was about to stand and dust himself off, he heard a car creeping down the alley, its tires crunching against the cracked, gravelly pavement. Damn. He'd waited too long. If he stood now, it would be apparent he had been hiding behind the dumpster. If he stayed put, there was a slight chance the car would roll on by.

Sam tried to calm his breathing even though the infuriatingly slow pace of the approaching cop car was pissing him off. *Just find me already or don't.* The sound of the creeping tires was close now—it was about to pass the dumpster. No blue and red lights. An unmarked car? Sam squinted when the hood finally rolled into view. Sure, police used all kinds of undercover makes and models, but he was sure no cop in Bennet County drove a Bentley.

Sam rose and stared into the relaxed face of Raj Buterab.

"Get in," a female voice said. Amelia leaned across Raj. Sam stepped out of the shadows, bolted around the car, and jumped into the front seat, bumping into Amelia and wedging her between himself and Raj. The Bentley drifted slowly down the alley. Sam could hear yells and chirping radios from the front of his building as red and blue lights colored the walls across the street.

"What the hell is going on, Amelia?" Sam asked softly.

"I should be asking you that," she whispered. "Your friend called me about an intervention. I was worried about you. What are the police doing at your apartment? What did you do?"

"Hello, Samson," Raj said.

"I gotta say, you're freakin' me out, Mr. Buterab." Sam looked out the back window as the sirens and lights in front of his apartment receded behind them.

Raj laughed softly. "You don't have to call me Mr. Buterab. I told you that before."

"You're freaking me out, Raj."

CHAPTER 20

THEY PULLED ONTO ROUTE 66, stayed in the right lane, and headed west at a cool fifty-seven miles an hour.

"Relax," Raj said. "To the extent possible, everything is unfolding as it should be. But there's been a glitch."

"I'm sure you are about to tell me what the hell is going on, Raj."

"Soon enough. Like I said, relax. I think you're in for an interesting evening."

Sam took a deep breath and stared straight ahead. He still clutched his briefcase. Papers stuck out of it, branding him as one of those sloppy, unprepared lawyers at the courthouse. He pulled the papers, photos, and the small bible out of it and held them on his lap. His fingers flipped the pages. He lit a cigarette and shut his eyes, his mind racing back over the last week, even the last years.

Some of it she was saving for you, until you grew up, which you have now done.

You ask good questions.

A chosen, or forgotten, people.

He flipped through his mother's old photos. The hippies in the parking lot. The happy group in his living room, his mother and others laughing while the tanned brunette kicked her leg high into the center of the group. The bearded man on his mother's right laughing hard, with a beer bottle in his hand. He saw it then. Raj Buterab, more than three decades ago. Arm around his mother. Whoa.

He reached back into his briefcase, his hand collapsing around his mother's thick, bound dissertation. He opened it.

Doctoral Dissertation of Marcela O. Young: Jesus, Resurrection, and the Occult.

Sam shut his eyes again.

Resurrected ones should never linger. It would cause all kinds of problems.

There's a lot you don't know, Sam, about the faith, about some of your mother's beliefs. Some of it she was saving for you, until you grew up, which you have now done.

Sam flipped back to his mother's old photographs. First, to the dancing woman with her back to the camera, the long, straight, black hair, and then to the photo of the hippies by the car in the parking lot. Young Raj Buterab with his beard. And, on the end of the group, the shorter, thin woman with the long, dark hair. She was beautiful then, as now, and hardly a day younger. Camille looked happy in the photograph, much happier than his mother, with her thin smile and slumped shoulders.

Raj took an exit, and they drove past the D-Day Memorial. Sam looked at the figures storming out of the amphibious landing craft. To Sam, the most striking thing about the D-Day Monument had always been their beautifully chiseled faces, the combination of terror and determination as they charged into the water. Each face was unique. Real people from different walks of life, facing death for people they would never meet. The statues sat on a groomed elevation from which, on a clear day, one could see the Lincoln Memorial, the Washington Monument, and the Capitol. Across the street, away from the city, the Memorial Place mansions—the community where Zebulon's body had been found—towered above the monument.

"This is your stop." Raj eased the Bentley into a spot in front of a townhouse. Sam had been on the roof of one of the multimillion-dollar homes for a political fundraiser he attended with an ex-girlfriend back when he first started at the office. "The best view of the DC monuments," their host had said.

"Where are you going?" Sam asked.

"Ring at 3301. I'll see you soon enough."

Sam neatly placed the files into his briefcase and slid out of the car, followed by Amelia. The Bentley eased away.

"This is some weird shit, Sam," Amelia said. "This isn't about your drinking, is it?"

"If it is, somebody has been spiking the shit out of my booze."

Sam and Amelia climbed the steps of the huge row house. Sam pushed the bell. Minutes passed. Then fast, heavy steps and what sounded like a hard landing at the bottom of the stairs. The door swung open.

"Dude." Barnabus looked at his huge Rolex. "About time."

Camille sat in the center of a tan patio couch on the open rooftop, one leg folded over the other like an actress on a television talk show.

"Hello, Sam."

Sam looked past Camille over the city. Briefcase hanging from his shoulder, he again felt like an unprepared lawyer—unsure of which document to use for cross-examination.

Sam looked at Camille. She sat straight, smiling slightly, a serpent once again.

"What are you doing here?" Sam asked. A simple question to stand in for a hundred more complicated others.

"Hiding out, I suppose. I'm scared. I want you to represent me."

"Represent you for what?"

"For murder. What else?"

No one spoke for a long moment as Sam searched Camille's eyes.

"Events are moving forward, Sam. They'll know my name within hours. The attorney-client privilege might protect me for a few days, but soon enough, the federal authorities will find me. This is the biggest investigation in the country. The normal rules won't apply. The FBI is in your apartment right now. Attorney-client or not, they'll find me. My number is all over your phone records. They'll learn about your past connection to Holy Angels.

They'll speak to Andrada. And they'll have the DNA from the Lucas crime scene you told me about. It's my profile on the chalice stem, not Andrada's."

Amelia glanced up and gripped her pen tightly—gestures that often accompanied an impulsive, and sometimes ill-advised, question to a client or witness. This time, Sam let it go.

"So, you killed Zebulon Lucas? What about the others?" Amelia asked.

Camille met Sam's eyes. They watched each other for a moment before she answered Amelia's question.

"I did what I felt I had to. I shouldn't talk about the rest right now, except privately with my lawyers. But I told you, Sam. I was never going to let anything harm Andrada."

"But the journal, all the bullshit? Why? You knew who Zebulon Lucas was before you met me? And my mother? Since I was a kid? What the hell is going on?"

Camille arched her back and returned Sam's gaze.

"Let's talk about problem number one first. I'm going to get arrested unless I turn fugitive, which I do not intend to do. So here's the thing, Sam. Since the chief says all the murders are related, won't they accuse me of being the Rosslyn Ripper? Your DNA friend is going to have to tell them what she knows, which will lead them to you and then to me."

"I'm afraid that process has already begun," Sam said. "But this whole shit-show, Camille. Why? Who are you?"

"First things first. I'm in trouble."

"Fuck that. Why are you screwing with me?" He pulled out the photograph of his mother with Camille and Raj Buterab. "Explain this. Now."

"We've got all the time in the world for those questions. I promise."

CHAPTER 21

"THERE'S ONLY ONE THING to do," Sam said. Barnabus and Amelia now sat on a long wicker couch across a coffee table from an identical couch occupied by Camille and Sam. "I'm going to make a couple of phone calls, and then you're gonna turn yourself in tonight."

"You're going to have to explain to me how that could possibly be the right move," Camille said.

"We can get you arrested without you admitting anything about actually killing Zeb. Juliana can help with that. Here's the thing—Zeb is the only murder not committed on federal property. It's a state case. The feds have no jurisdiction. In state court we have a much better chance to work things the way we want. If time passes and the feds figure out a way, as bogus as it may be, to label Zeb as a Ripper victim and charge you with all the murders, the case goes federal. And, believe me, we'll lose any semblance of control over it. They can't prove you did anything right now."

"I'll be in jail?" Camille said.

"Probably," Sam said. "At least for a while. What are your alternatives? Go on the run for life? You said you would never do that."

Camille stood and paced behind the wicker couch, back and then forth and again. Slowly. Sam could feel her mind churning, unsure, for once.

"I trust you," she said finally. "I'll do this if you say so."

Sam stood. "There's no going back from this call."

Camille nodded.

• • •

"Sparf."

Sparf answered his cell phone on the first ring, even on a Saturday night.

"Hey, Chad. I've got some information for you. You're gonna beat the feds to Zebulon Lucas's killer. But you gotta hurry."

A long silence ensued, but Sam could feel that Sparf believed him.

"You would never yank my chain about something like this." Sparf said it like a statement.

"No way. Get O'Malley, and get over here. My client is ready to self-surrender but no questions. You'll understand when Juliana Kim shows you what she has."

Sam could hear Sparf breathing. "Address?"

• • •

"They're close," Barnabus said.

A moment later, Sam heard sirens. The right ones.

"Locals. Sparf delivered."

Camille rubbed her neck with both hands. She took a large gulp from her glass. Her eyes met Sam's over the rim, and then darted away.

"Camille, tell me now. It's time. I need some fucking answers *before* they get here. You hired me well before Zebulon Lucas was killed, and it turns out you knew my mother, and you've known some of my clients for years. Why are you playing games with me? Who wrote the journal, and why'd you feed it to me like that? What's your game?"

They watched each other intently and Sam could feel her energy pumping towards him. He pushed back. He scrolled on his phone to Melvin's e-mail with the manifest from *La Liberación*. He scrolled down and down, slowly this time, until he found it. The same tight, disciplined cursive writing, the same writing from the manuscript. *Nombre: Angelica y Paul Paradisi. Edad: 18 y 10 Años. 2-1-58.*

As for ages, I told the truth for Paul, and made myself an adult. We had good, new names. Strong ones, reflecting our hopes.

"Explain, Camille." Sam's hands shook.

"There's no time."

"If you tell me the manuscript story is true, at least I'll know you're crazy, and I can use that to help you. But I do know that somebody named Salome Becker was killed in Argentina, and that these Paradisi kids boarded a ship the next day. I also know, as I'm sure you do, that somebody named Paradisi became a nun in Miami in the sixties. You really did a lot of work to concoct this shit, but why?"

Camille sighed. "This is a long conversation. I'm sorry I placed this hiccup in our path with this whole Rosslyn Ripper business. But I had no choice. The journal story is true, and was written by my sister, who was indeed born in Bariloche in 1942. I remember the very day she was born. I was five. Her name was Fifika Kritalsh. She changed it to Angelica Paradisi when she boarded the ship. I later took the name Camille Paradisi. My plan has always been to let you in on all of this. It's important for you to understand that."

"Paul's sibling was a woman? That makes you *Trinity?* Over seventy years old? Now at least I know you're batshit crazy. All of you."

"Father Andrada and I had been meaning to talk to you about this for years, but then she died, and things got sidetracked, and then the Rosslyn Ripper turned up at confession, and it seemed like a good reason to engage your services. For me to let you gradually learn about us, and for—"

"Why in the world were you always planning to speak to *me* about *anything?* Let's have it, Camille!"

"It needs to be explained slowly—"

"Now!" Sam yelled loudly enough that he could tell his voice carried off the roof and down Monument Street, blending with the approaching sirens. Camille flinched back in her seat, and then glanced sidelong at Raj who Sam suddenly realized had joined them on the roof. Raj raised his eyebrows thoughtfully and shrugged.

"Sam, I will say only one more thing. When all of this is over you need to speak to Father Andrada."

The sirens were very close now, perhaps rounding the corner. Sam's phone buzzed. *Sparf.* He ignored it. Barnabus stood at the edge of the rooftop porch, hands flat on the rail, leaning over to view the street three stories below.

"Let me get this straight," Sam said. "Before you get taken into custody, I need to know just how crazy you actually are. It may make a big difference in how we proceed. You're saying the whole Ripper part just kinda happened? You really believe that crap in the journal about being the descendants of fallen angels banished from heaven? This entire time, you've wanted to hire me to, what, sue God?"

No one spoke for a long moment.

Amelia jotted something on her pad and earnestly nodded once.

"The jurisdictional issue is going to be difficult," Amelia said.

Camille rested her eyes gently on Sam's, just like in their first client meeting, the first time she hired him.

"I've been thinking through the jurisdictional problem. I've got a few ideas. But first you've got to get me out from under this murder charge."

"You don't ask much, do you?" Sam said.

"Sorry for the inconvenience."

"You know I don't believe this, right?"

Camille only smiled.

"The fuzz has arrived," Barnabus said.

"I may have made the bail issue a little easier for you," Camille said. "You told me it was easier to get pregnant ladies out of jail, right?"

Sam looked Camille up and down, her thin legs, face, and hands, her stylish, loose-fitting clothes.

"More than seven months," she said.

Sam and Camille stood close now, out of hearing distance from Barnabus and Amelia, both of whom watched the street from the rooftop rail.

"Do you have any complications?"

"You want a complication, I'll get you one."

"Ever heard of preeclampsia?"

"As a matter of fact, it probably killed my mother, as Fifika wrote about in her journal. It also nearly killed Fifika herself."

"We gotta move," Barnabus said. Lights flashed below.

"You're still missing a big piece of it, Sam. There's so much more to tell. You'll learn everything. Get me out of jail, and we can get to work on our case."

Sam could hear dozens of vehicles approaching the front of the house.

Barnabus clapped a hand on Sam's shoulder.

"Told you, dude. Biggest case ever."

Moments later, Sam and Camille stood in the high-ceilinged vestibule downstairs. Sam expected shouts from outside and pounding fists, but instead heard only three slow knocks. Barnabus opened the door.

Chief O'Malley stood on the porch with Sparf.

"This better not be some of your bullshit, Young." Surrounding them on all sides were patrolmen with hands on their holsters. Reporters and cameras lined the street.

CHAPTER 22

KATHARTA BATEY READ SAM'S business card. "*Sam Young, Attorney and Counselor at Law. I've heard of you.*"

"I know." Sam and Amelia sat close to his new client in the jail visiting room.

Katharta perched in front of Sam on the short, fixed metal stool in the small visiting room. She had her legs folded one over the other. Her toe bounced in a rhythmic circle as she stared at her nails.

"There's something you should know right up front about my case." She reminded Sam more of a bored beauty salon stylist discussing local gossip than a prominent local businesswoman recently arrested for money laundering.

"Katharta, let's start with something else. You don't need to tell us all about what happened yet. I've read your press statements. I basically get it, at least enough for now. Tell me more about you, first of all. Are you okay? I know this has gotta be a shock to the system."

Sam knew Katharta had attempted suicide her first night in jail and had spent the last week in the mental health unit, where she had been barred from receiving visitors of any kind. Today—her second day in the regular jail population—had been Sam's first real chance to see her in person.

"I gotta tell ya, last week I thought my life was over. *Wished* it was over. You have no idea what it's like to go from having everything to having nothing, all in a few weeks. I couldn't . . . I don't know how to say it . . . it's like I couldn't stand being in my own skin. I hated it. Hated myself."

Katharta shook her head as if shrugging off a long-ago memory. Sam watched her carefully. Even in jail clothes and without makeup, or any of the trappings she sported in public, Katharta was a beautiful, mature woman. Regally so. She reminded Sam of a famous actress. Maybe Katherine Hepburn, slumming it as a prisoner in an old movie.

"Yesterday I was released from the nut-job unit and given a cell, a cellmate, some clothes and soap, and well—" Katharta paused, as if assessing her next statement cautiously to make sure it was fully true.

"Go on," Sam said.

"Your client Camille. She came in last night. She's the one who told me to call you. Since the second I met her I've felt better than I ever have in my life. And to top it off, my back seems suddenly cured. I've had terrible back pain for several years. On pills for it—that's a whole 'nother story. But anyway, I haven't had a pain pill, or my anxiety meds for that matter, in days, and my back feels great. And you know what else?"

Sam urged her on with a shrug.

"I have this sense of inner peace I've never felt before. It's like thank God she's my cellmate, even if outside the cell is constantly video recorded. I swear . . . I mean I'd actually pay to live in a cubicle with her for a few weeks. You must think I'm crazy."

"No." Sam closed his notebook. "I really don't."

"Oh, and Camille whispered to me to warn you that they are going to record your lawyer visits with her, so she can't talk about her lawsuit. Whatever that means. Anyway, you'd better get Camille out of here soon." Katharta leaned forward. "This morning she was vomiting, like, a lot. Last night she was shaking in her bed, like violent shivers. Like maybe she's having something like a seizure, and—"

Sam stood. "I'm on it. Really. As for your case, Katharta, you'll do six months at the country club where you can drive your own golf cart. Martha Stewart made it, so will you."

"I know."

"But there's something you can do for me. For Camille. She may need your help. You're going to be brought over to court to testify in the next day or so. When we go for bail."

Katharta stood, eyes wide. "You ask, you got."

"It won't be anything you wouldn't do anyway," Sam said. "Just tell the truth.

"I have a question. How did she cure your back?" Amelia said.

Katharta crossed her arms and gripped her own shoulders. "She just held me for a moment."

Amelia put a hand to her chest and stared at Sam.

The automatic door popped slightly open, signaling the end of Sam's visit.

"Sam," Katharta said, "you never asked what I wanted to tell you about the evidence against me."

"You were going to tell me you're guilty of what you're charged with. The fraud." He winked at her. "But I don't give a shit."

Sam walked calmly out of the jail, taking quick note of the number of press cameras and reporters behind the barrier. Three reporters. Two cameras.

"Mr. Young, Mr. Young! Will Camille testify?"

"Is Paradisi crazy?"

"Will she be out of jail tomorrow?"

Sam ignored their shouts, walking slowly past them with a nod. His Escalade glided up just as he reached the street, its occupants hidden by the newly darkened tint. Sam eased into the front seat and Amelia got in back.

Sam glanced back over his shoulder. Nguyen, sunglasses perched on his nose, fidgeted with an electronic gadget that hung from the side of his computer.

"Those medical documents better be good," Sam said.

"On it, boss," Nguyen said.

Sam sat back and listened to Nguyen's tapping computer keys as the Escalade cruised west on I-66. He scrolled through his phone for Alfredo Torres's number.

CHAPTER 23

"THE DEFENDANT'S MOTION FOR bail is worse than absurd," Sparf whined from the podium. "This defendant is under federal investigation for being a serial killer, and this court never gives bail for first-degree murder."

Sam could sense the differing emotions of the silent horde behind him in the gallery. The deputies had packed the rows tightly and allowed standing room all along the back and sides of the courtroom. Camille sat with perfect posture as usual, her face impassive. But she also had dark circles under her eyes, and her face seemed thinner than normal. She looked ill. Beaten down. Her radiance dimmed by only a few days of incarceration.

Sam watched Judge Linda O'Grady carefully. In a way, Judge O'Grady had been a terrible draw for Camille. She was a former prosecutor, deeply insecure about her own intellectual abilities, and angry about that. She was a successful example of a lawyer who knows he or she is behind the curve in the candlepower department and makes up for it by being angry and dismissive. She preferred moralizing lectures to legal analysis, and it was commonly believed that her habit of calling recesses at the end of legal arguments allowed her to go ask Judge Chin—a woman fifteen years her junior—how to rule.

On the other hand, by the way Judge O'Grady stared blankly at Sparf, maybe she was a decent draw after all. Three things about Linda O'Grady actually made her the right judge for Camille on the issue of bail. Sam remembered meeting her children once at a bar event. Polite, happy kids, both at great colleges, who saw their mother as a kind and hard-working soccer mom who made it as a judge without depriving them of an ounce of attention. In other words, she was a good mother, and insecure or not, she valued that above the respect of the arrogant assholes at the courthouse. Second, she wasn't smart enough to be absolutely sure that Sparf's arguments were correct, even though they were. Third, Judge Chin was on vacation.

Sam took a deep breath and waited for Sparf to finish his opening remarks. As always, he was long-winded and imperious. Unfortunately, he was also correct.

"The Virginia bond statute is very clear, Judge," Sparf said. "There's a presumption against bail for anyone charged with murder. Any irregularities, such as escape attempts, suicide attempts, or the like, could derail the prosecution of a potential serial killer. You should also know that after Paradisi was read her Miranda rights, when asked if she killed Lucas, she did not deny it. Did not explain how her DNA could have wound up at the crime scene."

O'Grady frowned. Sparf's comment on Camille's refusal to deny the offense would not be admissible at trial. Sparf, though, was trying to spin some leverage out of it for the bond motion and, of course, for the press. To put the pressure on O'Grady to deny Camille's release.

"I quote from Detective Zwerling's report. Quote: When asked if she killed Zebulon Lucas, Ms. Paradisi replied, 'Look at your own files and you'll figure it out.'"

"You haven't charged her with all four murders?" Judge O'Grady asked.

"Correct. DNA connects her to Lucas's killing, but one must also note—" Sparf paused for effect. "The killings stopped right after her arrest. We're reinvestigating the other three now. As stand-alone murders, the first three are all under federal jurisdiction. Once we establish the pattern, we can charge them all in state court."

"Once the pattern is established, won't the entire case, including the Lucas murder, go federal?"

Sparf paused. Any criminal lawyer knew that Sparf would unlikely be able to hold on to such a big case if the federal authorities had jurisdiction and wanted it badly enough. But Sam could feel Sparf's mind, with its rigid, methodical earnestness, rebel against the idea of giving up the Ripper case. By arresting Camille for Zebulon before the feds could get hold of her and reinvestigate the first three, he had gained an advantage, at least for now. "That is not how we wish to proceed."

"Okay, well let me ask you this. Is there any evidence at all that Ms. Paradisi is suicidal?"

Sparf glanced sideways. "No direct evidence of that, no. But it's always a risk in these cases."

"But she did turn herself in?"

"Yes."

"Mr. Sparf, I will hear Mr. Young out. You'll have your chance to argue at the end." Translation: *Sit down and shut up Sparf. You know damned well I am not releasing this nutty bitch. Never, nada, not on my watch.*

Sam stood. He looked briefly behind him at Nguyen and Barnabus, who sat together in the front row. Amelia sat on the other side of Camille.

"Ms. Paradisi calls Katharta Batey."

The door to the jail lockup swung open, and Katharta emerged in her orange jumpsuit. She sported a new hairdo and a girlish smile. She rubbed her wrists as she approached the stand, blinking, as if walking quickly into blinding sunlight.

"Ob-jec-tion!" Sparf called out in a low, bored tone, as if attacking Sam's evidence was a routine hassle. As if Sam wasn't wasting the court's time, and they could all be off to lunch. "Your Honor, the defendant's cellmate's testimony can't possibly be relevant. Nothing about this defendant's custody status or jail adjustment provides you with the legal basis to release her. Nothing."

Sparf was merely articulating the argument he had just made. The one he should have been saving for after the evidence.

"What is the relevance, Mr. Young?" O'Grady asked.

"Judge, this witness will testify to firsthand observations of Ms. Paradisi's medical symptoms, including regular and repeated vomiting, seizure-like shaking at times, and painful, blinding headaches. All these symptoms have been constant for the last thirty-six hours, and—"

"Fine," Sparf said. "I'll stipulate to all that." His nasally voice rose with a whiny annoyance. "It doesn't matter. I agree that Ms. Paradisi suffers from the symptoms Mr. Young describes. Let's move on."

Sam shrugged. Sparf was attempting to show disdain for Sam's legal position by suggesting that he should win the argument regardless of the evidence. Katharta stood, still blinking, in the center of the courtroom, obviously confused. Sam nodded to the deputy, who placed a kind hand on the small of Katharta's back and led her out of the courtroom as if escorting a date to their dinner table.

"Ms. Paradisi calls Dr. Alfredo Torres," Sam said.

Dr. Torres entered the courtroom in a crisp, black suit. Sam flipped through his notes as Torres strode confidently down the aisle, nodding at Sparf as if to an old friend as he passed. Sparf frowned.

"Please state your name," Sam said.

"Dr. Alfredo Torres."

"Tell the judge a little bit about your education and career."

Torres quickly ran through his unique resume, which included college in the Dominican Republic and medical school at the University of Virginia. Torres sounded like an impressive, if a bit nerdy, professor.

"Have you had the opportunity to review Ms. Paradisi's medical history, including records concerning her pregnancy and her family history, which have been marked as Defendant's Exhibit A?"

"Indeed, I have. Quite thoroughly."

"Have you had the opportunity to personally examine Ms. Paradisi?"

"Of course. I met with her at the Bennet County Jail two days ago. As instructed, I conducted a full examination."

Sam paused, pretending to examine some notes, and then

put the notes down. He held up an inch-thick file, motioning to the courtroom deputy, who approached Sam to retrieve the exhibit for Torres. He then handed a copy of the records to Sparf, who pretended not to care, accepting the file without looking at Sam. But he immediately began flipping through it. Sam's heart jumped, just a little, as Sparf's beady eyes began to scan the records.

"Dr. Torres, I am going to ask you to review Defendant's Exhibit A, and if it consists of the medical records you reviewed."

Torres sat quietly, reviewing each and every page of the record. Most witnesses would have answered the question after a brief glance at the documents, but Torres was making a point: he was very, very thorough. While Freddy flipped from one page to the next, Sam could not resist a quick probe into Nguyen's mind. Once a scattered, unhappy mess, Nguyen's thoughts now felt clean and contained. Like a small but fast-moving little stream bumping over polished rocks. Nguyen was not even nervous.

"These are the records I reviewed."

"Did you also interview an inmate named Katharta Batey— Ms. Paradisi's cellmate—concerning her eyewitness observations of Ms. Paradisi's symptoms?"

"I did. I interviewed her yesterday by telephone during an inmate call you arranged."

"Tell us, Doctor, based on your review of records, your personal examination of Ms. Paradisi, and your interview with Ms. Batey, did you make a diagnosis of Ms. Paradisi? Specifically concerning her pregnancy?"

"I did. Ms. Paradisi is seven and a half months pregnant. This is a first pregnancy for her. Her family history includes multiple female relatives, along with her mother and grandmother, who died during childbirth. In addition, she suffers from hypertension and has presented consistent symptoms of nausea and terrible headaches. Based on all of those factors, I have concluded that Ms. Paradisi has a severe form of a condition called preeclampsia, a complication of pregnancy, the cause of which is basically unknown. However, the condition renders childbirth much more dangerous than normal, for both child and mother. Because of the severe nature of Ms. Paradisi's preeclampsia, and the presence of what seem to be seizures, she runs a high risk of developing eclampsia, a related condition that renders childbirth extraordinarily dangerous. Life-threatening, in fact, both for child and mother."

Sam felt Sparf stiffen as he shifted through the records.

"Do you have a suggested treatment for Ms. Paradisi?" Sam asked.

"I do. I suggest an immediate delivery by C-section at the state-of-the-art maternity ward at Bennet County Hospital, or a similar facility."

Sparf started to rise to object, but a look from Judge O'Grady sat him back down.

"Would you, yourself, perform the delivery?"

"Yes," Torres said. "I have privileges at the hospital and have already spoken with the anesthesiologist who will assist me. I have made arrangements to perform a delivery by C-section as soon as Ms. Paradisi can be released. There are nurses standing by right now for an update."

"Dr. Torres, have you also examined the medical facility at the Bennet County Adult Detention Center?"

"I have."

"What is your opinion about whether or not the facility at the Bennet County Adult Detention Center is suitable for delivering Ms. Paradisi's child?"

Torres cleared his throat and looked directly at Judge O'Grady. "Your Honor, if that baby is delivered at the jail, then one or both of them is likely to wind up dead."

"Thank you, Doctor. Please answer any questions Mr. Sparf has for you."

Sparf stood and made his signature dismissive gesture of swiping a shoulder with a flick of his hand as if to dust off some lint.

"Would you agree with me that your prediction about the death of Ms. Paradisi or her child is not accurate if the correct doctor and equipment are brought into the jail?"

Torres looked nervously at Sam. Sam shrugged, a gesture seen by the judge and Sparf. It was the gesture of a lawyer telling his witness to tell the truth, even if it seemed to hurt the point.

Torres's shoulders slumped a little.

"That would be safer than without it."

"Any further witnesses?" O'Grady asked, indicating her growing impatience with the hearing. Torres hadn't even begun to leave the witness stand.

"Yes, Judge, I call—"

"Judge, may I be heard?" Sparf was picking up on O'Grady's cue, sensing that she might end the hearing early by buying into his legal argument that releasing Camille was a terrible move regardless of the evidence. "Paradisi has been charged with first-degree murder. As we all well know, she is also under major suspicion for being the most notorious serial killer in Bennet history. The idea of bail, the entire *idea* of it, is ridiculous. It's absurd. It's—"

"Mr. Young," O'Grady said, "I understand Ms. Paradisi's critical health condition, but I've always heard that medical care in the jail is quite good. Mr. Sparf's point concerning the code, and the potential that Ms. Paradisi has killed four citizens, is my problem here. You see that, right?"

"I do, and this next witness directly addresses that point. The defense calls—"

"Objection!" Sparf cried out. "If Mr. Young plans to call a witness about Ms. Paradisi's guilt or innocence of the offense for which she is charged, I need proper notice. I do not have my witnesses here—who would, I might add, make it obvious that she's guilty. This is improper—"

"Mr. Sparf." Even O'Grady, a lifelong prosecutor who kept prosecuting when she took the bench, saw the right ruling on this a mile away. "You can't use her guilt as an argument against bail and then object to evidence of innocence. I'll hear this witness."

A deputy opened the courtroom doors. Andrada strode purposefully to the stand, the most commanding presence in the room with his serene gaze and athletic physique.

"State your name, please," Sam said.

"Father Leo Andrada."

"What do you do for a living?"

"I am the pastor at Church of the Holy Angels in Bennet, Virginia."

"Do you know the defendant, Sister Camille Paradisi?"

"Yes, she began to work at Holy Angels in January of 2013. She serves as the Director of Religious Education."

"Do you, as part of your job, hear confessions?"

"Daily," Andrada said. "Not always as many as the younger priests, but one or two on most days."

"Did Sister Paradisi aid you in this regard?"

"Yes. Parishioners knew to make appointments through her, to make sure it fit with the rest of my schedule. She often greeted parishioners when they entered the church. She would lead them to the confessional, instructing them that they could choose to sit facing me or enter the door, which would place them behind me. Sometimes people do not want to face a priest during a confession. She also instructed them on the basics of confession, if needed, such as how to begin, and such things."

"Did you hear any confessions on July 3rd of this year?"

"Yes. I checked my calendar at your request. I listened to one."

"Do you now know that this is also the date of the third Rosslyn Ripper murder?"

"I do. I noted that fact the next day, when I read about the murder."

"Does your calendar list the name of the person who confessed to you on July 3rd?"

"No. Even if I knew the name, I wouldn't write it down, and in this instance I didn't know."

"Did the person sit facing you or behind a screen?"

"Facing."

Sam pulled a photograph out of a file and showed it to Sparf. Sparf shot to his feet.

"Objection! I thought this witness was called as a character witness for Ms. Paradisi, not a fact witness in this case. I have no idea where this is headed, but I object to relevance."

O'Grady looked at Sam for a response to the objection. Sam waited. He could see Sparf's wheels turning. Sparf had no idea how Andrada would answer, and he suddenly realized he wanted to know.

"Actually," Sparf said, "I withdraw the objection."

Sam glanced behind Sparf to the front row of the gallery to take a look at O'Malley, who had his arms folded. He looked cool, as usual. Inside, he was on fire. Sam made eye contact with him, absorbing the what? Anger? No, shame. At not finding this witness himself. Sam handed the photograph to the deputy, who then handed it to Andrada.

"Is that the man who came to confession?"

"Yes."

"Your Honor, please let the record reflect that Father Andrada has identified the photograph of Zebulon Lucas. Father, was Zebulon Lucas a parishioner?"

"No. We have no record of his ever actually attending church. One need not be a parishioner for me to provide confession though."

"Have the police ever interviewed you in connection with this case?"

"No."

Sam took a deep breath.

"What sins did this man confess to you?"

Sparf bounced to his feet, but Sam could sense that he was unsure of why, and how, he should attempt to bar this testimony. Just as he began to speak, Andrada looked squarely at Judge O'Grady and interrupted him.

"Your Honor, I refuse to answer that question on the grounds that it is subject to the priest-penitent privilege."

O'Grady frowned at Sam.

"Your Honor," Sam said, "he's already testified that he heard the confession of Zebulon Lucas. I submit to you that he has waived the privilege at this point. Secondly, Lucas is dead. I further submit that the privilege no longer exists."

Andrada smiled wisely at Judge O'Grady.

"Judge, I draw a distinction between testifying that a confession occurred and testifying about the substance of a confession. I believe the other legal privileges work that way too, do they not? And with all due respect to Mr. Young and to this court, I will not answer that question even if ordered to do so."

Andrada's elegant baritone filled the courtroom, and Sam could feel every head in the room nod with admiration.

As Sam hoped she would, O'Grady easily digested Andrada's point.

"He does not have to answer that question. It's protected by the privilege." Sam could sense her enjoying the glow from the approving gallery.

"Father Andrada, you said that Camille would sometimes instruct parishioners on the basics of confession. Would that include asking them to remove headwear?"

"It could, sure. Men generally don't wear hats during a confession."

"And if she informed a parishioner to remove a cap, let's say, would she hold it for him?"

"I'm sure she would, she'd do—"

"Objection—speculation." For Sparf, it was a soft objection, not bitchy or whiny, and very slow in coming. Deflated.

"Sustained."

"Did the man have a hat on during his confession?"

"No."

"Did you later become aware that he was killed last week?"

"Yes."

"Have you observed a photograph of the crime scene?"

"Yes, you showed me one."

"Was he wearing a hat in that photo?"

"Objection." An obvious one because there was no basis to ask Andrada about the crime scene photo. But Sam watched O'Grady, whose face wrinkled. She was wondering about confessions and hats.

"Sustained."

"Nothing further," Sam said.

Sparf stood, hand on his lips. Sam could feel his mind churning. Accentuate Sam's point, or let it go? But his eyes were on the future of the case. And then Sam felt a strong flicker of something from Sparf that buoyed Sam's hope that, despite the tough childhood and deep-seated anger, Sparf was a prosecutor for the right reasons. To get the bad guys. He cast his net exceedingly wide by Sam's standards, but he did not include people he thought were innocent. Sam then saw it clearly—Sparf decided he wanted the press to hear Sam's point stated clearly, for fairness, and, maybe, to cover his own ass, at least to himself. In the end, Sparf didn't care about O'Malley or his boss as much as he cared about being the earnest smiter of all that is selfish and mean. Good for the system. Good for Sparf.

"Father Andrada, do you have any idea if Ms. Paradisi actually touched Zebulon Lucas's hat, thereby inadvertently transferring her DNA onto it, and eventually making it appear that she may have actually been at the scene of his murder that night?" Sparf asked.

"No," Andrada said.

"That's all I have, Judge."

Pens scribbled and the tweets flew as Andrada left the courtroom, smiling kindly at Camille as he passed the defense table.

"One final witness," Sam said. "I call Juliana Kim."

Juliana entered the courtroom in a neat business suit. She carried a slim, black, leather folder. She nodded to Sparf as she approached the stand.

"State your name, please."

"Juliana Kim."

"Can you tell the court what you do for a living?"

"I'm a scientist at the Virginia Department of Forensic Science."

"And can you tell the judge a little about your education and experience?"

"Judge, I stipulate to Ms. Kim's qualifications as a DNA expert, if that's where this is headed," Sparf said.

"Thank you, Mr. Sparf," O'Grady said. "Ms. Kim is qualified as an expert witness in DNA analysis. Nice to see you again, Juliana."

Juliana, a regular witness for the prosecution, glanced up at O'Grady. "Always a pleasure, Your Honor."

Sam skipped over a few pages of his notes. Sparf and O'Grady were not going to make him jump through the basic hoops with Juliana.

"Have you had an opportunity to review the DNA certificates and underlying discovery materials pertaining to this case, Commonwealth v. Camille Paradisi?"

"Yes."

"Did you actually conduct the majority of the DNA tests in this case?"

"I did."

Sam nodded to the deputy, who walked over and received from him a thick stack of files. He then delivered them to Juliana on the witness stand. "Are these exhibits the DNA materials pertaining to all four victims of the so-called Rosslyn Ripper?"

Sparf rose halfway to his feet. "Objection, we don't use that term."

Juliana ignored him. "Yes."

"Now, with respect to the DNA profile obtained from the hat of victim number four, Zebulon Lucas, and the DNA profile taken from the blood of defendant Camille Paradisi, can you tell me what the results show?" Sam was skipping past the DNA education that Juliana would normally provide to a jury. O'Grady had heard it all before anyway. She didn't understand it, but she would certainly pretend she did. She understood enough to believe that if a cop scientist said DNA matched someone, it surely did, and that if a defense scientist challenged a cop's conclusion, he or she was obviously a paid hack.

"The profile from Zebulon's hat contains one allele—that's a genetic marker—at each of nine loci. Those are locations on the—" Juliana looked up at O'Grady.

"There's no jury here, Juliana. You can get straight to the conclusion."

"Thank you. The hat result shows one allele at each of the nine loci and nothing at the other six loci. As for—"

"Let me interrupt you briefly," Sam said. "Is that an incomplete result?"

"Yes. Every human's DNA has a pair of markers at all fifteen of the sixteen Powerplex loci, one from the mother, one from the father. This result is incomplete in that it lacks any markers at six of the loci. It happens sometimes, quite often really, with weak DNA results—when there's not enough DNA on a crime scene item."

"Is it not incomplete in another respect?"

Juliana looked up at the judge as if to stress the importance of this answer. But the answer was for the press.

"I thought so at first," Juliana said. "When I see only one marker at a locus, there are two possibilities—one is that there is an incomplete profile, like from a weak crime scene sample. Another is that the person received the same allele at that locus from his mother *and* from his father. When this happens, the sample is referred to as *homozygotic* at that locus. Here, I initially believed that this sample was incomplete with respect to some or all of the nine loci because I didn't believe it likely that someone would be homozygotic at nine loci."

"Why not?"

"Some people are homozygotic at one, two, three, or even four loci, but I had never heard of anywhere close to nine. The odds of it are, well, staggering."

"Do you still believe the hat profile is incomplete at the nine loci?"

"No."

"Why not?"

"Because Camille Paradisi is homozygotic at all fifteen Powerplex loci."

"And just briefly, what is the sixteenth loci?"

"It's a location used to determine gender. Males are XY. Females are XX."

"And?"

Juliana smirked. "She's a woman."

"What about the comparison?"

"Camille Paradisi cannot be eliminated as a contributor to the DNA profile found on Zebulon Lucas's hat. She matches at all nine loci—the same homozygotic marker at each."

Sam was pushing the testimony far beyond what a bail hearing would ever cover, but neither O'Grady nor Sparf nor anyone else in the courtroom—except, possibly, O'Malley, who had no standing in the proceedings—wanted to stop things now.

"How common is it for someone to be homozygotic at all loci?"

Juliana spoke past Sam straight to the gallery now. She was no longer in O'Grady's courtroom at a bail hearing. She was on a stage at a conference, educating the world.

"I was so curious about this I actually looked into it a good bit. The scientists I work with are, frankly, blown away by it. As far as we can tell, no human being has ever tested homozygotic at that many loci. If we could only do more research, we could find out just how utterly unusual this is."

"Could the results be fraud?"

"No. She's been typed with a buccal swab and a blood sample. It's real. The odds are simply too high for this to occur randomly. It's as if she has a mother, but no father. For a human being, I consider it categorically impossible."

"But Paradisi exists."

"No doubt."

Sam took a brief break, filled up a cup of water, and handed it to the deputy to hand to Juliana.

"One last point, Juliana—"

"Objection!" Sparf was now playing to the press as well on the point that he believed mattered. "All of these questions have been irrelevant. Fine—she's a genetic mutant, and ten mega-bazillion times more likely to have touched the hat than we ever thought. What in the world does this have to do with the bail hearing?"

"Your Honor, Mr. Sparf just told you that one of the reasons you should deny bail is that Ms. Paradisi is a serial killer. He has placed the strength of the state's evidence on this point at issue. I have just a few more questions, Judge. And these get straight to the point."

O'Grady's face wrinkled. Sam could tell she suspected a lot of his questions were irrelevant to the bail hearing, but she wasn't perceptive enough to realize she was right. Before she could figure it out, Sam filled the silence.

"Juliana, did you find any DNA profiles on victims one through three?"

"Yes."

"Tell us."

"I found four genetic markers at two loci on the bra strap of Joni West—victim number three."

"Could this incomplete profile belong to Camille Paradisi?"

"No, none of the alleles match, and the bra result is not homozygotic at either of the two loci for which I achieved a result."

"Did you have an opportunity to compare that partial profile with the profile of someone else?"

"Objection!" Sparf screamed this time. "Judge, if Mr. Young has conducted testing of a suspect unknown to us, it is not only inadmissible scientific evidence due to lack of notice, but it's probably an ethical violation, withholding evidence or something."

"Mr. Young, I'm not listening to testimony about DNA tests unknown to the prosecution. They gave you their results."

"I hear you, Judge. This question calls for an answer that comes entirely from the Department of Forensic Science's file, which the prosecution has. It's nothing new." Sam did not wait for O'Grady to rule. "You can answer the question, Juliana."

Sparf grunted and shook his head slowly from side to side while O'Grady stared straight ahead, blinking.

"Yes, I compared the bra strap profile to the only male profile contained within the Rosslyn Ripper DFS file. It matched perfectly at all four alleles at both loci."

"And what are the odds of this occurring by chance?"

O'Grady looked confused. Sparf was shifting around in his seat.

"One in several hundred chances that someone other than the male at issue left the DNA on the bra," Juliana said.

"And whose profile was it, the male profile you compared?"

"It was the profile of victim number four—Zebulon Lucas."

"What is your conclusion about whether or not Zebulon Lucas took part in the murder of Joni West?"

"The chances that he didn't touch that bra are one in several hundred. That night, she'd merely been walking home from the subway after a late day at work. That leads me to the conclusion that Zebulon touched her bra around the time she was killed. They had no prior acquaintance and didn't live or work near each other. Common sense, you know. I wouldn't convict someone on it, but you can pretty much figure it out."

Sparf stood up to object but ended up saying nothing. Instead, he started shifting through papers on his table, perhaps looking for Zebulon's profile before he opened his mouth.

Sam plowed ahead. "Do you mean to tell us that the Virginia DFS has had in its possession DNA evidence that shows it was extremely likely Zebulon Lucas took part in the murder of Ms. West, and no one has noticed it?"

Juliana smiled sweetly at Judge O'Grady, who now looked a little less enamored but didn't understand the evidence well enough to know how to feel.

"Things were happening so fast. There were different crime scenes, different files, and again, it was *only* a two-locus match. No one would ever think it was suitable for comparison. *I* did not even notice it, did not even think of it. The idea of Lucas being involved with the West murder simply never occurred to me."

Sam gathered his papers. "That's all I have."

Sam could feel Sparf's brain chewing through the evidence about Zebulon at the West crime scene. He had exactly two cross-examination choices with respect to this new information. He could approach Juliana and require her to show him the DNA profiles in his own file to see if they depicted a match between the bra and Zebulon. If he did so, and Juliana was right, it would do nothing but re-establish that he had never thoroughly looked at the evidence himself. His second choice was to do nothing. Juliana stared at him coolly, a sliver of a smirk that Sam knew to be a masked sign of fun.

"No questions," Sparf said.

Despite the fact that courtroom procedure dictated Sam speak first, Sparf began to argue his position as soon as Juliana stepped off the witness stand. He took a typical prosecutor's strategy, ignoring the bad and focusing on the good. His best point: The law.

"Your Honor, as I discussed earlier, a murder defendant should never be released on bail. The evidence also doesn't support the contention that Ms. Paradisi or her child are placed in danger by a jailhouse delivery. You have every right to order that a doctor of Ms. Paradisi's choosing be brought into the jail with the equipment he needs. If it's Dr. Torres, so be it. In any event, nothing that has happened at this hearing amounts to a reason to bend the rules. That being said—"

Sparf paused. Sam could feel the tension between Sparf and O'Malley sitting right behind him. The chief's eyes bore into Sparf's back, a smug look on his face.

"I believe this hearing has brought out factual issues which deserve," he paused again, "some attention. I plan to fully discuss this with the investigators in this case as soon as possible."

Sam looked at O'Grady. This is what it came down to. Guilt or innocence aside, would a judge like O'Grady break the obviously written law or lurch out on her own to help somebody? Normally, O'Grady utterly lacked that sort of creativity, even if the person who needed the help was a baby.

"I will hear from you, Mr. Young."

Instead, Amelia stood.

Sam sat down and looked at Camille for the first time since the hearing had begun. She leaned back, one hand on her stomach, the other gripping the armrest of Sam's chair. Their eyes met. The normal energy was gone, replaced by an inward-looking despair. He could feel her squeeze the arm of his chair. Her wrist, always thin, now seemed pale and bony—not like the appendage of a beautiful woman, but a desperate prisoner. Sam turned back to the podium.

"May it please the court," Amelia began in a soft, unassuming voice, almost too passive, too quiet for the moment. But as she began her argument, Sam's mind launched, somersaulting once on the way before hitting the judge at the same time as Amelia's words.

"Judge, I am handing forward three additional exhibits for your consideration during my argument."

The deputy retrieved the exhibits and delivered them to the judge, who merely stared at Amelia with a pleasant, anticipatory look on her face. She reached for the files mechanically.

"Mr. Sparf mischaracterizes our position by claiming we seek bail in this matter. What I am asking for is not bail, but a furlough, a temporary release for an important reason, which the Circuit Court of Bennet County has granted eighty-six times in the last ten years. If you will please look at Defendant's Exhibit B."

Amelia paused. Sam peered into O'Grady's eyes as she picked up the exhibit.

"Exhibit B is a list of every furlough granted in the past ten years. Seventy-five of them have been temporary releases for an inmate to attend a family member's funeral. Ten of them have been to attend important family events such as graduations, and one of them was so that eighteen-year-old robbery defendant Russell Hackmann could play in the Regional Basketball Championship for Yorktown High School. If there are two things we can agree on here, it would be that one, this court routinely grants furloughs, and two, this court routinely grants furloughs for reasons far less important than the life of a child."

Amelia paused again. She waited for O'Grady's eyes to leave the exhibit and return to her. Sam focused intently on O'Grady without staring at her too hard.

"How long a furlough?" O'Grady asked. Sparf sighed loudly with annoyance.

"Only until Dr. Torres clears her as safe to return to the jail. Exhibit C is a letter from John Joseph Rogers, the head administrator of Bennet Hospital. He estimates that the cost of temporarily outfitting the Bennet County Adult Detention Center with the proper staff and equipment to safely deliver Ms. Paradisi's child on an emergency basis by C-section would be approximately two hundred eighty thousand dollars. All of which, as I am sure Mr. Sparf would agree, would have to be paid from the state's criminal fund, if you ordered such adjustments to be made."

Sparf sighed deeply but not ostentatiously.

"Finally, Judge, Exhibit D is the defendant's proposed delivery plan, which includes transportation of Ms. Paradisi this evening, by a properly equipped ambulance, to Bennet County Hospital. I have attached the names and social security numbers of everyone involved, from the ambulance tech people, to the driver, to the staff, and the nurses who will take part in the delivery. All the parties are aware that they would be escorted by Bennet County Sheriff's Department vehicles, and that as many deputies as the court so orders will be permitted to secure the maternity ward in any reasonable manner they see fit during the delivery. Once Dr. Torres declares Ms. Paradisi fit to travel, the same personnel, under the same circumstances, will return her to the jail."

Amelia paused again and shuffled through some papers on the podium. Sam felt O'Grady's mind turning over slowly. She wasn't bold enough to decide quickly on her own what the Zebulon evidence meant. But she knew Sparf was. If he thought the evidence warranted further investigation, so did she.

"I have a question," O'Grady said, her face slightly contorted as she glanced back and forth between Sparf and Amelia. "Was your evidence designed to demonstrate that Ms. Paradisi is innocent? Or that Zebulon Lucas had it comin'?"

"Our evidence was designed to show that Chief O'Malley and his investigators need to take a *thorough* look at their case," Amelia said. "My final point is that all of the personnel and equipment required by the defendant's delivery plan will cost the state absolutely nothing, as Ms. Paradisi has insurance and private funding to cover all expenses if the services are provided pursuant to this plan. She cannot make the same commitment if the court orders the hospital maternity ward to be transplanted into the county jail. For that, the hospital requires a full, up-front payment. To conclude, there is simply nothing for the prosecutor to worry about here. Ms. Paradisi is a sick woman who will be under heavy guard, and whose DNA profile is formally filed as an exhibit with this court. As the court well knows, its anomalies render it the most unique human DNA profile ever found. Given that, and the publicity of this case, no person could escape justice under our plan, even if the sheriff's office fails to maintain proper security, and—"

"All right." O'Grady held her palm aloft to Amelia. "I have considered the evidence and the arguments of the counsel." She shuffled some papers on the bench and appeared befuddled for a moment, looking around as if she were a mere spectator at the hearing and not the focus of more than a hundred onlookers.

"Ms. Paradisi, I am going to order you furloughed this evening at seven for the purpose of delivering your child at the direction of the medical personnel described in the defendant's delivery plan. I order your immediate return to the detention center upon your clearance by Dr. Torres."

Judge O'Grady, herself again, now looked sternly at Sam, as if he had been the lawyer conducting the argument. Sam left her mind, wanting her to be herself. He wanted to hear some harsh, even biting words towards Camille. A typical anti-defendant rant by O'Grady would help show a lack of bias to the appeals court if Sparf tried an emergency appeal of O'Grady's decision to furlough Camille.

"Mr. Young, a minimum of twelve deputies will accompany Ms. Paradisi and remain in the closest reasonable proximity possible during the procedure." She began to stand, as if to adjourn, but then plopped back into her chair and looked around the courtroom, seeming to take in the size of the silent crowd behind the lawyers for the first time. Then she lightened the mood by speaking to O'Malley.

"Chief, I heard about what happened the other day with the assault. Glad to see you out and about."

O'Malley stood from his seat in the gallery, sporting his wide, political grin. The one he used for press conferences.

"Oh, I've been punched before, Judge. Part of the job.

Apparently the fella thought I wasn't working hard enough to find his daughter's killer."

"Well, apparently, he was wrong," O'Grady said. She then eased off the bench.

Typical O'Grady. The nonsensical comment, which suggested that O'Malley had solved the Ripper case, was belied by the evidence she had just heard.

Sam turned around. The reporters, scattered randomly throughout the courtroom, scooted past the legs of their fellow spectators to get to the door as fast as possible. As he gathered his materials, he sensed O'Malley lurking behind him. He turned to face the chief. Sure, O'Malley was selfish. Sure, he was driven. But, like Sparf, he wasn't one to convict an innocent person. And Sam saw something else. Unlike Sparf, O'Malley wouldn't work too hard to convict Camille if he thought she were only guilty of killing Zebulon. Not if she killed Zebulon because he had been the Rosslyn Ripper.

"What gives, Young? You couldn't have alerted me about Zebulon's DNA before?"

Sam shrugged. "I have my reasons. You don't know what it's like in my world."

Sam and Amelia stood together, watching Sparf as the courtroom emptied. He still faced the well of the courtroom, perfectly still. He held a sheet of paper in each hand, looking from one to the other. His posture was not that of the young, goofy Sparf or the adult, meticulous Sparf. He stood in the solid, unselfconscious pose of a leader weighing a serious matter.

CHAPTER 24

AMELIA, SAM, AND NGUYEN SAT at the bar at Harpoon Hannah's, watching the clock as well as the Fox news coverage of the demonic nun case. They touched on all the main points, the strange genes, even the odd religious overtones. The cameras still focused on the front of the Bennet Detention Center, from where the pregnant nun with a mother but no father would emerge in less than an hour.

"So what's your assessment of the case against Camille on Zebulon?" Nguyen asked.

"That's easy. They have one. The crime scene techs say the hat must have been replaced on his head after he was killed. Her DNA is on the hat, which they can say shows she probably placed the hat on his head after he was killed, thereby suggesting she killed him. She fled the scene. They know Andrada can establish that she had been onto Zeb as the Ripper. She could try self-defense, and sure, could be acquitted. But they have a case if they want to have one. Whether they technically have a case isn't the question."

"What is?"

"Justice, Nguyen. Some prosecutors care about it. Some don't."

Sam's phone buzzed. He peered at it. "It's Sparf."

"I bet he's appealing the furlough order, ten bucks," Amelia said. "He'll get O'Grady reversed on the papers."

"No bet," Sam said. "I'd be stealing your money." He picked up the phone. "This is Young."

"You know I could win this ruling on appeal," Sparf said with his usual quick, clipped analysis. "O'Grady would have to halt the release if I filed for it, and the appeals court would have to rule for me. Frankly, I don't know what O'Grady was thinking today."

"I'm listening."

"I'm not appealing. The feds called today after the hearing. They asked again if they could take Paradisi into federal custody. I told them to shove it."

"Thanks, Chad. How long will that hold them off?"

"I got a murder charge on her so they'd have to go to Main Justice and get politics involved to get hold of her. But hey, I also took another look at this case based on today's hearing. I'm thinking a different way about it now. O'Malley's following up on some of your information, but if it checks out, I'm thinking, you know, Paradisi isn't much of a suspect for the first three murders."

"True."

"There's no federal jurisdiction over just the murder of Zebulon. He wasn't killed on memorial grounds. The feds will have to back off unless they can build a case on the first three. But I gotta say, they seem to want her, badly. A deputy attorney general yelled at me on the phone."

"They could still at least charge her with the other three, though."

"Sure, but after today, that would look pretty stupid if you ask me. I think your girl's in the clear there. But don't think for a second I buy that DNA transfer on Zebulon's hat BS. I think Paradisi was at the crime scene. The thing is, unless I find more, I'm not convinced her involvement with his death means she committed murder. I mean, if he really was the Rosslyn Ripper, who's gonna believe she didn't kill him in self-defense?

Paradisi's in the Ripper victim demographic, plus she turned herself in. I'm not convinced there's a case there."

Whoa! Sam's mind drifted back over the years to the young Sparf. The kid with the funny haircut, stoically dressing in the junior high locker room after somebody had dumped a cup of piss on his head. Sam had sat on the bench in front of his own locker, watching Sparf's hollow eyes as he delved deeper and deeper into himself to escape. Sparf tied his shoes while the urine still glistened on the side of his face. But through it all Sparf was a smart guy, and maybe the adult Sparf shared something with Sam they had come to in different ways.

Fuck the feds. Fuck the bosses. Fuck 'em. Good for Chad.

"Chad, for what it's worth, you are one hell of a good prosecutor."

"I need a few days. But if all this stuff checks out, I'll likely drop the case next week. And by the way . . . "

"Yes?"

"Fuck you, Young."

• • •

Wooden sawhorses, manned every twenty feet or so by a cop with a baton, penned the crowd, press included, away from the entrance to the detention center. The officers faced the horde of people and cameras, backs to the detention center exit. O'Malley stood yards from the jail exit talking to Deputy Plosky, who wore street clothes—his signature tight shirt and Western-style jeans. Plosky also wore a badge around his neck and a pistol at his side.

Plosky waved Sam past the barricades, and he approached the two of them.

"A nutty-ass detail, thanks to you, Young," Plosky said as Sam reached him. Sam did not respond. O'Malley lectured Plosky on detail protocol, how to position the eleven deputies he would be commanding and the like.

"Chief, I've been doing this for thirty-two years," Plosky said. "Relax."

O'Malley shook his head and walked away.

"Hey, Sam, Irwin Junior got accepted to Virginia Tech. He's doing great. Told me to tell you hi."

"Of course he's doing great. He's got you for an old man."

Plosky looked down. "Your girl will be just fine. As long as there are no surprises, this will be easy, easy. Now, let's get her to the hospital." Plosky signaled to another deputy, who spoke into a walkie-talkie. Minutes later, the double doors swung wide and Camille, flanked by deputies, emerged in handcuffs. The crowd roared, a combination of cheers and curses.

"Follow me." Plosky led them towards the waiting ambulance, which was surrounded by police cruisers on all four sides.

Camille's gaze was on the ground when she emerged, walking slowly, her cuffed hands in front of her. A deputy held each arm, and three more walked behind her.

Sam waited with Plosky by the back of the ambulance as Camille and her guards slowly crossed the pavement between them and the jail entrance. When she got within reach, he and Plosky each lightly grabbed an arm to facilitate an easier climb into the ambulance. Sam gazed along the sawhorses behind her and marveled at the random assortment of yelling and gesturing citizens and reporters. Cameras rolled from every allowable angle. When Sam touched Camille, her emotions pumped into him. They were warm and soft. Happy even.

Just as Camille placed a foot on the first metal step leading into the ambulance, Sam felt a burst of warm, pungent liquid, which he at first bizarrely took to be gravy, splatter the side of his face. Then he felt Camille go limp.

Sam looked at Camille just in time to see her body collapse into Plosky's arms. A man stood in front of the sawhorse barricade, hunched over and screaming in their direction. It only took the second between when Sam focused on the man and when the man was torn apart by bullets for Sam to see that he knew the guy. In the same second Sam also realized how utterly badly he had screwed up by not calling O'Malley. Of course, Jerome Johnson had screamed what anyone would expect him to scream. *Murderer.*

In Sam's memory, Johnson's body would always appear, like in the movies, to have stayed standing for just a moment while bullets riddled it, as if, though he was dead, the world wanted to feel his effect for an extra second or two. Whether that actually happened or not, Johnson crumpled to the ground, dead. His gun bounced and skittered away across the pavement. Sam knelt and placed his hands on the sides of Camille's head. Plosky, still screaming, arms under her armpits, held her just off the ground. Sam had never been in combat, never been to medical school, never been trained in first aid. But no training was needed to know what could be done to save Camille. Nothing. The small hole in Camille's temple looked, and indeed felt, almost surgical. But the gaping exit wound behind her ear gushed blood and brains. Camille's eyes were empty saucers. She was dead.

Deputy Plosky, in the immediate wake of the security debacle that would likely cost him his job, kept his head. Obviously recognizing the futility in providing any life-saving aid to Camille, he focused on the matter at issue.

"*Her baby! Her baby!* We need to get to the hospital!"

In the midst of the shouting observers and influx of what seemed like hundreds of police officers on the scene, Sam and Plosky lifted Camille's body into the ambulance, which sped off pursuant to Plosky's desperate orders.

They were led and followed by dozens of police cars, sirens wailing. Sam kept his hands pressed on Camille's head wounds as they drove, but nothing much more tried to escape through his fingers. Within five minutes the doors sprung open and two medics placed Camille on a gurney and rushed her through the automatic doors and into the emergency room. Plosky and Sam stood together on the street. Sam felt the side of his own face and realized it was thickly matted with blood.

"It wasn't your fault," Sam said. He watched the man cry for a while before he responded.

"I know," Plosky said. "It was yours."

Sam and Plosky sat next to each other on the curb, covered in blood, not speaking for what felt like half an hour. Occasionally Sam looked at his phone. Texts flew in from friends and colleagues, but he ignored them. Finally, his phone buzzed and when he saw who it was, he decided to answer it

"This is Young."

"Dude," Barnabus said. "We gotta hurry."

Sam shut his eyes. "You must not be watching TV. Camille's been shot. She's dead."

"Oh, I was watching. I'm inside the hospital now. That's how I know we gotta hurry. They saved Camille's baby. It's being rushed up to intensive care."

"Then what the hell are you talking about? Hurry for what?"

"You fully well know, dude. Look, I can get to Camille's body in the morgue, but that does us no good without a legal-like way to actually get her out of here. Only you can figure that out. But we gotta get her body outa there."

"What are you up to, Barnabus?"

"Call that undertaker friend of yours and get him to meet me in the delivery area, Lot 3A, as soon as he can be there."

"Barnabus—"

"Samson, I don't like telling you what to do, but who's payin' the fee here? Please, just do it." Barnabus hung up.

Without thinking, Sam hit a number on his phone.

"Yeah?" a thick, scratchy voice said.

"Get sobered up, my friend. I need your help."

Silence, then attention. "Anything for you, man."

"Thanks, Acorn."

CHAPTER 25

SUSPECT NUN IN ROSSLYN RIPPER CASE MURDERED

By Lexi Shapiro

Sam put down the paper. He and Raj sat in the lobby of the Virginia Department of Forensic Science, which also housed the Office of the Medical Examiner. Sam studied the old man's face. Raj held his eyes half shut, as if praying.

"Raj, about Camille and my mother."

"What about 'em?"

"What do you mean, what about 'em? How'd you meet them? And why'd you never tell me you knew my mother?"

"They were nice young women I met long ago, Samson. That's all you need to know for now. We'll talk more later."

"Good morning, Sam," O'Malley said, startling Sam out of his intense focus on Raj.

"Chief?" Sam was surprised to see O'Malley in the morgue lobby in street clothes—sweat pants, T-shirt, and sneakers. He held his police creds and his wallet in his hand. He did a double take on Raj.

"What are you doing here, Buterab?"

"Good morning to you, too, sir."

O'Malley did not respond. He turned to Sam.

"Where's the next of kin?"

"I guess this is all she's got," Sam said.

O'Malley sighed. "Good grief. I don't care at this point. You gentlemen ready?"

They followed a young clerk down a hallway. Sam's phone buzzed with an incoming text.

"Her body is in a refrigerated drawer," the clerk said. "I'll pull out the drawer, and all I need you to do is take a quick look at her and tell me whether it's the body of Camille Paradisi."

The clerk swiped his way through a door and into a small room with about ten large metallic drawers against the far wall. She placed her hand on the drawer and pulled.

The four of them stared into an empty drawer.

"Wait here." The clerk quickly left the room and moments later returned with an elderly Indian man wearing a nametag identifying him as Dr. Lail. He opened every drawer on the wall, checking paperwork on the plastic clipboards hanging from a peg on each one.

"There has to be some mistake. The body was in this drawer last night. I closed it myself." He examined the clipboard, and Sam could see he was looking at his own set of initials from the night before. "This building, and this room in particular, is absolutely secure. No one can get in without swiping one of these badges, and only five people have the badges. Not to worry, Chief, she's here somewhere."

Lail awkwardly ushered the clerk out of the room. "We'll be right back."

"I'm detaining your ass, Young," O'Malley whispered.

"For what?"

"Not sure yet, but until we find that body, I'm assuming this is some of your bullshit."

"I'm sure they'll find the body," Sam said. "We both know she's dead. Besides, this is on you—not me."

"Me?"

"You're the chief. It's your department. You definitely don't want the press finding out you misplaced the body, even for a few minutes. I mean, after you released Johnson, failed to protect Paradisi, and missed the obvious facts in the Ripper case? Besides, why would I take her body? And how?"

The chief laughed softly.

They could hear Lail's yells coming from down the hall.

"Get the hell out of here, Young," O'Malley said.

• • •

Sam sat behind the wheel of the Escalade in the parking lot of the Department of Forensic Science. He watched Raj walk slowly across the parking lot towards his shiny Bentley. Sam looked at his phone. Sparf three times. Amelia. Juliana. Nguyen. Lexi Shapiro. He put the phone in his pocket and felt the side of his face, remembering how Camille's warm blood had splashed against it.

"Samson."

Sam broke out of his trance and saw that Raj had pulled his car up next to his, driver's window to driver's window, apparently wishing a last word.

"Yes?"

"We won't be seeing each other for a while."

"Okay."

"Wanted to say goodbye, for now. You're a heck of a lawyer, Samson. I've always cared about you. I'm proud of you. You know, once things settle down, let's get together. Talk some things through. Once you kinda sort things out. Learn a few things. "

"When?"

Raj smiled. "At the opportune time. For now, see you around, Samson."

Raj eased away in the Bentley.

Tap. Tap. Tap.

Sam rolled down the passenger-side window.

"What are you doing here?"

"I work here," Juliana said. "You okay?"

"I think so."

"For what it's worth, I've been on a phone conference all morning. About the DNA and the statistics and whatnot. Just between us, the FBI is fixin' to declare the case solved. Zeb was the Ripper. Paradisi killed him. Now she's dead. As far as they're concerned, it's wrapped up."

"You were right all along," Sam said. Juliana smiled. "As usual," he added.

"Oh my God, my voice mail was full this morning with reporters wanting to ask me about the mother-but-no-father thing. It's crazy."

He and Juliana watched each other closely for a moment.

"Sorry about your friend, Sam."

"See you soon."

Sam pulled the Escalade out of the parking lot and headed south. His phone buzzed. This one he needed to take. Ten minutes later he arrived in front of R and S Moving and Storage. One of the automatic bay doors began its slow rise as the Escalade approached it.

Inside, Acorn, wearing a black suit, stood next to his hearse with Barnabus and Steve Buterab. All three men regarded Sam with folded arms.

"I fucked up, Cochise," Barnabus said. "Somehow I got the wrong body." A blue plastic hospital body bag lay on the round poker table in the center of the otherwise empty warehouse. Barnabus approached the table and, with his pudgy fingers, fumbled with the zipper, then yanked it down about twelve inches, just enough for Sam to see the face of Camille's killer, Jerome Johnson.

"Am I good, Sam?" Acorn said. "This is sketchin' me out, man."

Sam took a deep breath. "You're good."

Acorn quickly got in the hearse and backed out of the warehouse while Sam, Barnabus, and Steve regarded Jerome Johnson.

"I coulda sworn Camille was in drawer seven," Barnabus said. "I even checked it late last night. This morning I just loaded the bag. Seriously, what are we gonna do about him?" Barnabus gestured towards Johnson.

"I'll take care of it," Steve said. "I suggest you guys get out of here, and maybe, you know, don't be in touch for a while." Steve walked across the empty warehouse and disappeared into the room that Sam had always taken for his office.

"You know, the level at which you're full of shit is utterly staggering," Sam said. "You took both bodies. Where's Camille's?"

Barnabus put on his puzzled expression. "If I were to answer that question, you may think I have some knowledge of illegal activity."

"Why steal her body, dude? I don't get it."

"Yes you do, dude. You so fully do. Stop pretending to be a pussy. Look, man, I'm just following orders. I'll be in touch." Barnabus turned and walked slowly out of the warehouse, Sam trailing behind him.

"I saw her brains fall out of her head, Barnabus. They sprayed the side of my face. *She's fucking dead!*" Sam realized he was yelling.

"Yes, she was," Barnabus said. "I told you I'd be in touch."

"When, Barnabus? When will you be in touch?" But Barnabus was walking towards his car. For the first time in their relationship, Sam felt the force of Barnabus's personality as it really was. Endearing? Maybe. Goofball? No.

"You know when, dude," Barnabus called over his shoulder.

Sam drove and drove, only to end up in the empty Holy Angels parking lot after dusk. Across the lot he saw that Andrada's light was on. He really did not know what he was doing there. Or what he was doing next. He held his mother's photograph of the old group of friends in his hand. Camille on the end, looking barely a day younger than the moment she was killed almost thirty years later, Raj in the middle, an overgrown teenager compared to the wizened old gangster Sam knew now, and his own mother. Exactly the way he remembered her.

"Sam."

Sam jumped, startled by the presence of Father Andrada by his window. "Father?"

"Why don't you come in for a drink?"

CHAPTER 26

"SCOTCH?" ANDRADA STOOD BY the rolling bar in the sitting room of the main house.

"I'll pass," Sam said.

"No, I think you'll have one."

Sam watched the man pour two drinks. His face looked old, but his movements were quick and dexterous, an athlete's movements. Andrada took a long gulp. They regarded each other.

"I've got to say, Father, you don't seem particularly broken up about Camille. Your closest friend was shot dead yesterday. She was practically like a daughter to you, wasn't she?"

Andrada smiled at Sam. "What I'm worried about is how to persuade the government to allow me to have custody of Camille's daughter. An uphill battle for an old man. Maybe you can help? I'm willing to tell you everything. But somewhere inside, you already know it. Unlike most, you have the *capacity* to believe it, a unique capacity. Want to give it a try? Pretend with me at least? First off, Camille is not like a daughter to me, and if you allow yourself to have a little faith, you'll see you already know she's my older sister."

Sam drained half of his glass. "Do you realize I have no idea what you're talking about?"

Andrada watched Sam carefully, and he could tell the old man was waiting for him to speak. Their eyes met. The mirrored image. One brown, one green.

"You want me to believe that Trinity and this Fifika Kritalsh are descendants of the fallen angels cast out of heaven. Camille is over seventy years old. The journal is true. You, of course, with your dark moods and normal aging, are Paul Kritalsh, later Paul Paradisi."

"Indeed. And Buterab?"

I've always thought of you as kinda like a son.

"My father."

"And?"

"You and Camille, or Trinity, or whatever you want to call her, decide to hire me to try to stop the serial killer, thereby connecting with me in the hopes of seeking my services in their lawsuit against God. The whole thing is preposterous, not least of all why you would choose me. I don't believe in any of that religious shit, even the parts that are more believable than this. Most of all, why would any of you deceive me like this?"

Sam finished his drink, and the two were quiet for a long moment. Sam felt awkward, much like during the silence that sometimes followed a client's preposterous story. Andrada's eyes probed Sam's playfully now.

"So what happened to Trinity between running away from home in Bariloche and showing up outside the cathedral in Miami?"

"That's another whole story. You'll need to learn it someday if you take the case."

Andrada stood and refilled both glasses. When he returned to his seat he held an inch-thick envelope. He handed the envelope to Sam. They finished their drinks in silence.

"The rest of Fifika Kritalsh's journal. The remainder of the contents are rather self-explanatory. Do what you want, Samson. Follow this up, or don't. Stay in touch, or don't. Either go for it or leave it alone and continue on your way. But ask yourself this. If given a choice between this story being true or being hogwash, which do you prefer? I think I know. Good luck either way. Finish the journal. You'll figure it out. I gotta say, I think you already know."

● ● ●

Sam stood by the Escalade in the empty church parking lot. He put his cigarette out on the pavement and opened Andrada's envelope. He expected a cryptic priest's note, an overdone religious analogy, or a tidbit of obscure information that got him part of the way there—but then again, hardly close. He focused on the same tight cursive writing he had been looking at for weeks. Sam flipped through the journal and saw that the entries were made only every few months, but went on through the '80s. Under the journal he found a check for sixty thousand dollars and an Internet printout from Expedia.com. A round-trip ticket in Sam's name. Montreal. Havana. Leaving the next day.

CHAPTER 27

SAM'S FINGER CLICKED STOP. The video clip depicted the murder differently than he remembered it. Her body had dropped so much faster. He had moved so much slower. At one point, the ABC 7 camera zoomed in on Sam feeling the back of Camille's head, and the viewer could see a thick chunk of blood and brain ooze onto his hand and through his fingers. Sam was expressionless as he held Camille, even while Plosky's screams dominated the audio.

The old women were long gone, maybe sitting out of Sam's view in one of the cafés lining the Plaza Vieja, or strolling together down a side street, still listening to their friend rehash some old argument with her long-dead husband. Their chatter was beyond his reach. Sam glanced along the tables at the various cafés along the wide plaza, his mind gliding above the noise but fishing nevertheless. Like an eagle? No, a seagull, looking for a bit of dead fish or trash to swoop down and scoop up? Sam was still unclear on whether Andrada conceived of Sam's trip as a continuation of his, what, investigation? Or as merely a well-deserved vacation. He crushed out his cigarette and gazed across the center of the plaza.

Slow time. Observe.

Sam reached into his briefcase and pulled out the journal—staring at the writing that had always seemed familiar, but, in any event, was new. In his memory, he never could get it straight whether he saw her first or recognized the writing first. He did remember that he was holding the birthday card from his mother—her last card to him before she died—when he sensed her approach. His eyes were transfixed on the handwriting in the card. The tight cursive felt bound up with nurturing love as opposed to the menace and mystery the writing in the journal seemed to scream. But it was her writing all the same. He reached into his briefcase and pulled out his mother's bible, realizing he had never really examined it before. He flipped through it. Spanish. He held on to it for a long moment, staring across the plaza. His thumb tickled the red-rimmed pages. Then he flipped to the first page and saw her writing again.

Nombre: Fifika y Paul Kritalsh, Buenos Aires, 21-2-57.

At first he thought the trio of old women were back. But even before his head swung to the three approaching from straight across the plaza, he felt their focus on him, and knew they could not be strangers like the old women. The three woman, two young and one older, wore sundresses, one red, one white, one black. They strode slowly, parting the pigeons as the others had done. But when her eyes met Sam's, the young woman in the white dress broke into a run just as Sam realized he was doing the same. In seconds they embraced without speaking though the woman's mantra came into his head with perfect clarity.

I'm sorry. I love you. I'm sorry. I love you. I'm sorry. I love you. I always meant to tell you. Again and again and again until Sam absorbed it.

It's not your fault, Mom.

Sam was not sure how long he and his mother embraced before he turned to the other women, who had now reached them.

"Aunt Trinity," he said. Camille smiled at him and touched his arm.

"And I guess that makes you Grandma," Sam said to the older lady. Unlike Aunt Trinity, and more like his mother,

Fifika, his grandmother carried herself with a certain slumped-shouldered sadness—a melancholy that had always been part of his mother's personality.

The three stood quietly for a moment at the center of the largely empty plaza.

• • •

"So, I gotta ask. Where's Fidel?" Sam said.

"He doesn't get out much these days," Fifika said.

The waiter delivered four glasses of red wine. Trinity lifted hers for a toast. Fifika made eye contact with Sam and followed suit. His grandmother held her glass with two fingers, as if unsure of the timing or purpose of the toast, which so obviously was meant to seal a bargain.

"Ready for the case of the ages?" Trinity said.

"To my wonderful son, and the opportune time," Fifika said softly, with the thoughtful, yet hesitant edge in her voice Sam remembered so well. For the first time Sam realized that Trinity and Fifika looked a lot alike except in complexion; Trinity the Trinity tanned and his mother pale and freckled. Trinity smiled mischievously, her eyes dancing with excitement. Sam's mother, though, was sad and serious. How odd was this pairing, his somber mother and his crafty aunt? And would he ever learn, or indeed believe, who they were and what they had been through?

"You'll find out more as we go along," Fifika said, answering the unspoken question.

"To the biggest case ever, dude," Trinity said, mimicking Barnabus's voice. Sam looked as far as he could into the eyes of Fifika Kritalsh and raised his glass.

CPSIA information can be obtained
at www.ICGtesting.com
Printed in the USA
FFOW04n1334140416
23187FF